PAINT IT BLACK

The interior of the club is dark, lit by low-wattage rose-colored bulbs so the human attendants don't trip and fall as they work the room. There is a lot of black velvet drapery, antique statuary and Victorian furniture in evidence. But the first thing that catches my notice are the people hanging from the ceiling. Some are men, some are women, some are children. Almost every major ethnic group seems to be represented. They are all naked and suspended by piano wire from hooks fixed in their flesh. Some are wrapped in barbed wire. Some have been flayed, peeled to expose the muscles that lurk beneath their skin. All of them are alive.

Something warm and wet strikes my hand. It's blood. I look up to see a partially skinned young man suspended directly overhead. The skin on his legs and feet has been carefully pared away, leaving only the bone. He smiles down at me like a medieval martyr, his eyes going in and out of focus as he speaks.

'Welcome to the Black Grotto, milady.'

The other human chandeliers take up his greeting, their voices slurred and dreamy.

'This is my kind of place,' purrs the Other.

*Also by the same author
and available from New English Library:*

In the Blood
Wild Blood

Paint It Black

Nancy A. Collins

NEW ENGLISH LIBRARY

First published in Great Britain
in 1995 by Hodder and Stoughton Limited
A division of Hodder Headline PLC

A New English Library paperback original

British Library Cataloguing in Publication Data

Collins, Nancy A.
Paint it Black
I. Title
813.54 [F]

ISBN 0 450 61010 1

Typeset by Phoenix Typesetting, Ilkley, West Yorkshire.

Printed and bound in Great Britain by
Cox & Wyman, Reading, Berks.

Hodder and Stoughton Ltd
A division of Hodder Headline PLC
338 Euston Road
London NW1 3BH

This book is dedicated to the memory of my good friend Dave Ryan (1953–1992).
Smoke 'em if you got 'em, dude.

Author's Note

Portions of this novel, in a slightly different form, first appeared in chapbook form as *Cold Turkey*, published in 1992 by Crossroads Press.

PRELUDE

    Particularly
When something like a dog is barking
When something like a goose is born a freak
When something like a fox is luminous
When something like a tortoise crystallizes
When something like a wolf slides by
All these things are harmful to the health of man.

                Hagiwara Sakataro, 'Harmful Animals'

It's a beautiful world.

I look out across the predawn rooftops. Most of the buildings are still dark, except for scattered windows that mark early risers and insomniacs. The moon is down and the sun has yet to make its appearance, leaving the city to a darkness that is deeper than midnight. Now is the time for the changing of the guard.

I look down on the streets from my perch and watch the night things begin their retreat. I don't mean prostitutes and drunkards and other so-called 'night owls'. I refer to creatures that are genuinely nocturnal. Things that shrink from the first touch of the sun's rays for fear of burning.

A succubus wearing the outer appearance of a crack whore is bartering with a drunken older man. The succubus lifts its head, nostrils flaring as it scents the coming dawn, and speeds up the transaction. The older man seems pleased that he is getting such a good deal on pussy as they stagger into a darkened alley. I doubt he'll think it's such a bargain when, in the middle of his five-dollar fuck, the whore's body starts revealing razored mouths in places he never dreamed of.

I spot a pack of *vargr* making their way down a connecting street. The early hour and the accompanying darkness have made them bold, and they run in their skins. They are young, at least by werewolf standards, and still given to such acts of rebellion. They lope along, two abreast and three deep, almost on all fours. They snap and growl and bark at the shadows. Any human unlucky enough to encounter them might, at first glance, mistake them for a pack of feral dogs – household pets gone wild. But once they stood up on their hind legs, baying to signal an attack, the illusion would be torn asunder and the truth revealed.

For all the good it would do their victim. The werewolves pass by quickly, headed in the direction of the abandoned warehouses lining the river front where they make their den.

Not long after the *vargr* run past, a homeless man emerges from a piss-soaked doorway. He is dressed in rags, his feet encased in busted-out boots stuffed full of newspaper. I study him more closely, thinking he might be a seraphim in disguise. But no, he is a genuine vagrant. He is probably old, but it is hard to tell for sure because of the grime caking his hands and face. He might be black, maybe not. He is clutching an empty vodka bottle in one hand and muttering aloud to himself. He tilts back the bottle, tonguing the neck for one last drop. His brow furrows when he realizes it's empty and, in a sudden burst of rage, he shrieks an obscenity and hurls the bottle to the curb. The sound it makes as it breaks is impressively loud in the predawn silence.

The bum seems to find a certain pleasure in making noise and continues to do so. He rants at the top of his voice, his ravings bouncing off the surrounding buildings like a handball. He finds a garbage can to knock over and kick. A bottle or two to dash against the curb. Just as he seems to be losing steam, there is the sound of leathery wings and he is gone.

I look up in time to spot a large black shape silhouetted against the dark sky. It looks to be carrying something almost as large as itself in its talons. No doubt a diligent gargoyle matriarch out hunting for prey to feed her hungry chicks.

As the sky begins to slowly lighten, I spot my own prey. It moves swiftly, clinging to the shadows as it hurries to its nest. Its pallid features and blood-red eyes make me want to puke. I hate these creatures more than all the other Pretending races combined. The very sight of them makes my palms itch and my gut tighten. All I want to do is drive my silver switchblade deep into their worm-fed hearts. Fucking lousy bloodsuckers.

I do not want to lose the vampire's trail, so I abandon my perch. I grin in anticipation of the slaughter that is to follow, the morning breeze chill against my exposed fangs. Without further delay, I crawl headfirst down the side of the four-storey building I've been using as my observation tower and hurry after my victim.

It's a beautiful world.

From the diaries of Sonja Blue

Part 1

When the Dead Love

I am the Vampire at my own veins
   one of the great lost horde
doomed for the rest of time, and beyond,
   'to laugh – but smile no more.'
                    Baudelaire, 'Heauton Timo Roumenos'

1

I see the world through ancient eyes.

They are not the eyes of an old man, dimmed by age and clouded by cataracts. And while my mind is filled with memories, unlike humans, I never find myself lost in the tangle of interconnecting association or the fog of recollection.

My time on earth has been tenfold that of the oldest human. I am ancient. But I am not old. I stand outside the time stream that ages mortal flesh, making bones brittle as glass, teeth crack like chalk. I need never fear that my world will telescope downward to what little light and sound can be strained through failing sensory apparatus.

I look upon some of the aged creatures I myself have personally known and sported with in years past and marvel at their irretrievable descent into decay. A breast that was once as succulent and firm as a fresh melon is now a withered dug, hanging flat and wrinkled. A penis, once proud and full of the malt of life, is now only good for the elimination of waste.

This is mankind's heritage. Its destiny. All of humanity's triumphs and advances — its art, science, technology, and philosophy — reduced to a lump of sweating flesh, straining on a nameless bed. Being mortal as individuals, humans seek to embrace eternity as a species. And while I consider such attempts at 'immortality' laughable, through their relentless breeding they *have* succeeded in maintaining a certain continuity throughout the centuries.

I have kept a journal for seven hundred years. There are literally thousands of volumes, stored in a hundred different hiding places scattered over three continents. I have no genuine memories of my life as a human, except for those preserved in faded ink on these crumbling pages. The sentiments, dreams, and fears expressed in those earliest entries belong to a creature forever beyond my ken, thanks be to the forces that made me.

Still, humans have their uses. Of course they provide my kind with sustenance; that deep red vintage that is so much sweeter when stolen from its host. That much goes without saying. But there are other, more subtle, more . . . *rarefied* pleasures to be had at their expense.

Allow me to elaborate . . .

There are several nightclubs in this city that cater to those humans whose personal tastes, like those of my own kind, have nothing to do with procreation. There is one club in particular — The Ossuary — I enjoy frequenting. It's located in the meat-packing district. In fact, I was there just last night. The exterior of The Ossuary is very unprepossessing, no different from the rest of the drab warehouses lining the street. But the interior is, by human standards, quite inspired. The walls are painted matt black and festooned with the bones of the various beasts who have met their fate at the hands of the neighbors. The boiled, peeled, and bleached skulls of creatures bovine, porcine, caprine, and equine stare blankly at the prancing hairless primates responsible for their destruction, bearing mute witness to the rituals of orchestrated pain and degradation played out before their empty sockets.

Entry to The Ossuary's dank pleasure rooms is expensive — the cost of membership runs in the low four figures. One-time 'tickets of passage' for curious visitors can cost upwards of fifty dollars apiece, and there's always a line to get in. The bouncer nods his head in recognition as I move to the head of the line, stepping aside to allow me passage. They know me here, as I am known in dozens of similar establishments throughout the rest of the Americas, Europe, and Asia.

I breeze past the combination dressing-undressing room, where the club's regulars change into their preferred costumes for the evening's entertainment. I have no need for such theatrics. The thump of the disco and the smell of dry ice make me smile, ever so slightly, in anticipation of the night's hunt.

The cavernous main room is filled with people, both well dressed and naked, milling about under the strobe lights. Beautiful fashion models, made trim and perfect by strict diets and surgery, move amongst tattooed and creatively pierced grotesques.

A stylishly dressed businessman, looking like he's just vacated a Wall Street brokerage house, his power tie loosed slightly at the collar, leans against the bar, watching the massive video screen suspended from the ceiling that shows vintage Times Square porno loops, groping the tightly trussed rear of a transvestite between sips of draft beer.

Studding the main room are several tableaux areas: a rack; a man-sized doghouse, complete with food bowl; a mirrored jail cell; manacles and

stocks of every description. Some of the equipment
is available for use by patrons, for a nominal fee.
The snap and crack of whips, rods, and paddles on
wriggling backsides fills the air.

I scan the assemblage for potential prey. I spot
a beautifully coiffured blonde sitting on a bar
stool, staring imperiously into space as a drudge
licks her boots clean, a second slave kneeling before her so he can suck her fingers, one at a time.
I contemplate her for a moment, then pass on. While
taking one such as herself would no doubt prove
amusing, I seek a different diversion for my night's
pleasure.

I watch dispassionately as a young girl dressed
only in leather boots and a blindfold is strung
up by her hands. As she balances precariously on
tiptoe, her partner dribbles hot wax onto her exposed buttocks. She whimpers and wiggles her bottom
most becomingly. The master puts aside his candle
and produces a whip, the head of which he inserts
into his compliant slave, lifting her off her feet.
She shrieks and moans at this violation, her hips
bucking to the beat of a Cure song.

A naked man with a junior executive's paunch
stands off to the sidelines, watching the couple. He
pulls on his semi-hard penis with his right hand,
but elevation remains elusive. Bored, he turns his
voyeur's gaze — as empty as those of the animals
mounted on the walls — to a heavily tattooed fat
man kneeling before a tiny Oriental woman armed
with a cat-o'-nine-tails, his penis clamped in the
jaws of a household mousetrap.

A man dressed in unconvincing drag emerges from
the dry-ice smoke of the dance floor, his wig askew,
funeral crêpe wrapped about his exposed penis,
lead fishing weights hanging from his testicles.

He smiles at me, his eyes unfocused and unreadable, even to me.

I find what I'm looking for in a young couple
dressed in leather bondage gear. The female wears
a brassiere with holes cut in the center that allows
her pierced nipples to protrude, and a peaked cap
reminiscent of those once favored by the Gestapo.
The male wears a halter studded with chrome spikes
that displays his tattoos to their best advantage.
A leather bondage mask hangs from his belt. Both
wear tight-fitting leather chaps that expose their
pale ass cheeks. With their blond hair, tanned good
looks, and complementing bodywork, they could be
easily mistaken for fraternal twins. Perhaps they
are.

The male seems a bit dubious at first, eyeing the
scar that twists the right side of my face into a
perpetual sneer and my ruined eye. I might not be
physically attractive enough to suit his tastes,
but I appear to have the necessary wealth. In the end
they prove pathetically easy to snare – all it takes
is the promise of free drugs and a night of excess
at a fashionable address. As we leave, I probe their
minds, expertly tweaking their pleasure centers
while dampening their sense of self-preservation.
The humans that frequent these clubs are far from
cautious by the normal standards of the herd, but
I still find it prudent to lull them into a false
sense of security.

It is early morning, and as the club prepares
to seal its doors against the coming dawn, the
city's butchers can be seen starting their day's
work, unloading freshly slain sides of beef and
pork from refrigerated vans. High-pressure hoses
sluice the blood from the loading docks into the
gutters, where it mixes with the vomit, urine,

and used condoms from the night before, filling the air with the fragrant aroma of spent meat. I find it most invigorating.

The leather-clad couple ooh and aah appreciatively at the sight of my vintage Rolls and the uniformed driver that awaits my return. We climb inside and I offer my new playthings cocaine and champagne in copious quantities as we roll through the city's predawn streets. They indulge themselves to excess, giggling and snorting and groping one another as I watch, smiling quietly.

The male fixes me with a questioning gaze, his eyes made hot and wet by drugs and my manipulation of his brain chemistry. 'So, what's your particular kink, buddy?' He smiles slowly, knowingly. 'You like to watch? Is that it?'

He slides his gloved hand between the female's thighs, massaging her mons veneris.

I return the drunken idiot's clueless grin. 'Yes. I like to watch.'

They are duly impressed when we arrive at our destination: a stylish loft apartment that utilizes the entire top floor of what was once a furrier's warehouse. The interior is an austere variant of art deco, all shining chrome and black marble decorated here and there with expensive Persian carpets, atmospherically lit by cunningly arranged track lighting.

I shrug out of my coat and smile comfortingly at my playthings. I take my place in an overpadded leather easy chair, light a French cigarette, and cross my legs. I gesture to a corner of the room with exposed brick walls, bare metal pipes, and a stained concrete floor. Handcuffs are attached to one of the radiator pipes and leg manacles are set into the wall, and a metal trapeze hangs suspended at eye level from the rafters. An array of punishment devices hangs from a row of pegs.

'Why don't you show me what you do best?'

The leather-clad couple exchange glances and shrug. As far as they are concerned, I am a jaded, somewhat physically repugnant jet-setter with too much time and money on my hands.

The male removes his bondage mask from his belt and slips it on. With its zippered mouth and eyeholes, it resembles a leather scarecrow's face. The male grabs the female by the hair and drags her over to the pipe, where he handcuffs her with her arms over her head, her buttocks pointed in my direction. The male selects a cat-o'-nine-tails and, after a couple of experimental snaps, brings it down on his partner's ass. The female squeals and wriggles as the male rains blow after blow onto her upturned derrière, leaving angry red welts across the creamy expanse of her jiggling cheeks.

I yawn.

This seems to aggravate the male, although it's hard to tell with the bondage mask on.

'What's the matter? Isn't this good enough for you, scarface?' he snaps, turning from his trussed partner to glower at me.

I pretend to let his insult go unnoticed. 'You haven't even broken the skin!' I sniff. 'I want the Real Thing, not this candy-coated pretense!'

The male mutters something to himself and returns his attention to his slave, smacking her unprotected backside with even greater ferocity. The female shudders and weeps, struggling against her restraints as blood fills the paper-thin cuts striping her ass.

After a few minutes of this, the male stops to change hands, shaking the blood from the whip. He

turns to fix me with a challenging stare from behind the safety of his mask.

'Is *this* real enough for you, you one-eyed
bastard?' he snarls, slapping his partner's blood-
smeared flank with the flat of his hand.

'You're not even close,' I smile. 'Here, allow me
to show you how it's done.'

He stands aside, hands on his hips, expecting me to
get up and take the whip from him. Instead, I simply
force my mind into his skull.

The male's body twitches as I penetrate him between the eyes, his limbs convulsing involuntarily
as I seize control of his nervous system. As far
as he is concerned, he has been suddenly, inexplicably struck blind, deaf, and dumb. I am the
only one who can hear him screaming inside his
head.

I give him back his eyes and ears, but I don't allow
him to open his mouth. Screaming is not allowed. Not
yet.

The female turns to look at what she believes is
still her partner, her eyes confused. 'Frankie?'

The male grabs a handful of the female's long,
flowing blonde hair. I pause long enough to savor
its silkiness against borrowed fingertips, then
proceed to pound the captive woman's head repeatedly against the steam pipe.

At first she's too startled to respond. By the
second blow she begins to struggle and swear. The
punishment my surrogate is meting out is not the kind
she craves.

'Frankie! Stop it, you fucker! You're *hurting* me,
damn it!'

I have my plaything slam her head into the pipe a
third time. A fourth. One of her retinas has become
detached. Blood streams from her nostrils, making

the bottom of her face look like a clown's mouth. The female goes limp by the sixth blow, cranial fluid leaking from her ears and the corners of her eyes.

Humans have so many foolish preconceptions concerning my kind: that we cannot walk in the light of day; that we burn at the touch of religious icons; that we survive on a diet of human blood. That last bit is true, in part. Yes, blood is indeed the life. But to feed on blood alone — do humans subsist on nothing but bread and water? Of course not. For those of us with a more *refined* palate, there is the gourmet delight found in human suffering. It is to blood what crack is to table wine.

However, it is not the female's pain that thrills me, delightful though it may be. It is the anguished horror of her partner I feed on, as I force his body to batter his lover's skull into an oozing mess of matted hair and bone fragments. There are no words in the mortal lexicon to describe the exhilaration and gratification I receive from such raw, unfiltered emotions.

The female is dead, or so close to death it doesn't really matter. I have the male release her and stand before a mirror mounted on the wall. As he watches, locked within his own flesh, more helpless than the day he was born, I command his hands to snap the nostril holes of his mask shut. Then I zipper the mouth shut.

I feel the surge of panic swell within him as he realizes what I plan to do. The screaming inside his head doubles in intensity, echoing within his skull, as I seal first the right eye, then the left, leaving him to darkness.

Even after everything is sealed, the mask is far from airtight. It takes the male over half an hour

to suffocate. I sit in my chair and watch, savoring
the alternating surges of fear, terror, rage, and
despair, as the dying human first realizes then
rejects his fate. His last cogent thought is that
the police will kick open the door and rescue him
in the nick of time, just like on TV. Then he dies.

I frown at the dead man's body, then at the battered corpse of the female, still tethered to the
radiator pipe. I had hoped this would be enough,
but it is not. I close my eyes, trying to block
her image from my mind, but it is to no avail. I
can still see her. Something in my chest aches,
reminding me of my emptiness.

Dawn is close at hand, but I do not fear the intrusion of its rosy fingers, here in the mirrored
security of my Rolls. I am not a lowly revenant,
scuttling from the sun's rays for fear of being
reduced to a pile of oozing sores. I evolved past
such worries decades before the invention of the
steam engine.

My powers are somewhat diminished during the
daylight hours, that is true. And, like all of
my kind, I find it necessary to lapse into a
death-like 'sleep' in order to restore my vitality
and heal wounds dealt me in combat. But I am far
from helpless, as the legends would have humans
believe.

My driver cruises the streets of the Lower East
Side. He asks me if I have a destination in mind –
I almost give him an address of a low dive in Five
Points, then I remember that the neighborhood was
demolished close to a century ago. Too bad. There
was a brothel there operated for and by children
that provided me with great amusement now and again.
Instead, I direct him to Allen Street.

The whores who ply their trade along this particular boulevard are, at best, careworn. Most of them are crack or heroin addicts, the ravages of their addictions obvious even to the most obtuse of human gazes. Even if I was prone to the human sexual urge, I would never dream of mating with one of these horrors. They are rarely beautiful, and often they aren't even women. But they are expendable and when one of them disappears no one notices. That is what I find most attractive about them.

I see what I need and I order the driver to stop the car. A small knot of whores stand in a doorway, fidgeting expectantly as they eye the Rolls. The night must have been slow — or their drug consumption immense — if they are still loitering on the streets this close to daybreak. One of them, a redhead dressed in a polyester miniskirt that reveals her unwashed legs almost to her crotch, saunters forward as I power down the window.

'Lookin' for someone, mister?' she coos, her breath redolent of gum disease, as she bends down to look into the interior of the car. When she smiles, I see that she is missing most of her lower teeth.

I say nothing, stabbing a finger over her shoulder at one of the girls standing behind her. She is tall with dark hair and high, vaguely Indian cheekbones. She is too thin and too dirty, dressed in high-cut denim shorts and a halter top, but she will do for now.

The redheaded whore swears and moves out of the way to let the other girl by. I open the door and she hops in with an excited squeal that could almost pass for delight. The Rolls is already pulling away before the door closes, but not before I

25

have reached inside the tiny, crabbed minds of
my victim's compatriots, erasing what memory they
hold of either me or the car.

'My name's Cheryl,' the whore says, rubbing the
front of my pants with all the finesse and speed of
a Girl Scout trying to make a fire without the aid
of matches. When I look at her I can see the virus
gestating within her, eating away at the T-cells in
her blood.

I slap her hands away and I see fear spark in her
eyes as she gets her first good look at my face. I
reach inside my jacket and produce a roll of twenty-
dollar bills the size of an infant's doubled fist.
The whore's eyes widen and she licks her lower lip.

'Do you want this?'

'Yeah. 'Course I want it. What I gotta do t'get
it?'

'Nothing much. All you have to do is come home with
me and play a little game.'

'What kinda game?' She bites her lower lip but
does not move her eyes away from the money.

'Dress up.'

My renfields have the costume laid out in anticipation of our return. I lead the whore into a large
room, empty except for a marble table lit from below by a mauve light. The whore frowns down at the
leather jacket, stained T-shirt, ripped jeans, and
scuffed engineer's boots, obviously perplexed. She
had, no doubt, been expecting something far more
exotic.

'Is this it? Is this what you want me to wear?'

I say nothing, but simply smile. She shrugs and
peels out of her working clothes. The room is cold
and I watch with detached interest as her flesh
creeps and her nipples harden. She is awkward and

it takes her a few minutes to complete the change. Finally she shrugs into the leather jacket, which creaks with her every movement.

'So, do I look okay? Is there anything else?' she asks, holding her arms up and out, modeling the costume for me.

'Just two things. You'll find them in the inside breast pocket of the jacket.'

The whore sticks her hand inside the jacket and removes the items, looking puzzled. 'A pair of mirrored sunglasses and a switchblade?'

'Put the glasses on. Put them on now.' The excitement is starting to stir within me, and the words come out as a breathy whisper.

The whore is confused, perhaps even a little frightened, but she is unwilling to forfeit the money I promised her. She puts on the glasses.

She is dirty and smells of rank jism and vaginal secretions. Her hair is too long and oily. Her motions lack grace and suppleness. But there is a resemblance, tenuous as it may be, and that is enough. She is not the one I want, but she will do for now.

I move closer to the whore, my arousal growing acute as the image of the one I want shimmers behind my eyes. The one this pathetic piece of human waste is standing in for.

'Show me the knife.' It is all I can do to keep the shiver out of my voice.

'What?'

'The knife! Show me the blade?'

'Huh?'

'Just *do* it!' I snap, grabbing the girl by her shoulders. Not too tightly, but roughly enough to spark the fear again.

The blade leaps from its hilt, like a minnow darting through shallow water. The whore holds the

knife cautiously, but not without some familiarity,
I notice. Perhaps she and the object of my desire are
not so disparate, after all.

'Now what?'

'Stab me.'

'What? Are you fuckin' *crazy*?' The fear recedes,
to be replaced by indignation. This is kinkier than
she had bargained for. She'd figured me for some
deformed pervert, one who wanted to be pissed on or
made to roll around in her shit. But this is too
much. Even Allen Street whores, apparently, have
their limits.

'Stab me!'

I have lost all patience with this trollop. If she
will not give me what I want, then I shall use force.
I grab her by the throat and her eyes bug out as she
realizes I mean business.

She raises her hand. I catch a glimpse of metal
as her fist smashes into my chest. There is a cold
sharpness as the blade enters me. I continue to
squeeze her throat. Again she stabs me. And again.
Blood sprays from my wound, spattering both her
face and mine. I close my eyes in order to savor
the illusion that it is not she, but my beloved who
is ramming the knife into my heart again and again.
The fear that radiates from her as I slowly choke
the life from her is amongst the best I have known
in recent years. I groan in ecstasy as I hold her
death cry in the palm of my hand.

I open my eyes, half expecting to see my beloved's
face before me, contorted in death. Instead, all
there is is a dead whore, her blackened, swollen
tongue protruding lewdly between painted lips. The
sunglasses have come loose during her struggle,
and are dangling from one ear. The dead whore's
eyes, filled with burst blood vessels, start from

their sockets like those of a grotesque insect. Disgusted, I let the corpse drop.

I realize that the switchblade is still lodged in my chest. I stare down at the hilt protruding between my ribs. My white silk shirt is now the color of port wine. Chuckling to myself, I pull the knife free.

I close my eyes again and see my love moving like a panther tracking its prey, her eyes burning in the darkness. She wants me. Her passion radiates from her like a dark halo. But what she lusts after is not my touch, my kiss, my seed. No, what she desires is my death.

When I look into her mirrored eyes I know fear and joy. So beautiful. So deadly. I stand in awe of her; my lovely, lethal masterpiece.

Is this how Pygmalion felt when his Galatea stepped from her pedestal? Granted, he did not have to worry about his creation chasing him about the studio, armed with a hammer and chisel, bent on his murder. And she came close, so very close, to killing me the last time we were together. I have suffered countless mutilations during my seven centuries of existence, including amputation, but I shall carry the wounds she dealt me forever.

She split my face open with a silver knife. And I loved it.

I touch the scar that pulls the right side of my face into a rictus grin and think of my fatal beauty. I close my remaining eye and I see her standing there, naked except for the mantle of power that crackles about her like fox fire, and the scar over my heart puckers.

Gods of the Outer Dark, help me.

I love her.

And that is why I must destroy her. Again. And again. And again. Until I am certain I can bring myself to do the deed for real.

> *From the journals of Sir Morgan,*
> *Lord of the Morning Star*

2

William Palmer woke the same way a swimmer emerges from the sea, gasping for air. He lay flat on the bed, staring up at the cracked plaster ceiling for a long moment before really seeing it, the last of the dream bleeding away from the corners of his eyes.

Dream. Thank God. Just a dream.

He'd been dreaming of the house again. The house called Ghost Trap. It had been built earlier in the century by a gifted, if demented, architect who had designed it to keep him safe from the vengeful spirits of his slaughtered family. The mansion was a crazed conglomeration of rooms without windows, blind stairways, secret passageways, and other mad fancies, using non-Euclidian geometric principles that not only confused the restless dead, but disoriented the living as well. For someone such as Palmer, possessing psionic abilities beyond those of normal humans, Ghost Trap was the psychic equivalent of the La Brea Tar Pits.

Nearly three years ago, Palmer had found himself lost in Ghost Trap, at the mercy of the dead that roamed its empty halls. He'd entered in search of his friend and lover, Sonja Blue; the woman who had helped him learn to deal with psychic powers – and had dragged him into her battle with the master vampire, Morgan.

He'd survived that night in Ghost Trap, but just barely. He'd lived to see the horror house consumed by flames, releasing its damned occupants once and for all. Ghost Trap was no more. Yet it still lived within his mind, playing host to his nightmares.

Palmer stared up at the ceiling fan mounted over the bed,

watching the rotors beat the heavy, humid air in near-silence. No doubt the stickiness and heat had contributed to his bad dream. It was too uncomfortable to be sleeping inside, but the mosquitoes were too fierce this season for him to try using the hammock on the front porch.

He sat up, pushing aside the sweat-drenched sheets. He wasn't going to get back to sleep, at least not for a while, anyway. He swung his feet onto the floor and stood up with a groan, catching a glimpse of himself in the mirror opposite the bed. He ran one hand across the ritual tattoo that covered his entire chest. It was of Mayan design, as were the jade plugs that stretched his earlobes. It depicted the symbol of the House of the Jaguar Lords.

Palmer didn't hold with past-life regression therapy, channeling, Space Brothers, or any of the other New Age crap. It just happened that he was the reincarnation of a pre-Columbian Mayan. He had once been one of the six-fingered wizard-kings of the *Chan Balam*, who saw their deformity as a sign of godhood. He was also an ex-private investigator, a pardoned felon, a telepath, and proprieter of a successful specialty export business.

Palmer moved towards the hallway, only to freeze when something the size and shape of a large tarantula skittered out from behind the door. He let out a sigh of relief when he saw what it really was – a mummified six-fingered hand, amputated at the wrist.

'Damn it, Lefty! You nearly gave me a heart attack!' Palmer chided, nudging the thing with his foot. He'd grown fond of the gruesome relic over the months. It really wasn't so surprising that he should develop an attachment to it. After all, it had once belonged to his previous incarnation.

Palmer padded down the hallway, naked except for a pair of boxers, Lefty skittering after him like a faithful pet. He paused at the nursery, quietly opening the door so as not to wake Lethe.

I really should stop calling it the nursery, he thought to himself, not for the first time. *She's really too old for that.*

It took him a second or two to locate her amidst all the stuffed animals and dolls she had in bed with her, then he spotted her hair, as dark and sleek as a sable's pelt, peeking out from between a Raggedy Ann and a Paddington Bear. As he watched, she mumbled something in her sleep.

He was going to have to get her some new clothes pretty soon. She'd already outgrown the ones he bought less than a month ago, having shot up another three inches, literally overnight. Palmer's eyes wandered to the closet door he used as Lethe's official growth chart and the series of overlapping pencil marks with crabbed notations as to date and age. As of her last measuring, she stood close to five foot one. Not bad for a child who had yet to reach her third birthday.

One of the shadows near the foot of Lethe's bed detached itself and moved towards Palmer. Two points of golden light, set about the height of a man's eyes, suddenly blinked on.

'Don't worry, Fido. Nothing's wrong. I was just checkin' in,' Palmer whispered.

The hulking apparition, looking more like a mound of dirty laundry sculpted into the form of a human being, nodded dumbly and returned to its silent vigil. During the two and a half years Palmer had spent in the company of the seraphim, he still had no idea what the creature thought – or if it thought at all. While it was obviously appointed to guard Lethe, it had never once attempted to communicate with him – at least on a level that he could understand.

Satisfied everything was under control, Palmer continued on his nocturnal perimeter check. He paused at the door that led to the patio, with its expensive Spanish tile and a small three-tiered fountain that constantly burbled to itself.

Palmer stepped outside; the humid Yucatán night was no relief. It felt as if the world's largest dog was breathing on him. Palmer wiped at the sweat on his brow and upper lip as he peered up at the moonlit sky.

Where are you? his mind whispered into the night.

Nancy A. Collins

The sound of a radio scanning through a thousand different competing signals filled his head. Some were fairly strong, others weak. Some were in languages he understood, most were not. Some were angry, some were sad, some were happy, but most were confused. The signals blurred and clashed, waxed and waned.

Where are you? He boosted his own signal, hoping to cut through the drift of muted voices that filled the ether. This time he was rewarded with a response – a voice made faint and blurry by distance, but still recognizable.

I'm here. In New Orleans.

He smiled at the sound of her voice in his head; even though she was not there to see it, he knew she felt it.

When are you coming home?

Soon. But I still have work to attend to here.

I miss you.

I miss you, too. She smiled then. He could feel it.

Any luck?

No sign of him yet, but I have a few hunches as to where he might be hiding. How is Lethe?

Fine. I guess.

Glad to hear everything's okay. I have to go now—

Sonja? Sonja, we need to talk . . . Sonja?

There was no reply, only the squawk and squelch of the minds of a million strangers babbling into the void.

34

3

I have to give the dead boy credit; he has the trick of appearing human nailed down tight. He's learned just what gestures and inflections to use in his conversation to hide the fact that his surface glitz is not there to disguise shallowness, but an utter lack of humanity.

I've seen enough of the kind he imitates: pallid, self-important intellectuals who pride themselves on their sophistication and knowledge of what's 'hip', sharpening their wit at the expense of others. Like the vampiric mimic in their midst, they produce nothing while thriving on the vitality of others. The only difference is that the vampire is more honest about it.

I work my way to the bar, careful to keep myself shielded from the dead boy's view, both physically and psychically. It wouldn't do for my quarry to catch scent of me just yet. I hear the vampire's nasal intonations as it holds forth on the demerits of various artists.

'Frankly, I consider his use of photomontage to be inexcusably *banal.* I've seen better at Olan Mills's!'

I wonder who the vampire stole that particular drollery from. A dead boy of his wattage doesn't come up with bons mots and witty remarks spontaneously. When you have to spend a lot of conscious energy remembering to breathe and blink, there is no such thing as top-of-your-head snappy patter. It is all protective coloration, right down to the last double entendre and Monty Python impersonation.

It will be another decade or two before the vampire dressed in black silk and leather with the stainless-steel ankh dangling from one ear and a crystal embedded in his left nostril can divert his energies to something besides the full-time task of ensuring his continuance. And I doubt this dead boy has much of a chance of realizing that future.

I wave down the bartender and order a beer. As I await its arrival, I catch a glimpse of myself in the mirror backing the bar. To the casual observer I look to be no more than twenty-five. Tricked out in a battered leather jacket, a stained Circle Jerks T-shirt, patched jeans, mirrored sunglasses, and with dark hair twisted into a tortured cockatoo's crest, I look like just another member of Generation X checking out the scene. No one would ever guess I'm actually forty years old.

I suck the cold suds down, participating in my own form of protective coloration. I can drink a case or three of the stuff without effect. Beer doesn't do it for me anymore. Neither does hard liquor. Or cocaine. Or heroin. Or crack. I've tried them all, in dosages that would put the US Olympic Team in the morgue; but no luck. There is only one drug that plunks my magic twanger nowadays. Only one thing that can get me off.

And that drug is blood.

Yeah, the dead boy is good enough to have fooled another vampire. But he didn't.

I study my prey speculatively. I doubt I'll have any trouble taking the sucker down. I rarely do, these days. At least not the lesser-evolved undead that still lack major psionic muscle. Sure, they might have enough mesmeric ability to gull the humans in their vicinity, but little else. Compared to my own psychic abilities, the art-fag vampire might as well be packing a peashooter. Still, it isn't smart to get cocky. Lord Morgan dismissed me in such a high-handed manner, and now he's missing half his face. That's what you get for being smug.

I shift my vision from the human to the Pretender spectrum, studying the vampire's true appearance. I wonder if the black-garbed art aficionados clustered about their mandarin, their heads bobbing like puppets, would still consider his pronouncements worthy if they knew his skin was the color and texture of rotten sailcloth. Or that his lips are black and shriveled, revealing oversized fangs set in a perpetual death's-head grimace. No doubt they'd drop their little plastic cups of cheap blush and back away in horror, their surface glaze of urbanite sophistication and studied ennui replaced by honest, old-fashioned monkey-brain terror.

Humans need masks in order to live their day-to-day lives, even amongst their own kind. Little do they know that their dependence on artifice and pretense provides the perfect hiding place for a raft of predators. Predators such as the vampire pretending to be an art fag. Predators such as myself.

I tighten my grip on the switchblade in the pocket of my leather jacket. *Midnight! Time to drop your masks!*

'Uh, excuse me?'

I jerk around a little too fast, startling the young man at my elbow. I was so focused on my prey I was unaware of his approaching me. Sloppy. Really sloppy.

'Yeah, what is it?'

The young man blinks, slightly taken aback by the brusqueness in my voice. 'I, uh, was wondering if I might, uh, buy you a drink?'

I automatically scan him for signs of Pretender taint, but he comes up clean. One hundred percent USDA human. He is taller than me by a couple of inches, his blond hair pulled back into a ponytail. There are three rings in his right ear and one in his left nostril. Despite the metalwork festooning his nose, he is quite handsome.

I am at a loss for words. I'm not used to being approached by normal people. I tend to generate a low-level psychic energy field that most humans find unnerving, if not antagonistic. In layman's terms, I tend to either scare people or piss them off.

I shoot my prey a glance out of the corner of my eye. Shit! The bastard is starting to make his move, hustling one of the more entranced hangers-on.

'I realize this is going to sound like a really dumb come-on,' he says, shooting me an embarrassed smile. 'But I saw you from across the room, and I just had to meet you. Please let me buy you a drink.'

'I, uh, I—'

The vampire is escorting its prey outside, smiling widely as it continues to discourse on postmodern art.

'There's something I have to take care of – I'll be right back! I promise! Don't go away!' I blurt, and dash off in pursuit of my target for the night.

I scan the parking lot, checking for signs of the vampire's passage. I pray I'm not too late. Once a vamp isolates and seduces a human from the herd, they tend to move quickly. I know that from my own experience at the hands of Sir Morgan, the undead bastard responsible for my own transformation.

The vampire and its prey are sitting in the back of a silver BMW with heavily tinted windows, their blurred silhouettes moving like shadows reflected in an aquarium. There is no time to waste. I'll have to risk being spotted.

The imitation art fag looks genuinely surprised when my fist punches through the back window, sending tinted safety glass flying into the car. He hisses a challenge, exposing his fangs, as he whips about to face me. His victim sits beside him, motionless as a mannequin, his eyes unfocused and fly open. The human's erect penis juts forward, vibrating like a tuning fork.

I grab the vampire by the collar of his black silk shirt and pull him, kicking and screaming, through the busted back windshield. The human doesn't even blink.

'Quit yer bitchin'!' I snap as I hurl the snarling vampire onto the parking lot gravel. 'Let's get this over with, dead boy! I've got a hot date!'

The vampire launches himself at me, talons hooked and fangs extended. I move to meet the attack, flicking open my switchblade with a snap of my wrist. The silver blade sinks into the vampire's thorax, causing him to shriek in pain. He collapses around my fist, spasming as his system reacts to the silver's toxin.

I kneel and swiftly remove the vampire's head from his shoulders. The body is already starting to putrefy by the time I've located the BMW's keys. I unlock the trunk and toss the vampire's rapidly decomposing remains inside, making sure the keys are left in his pant pocket.

I look around, but, remarkably, there are no witnesses to be seen in the darkened lot. I move around to the passenger side and open the door, tugging the entranced human out of the car. He stands propped against the bumper like a drunkard, his eyes swimming and his face slack. His penis dangles from his pants like a deflated party balloon. I take his chin between thumb and forefinger and turn his head so that his eyes meet mine.

'This never happened. You do not remember leaving the bar with anyone. Is that clear?'

'N-nothing h-happened.'

'Excellent! Now go back to the bar and have a good time. Oh, and stick that thing back in your pants! You don't want to get busted for indecent exposure, do you?'

I am buzzing by the time I enter the bar. I like to think of it as my *après*-combat high. The adrenaline from the battle is still sluicing around inside me, juicing my perceptions and making me feel as if I am made of lightning and spun glass. It isn't as intense as the boost I get from blood, but it's good.

Someone jostles me, and I look down at a drab, mousy-haired woman, her face set into a scowl. I pause, studying the schizophrenia that radiates from the woman like a martyr's halo. She is thinking of returning home and repeatedly stabbing her elderly parents as they lie in their separate beds, then setting the house ablaze. This is not a new thought. The scowling woman suddenly blushes, draws her shoulders in, ducks her chin, and hurries away, as if she has suddenly woken to discover herself sleepwalking in the nude. I shrug and continue scanning the bar for the young man who spoke to me earlier.

Give it up, he's forgotten you and found another bimbo for the evening.

I fight to keep from cringing at the sound of the Other's voice inside my head. I have managed to go almost all night without having to endure its commentary.

I find him waiting for me at the bar. I make a last-minute spot-check for any blood or telltale ichor that might be clinging to me, then move forward.

'You still interested in buying me that drink?'

The young man's smile is genuinely relieved. 'You came back!'

'I said I'd be back, didn't I?'

'Yeah. You did.' He smiles again and offers his hand. 'I guess I ought to introduce myself. I'm Judd.'

I take his hand and smile without parting my lips. 'Pleased to meet you, Judd. I'm Sonja.'

'What the hell's going on here?!?'

Judd's smile falters as his gaze fixes itself on something just behind my right shoulder. I turn and find myself almost nose to nose with a young woman dressed in a skintight black sheath, fishnet stockings, and way too much makeup. The woman's psychosis covers her face like the caul found on a newborn infant, pulsing indentations marking her eyes, nose, and mouth.

Judd closes his eyes and sighs. 'Kitty, look, it's over! Get a life of your own and let go of mine, all right?'

'Oh, is *that* how you see it? Funny, I remember you saying something different! Like how you'd *always* love me! Guess I was stupid to believe that, huh?'

Kitty's rage turns the caul covering her face an interesting shade of magenta, swirling and pulsing like a lava lamp.

'You're not getting away *that* easy, asshole! And who's this – your new slut?'

Kitty slaps the flat of her hand against my shoulder as if to push me away from Judd. I grab Kitty's wrist, being careful not to break it in front of Judd.

C'mon, snap the crazy bitch's arm off, purrs the Other. *She deserves it!*

'Don't touch me.' My voice is flat and blunt, like the side of a sword.

Kitty tries to yank herself free of my grip. 'I'll fucking touch you anytime I want! Just you stay away from my boyfriend, bitch! Now, let me go!' She tries to rake my face with her free hand, only to have that one grabbed as well, forcing her to look directly into my face. Kitty's features grow pale and she stops struggling. I know the other woman is seeing me – *truly* seeing me – for what I am. Only three kinds of human can perceive the Real World and the things that dwell within it: psychics, drunken poets, and lunatics. And Kitty definitely qualifies for the last category.

I release the girl, who massages her wrists, her gaze still fixed on me. She opens her mouth as if to say something, then turns and hurries away, nearly tripping over her own high heels as she flees.

Judd looks uncomfortable. 'I'm sorry you had to see that. Kitty's a weird girl. We lived together for a few months, but she was incredibly jealous. It got to the point where I couldn't take any more of it, so I moved out. She's been dogging my tracks ever since. She scared off my last two girlfriends.'

I shrug. 'I don't scare easy.'

He isn't afraid of me. Nor do I detect the self-destructive tendencies that usually attract humans to my kind. Judd is not an entranced moth drawn to my dark flame, nor is he a renfield in search of a master. He is simply a good-natured young man who finds me physically attractive. The novelty of his normalcy intrigues me.

He buys me several drinks, all of which I down without any effect. But I *do* feel giddy, almost light-headed, while in his company. To be mistaken for a desirable, human woman is actually quite flattering. Especially since I stopped thinking of myself in those terms some time back.

We end up dancing, adding our bodies to the surging crowd that fills the mosh pit. At one point I am amazed to find myself laughing, genuinely *laughing*, one arm wrapped about Judd's waist. And then Judd leans in and kisses me.

I barely have time to retract my fangs before his tongue finds mine. I slide my other arm around his waist and pull him into me, grinding myself against him. He responds eagerly, his erection rubbing against my hip like a friendly tomcat. And I find myself wondering how his blood will taste.

41

I push him away so hard he staggers backward a couple of steps, almost falling on his ass. I shake my head as if trying to dislodge something in my ear, a guttural moan rising from my chest.

'Sonja?' There is a confused, hurt look on his face.

I can see his blood, beckoning to me beneath the surface of his skin: the veins traced in blue, the arteries pulsing purple. I turn my back on him and run from the bar, my head lowered. I shoulder my way through a knot of dancers, sending them flying like duckpins. Some of the bar's patrons hurl insults in my direction, a couple even spit at me, but I am deaf to their anger, blind to their contempt.

I put a couple of blocks between myself and the bar before I stop to catch my breath. I slump into a darkened doorway, staring at my shaking hands as if they belong to someone else.

'I liked him. I honestly *liked* him and I was going to . . . going to—' The thought is enough to make my throat tighten in a gag reflex.

Like. Hate. What's the difference? Blood is the life, wherever it comes from.

'Not like that. I never feed off anyone who doesn't deserve it. *Never*.'

Aren't we special?

'Shut up, bitch.'

'Sonja?'

I have him pinned to the wall, one forearm clamped against his windpipe, before I recognize him. Judd claws at my arm, his eyes bugging from their sockets.

'I'm . . . I'm sorry . . .' he gasps out.

I let him go. 'No, I'm the one who should be sorry. More than you realize.'

Judd regards me apprehensively as he massages his throat, but there is still no fear in his eyes. 'Look, I don't know what it was I said or did back there at the bar that put you off—'

'The problem isn't with you, Judd. Believe me.' I turn and begin walking away, but he hurries after me.

'I know an all-night coffeehouse near here. Maybe we could go and talk things out there?'

'Judd, just leave me alone, okay? You'd be a lot better off if you just forgot you ever met me.'

'How could I forget someone like you?'

'Easier than you realize.'

He keeps pace alongside me, desperately trying to make eye contact. 'C'mon, Sonja! Give it a chance! I – damn it, would you just *look* at me?'

I stop in mid-step to face him, hoping my expression is unreadable behind my mirrored sunglasses. 'That's the *last* thing you want me to do.'

Judd sighs and fishes a pen and piece of paper out of his pocket. 'You're one strange lady, that's for sure! But I *like* you, don't ask me why.' He scribbles something on the scrap of paper and shoves it into my hand. 'Look, here's my phone number. *Call* me, okay?'

I close my fist around the paper. 'Judd—'

He holds his hands out, palms facing up. 'No strings attached, I promise. Just call me.'

I'm surprised to find myself smiling. 'Okay. I'll call you. Now will you leave me alone?'

When I revive the next evening I find Judd's phone number tucked away in one of the pockets of my leather jacket. I sit cross-legged on the coarse cotton futon that serves as my bed and stare at it for a long time.

I was careful to make sure Judd didn't follow me last night. My current nest is a drafty loft apartment in the attic of an old warehouse in the district just beyond the French Quarter. Apart from my sleeping pallet, an antique cedar wardrobe, a couple of Salvation Army-issue chairs, a refrigerator, a cordless telephone, and the scattered packing crates containing the esoteric curios I use for barter amongst information and magic brokers, the huge space is practically empty. Except for those occasions when the dead come to visit. Such as tonight.

At first I don't recognize the ghost. He's lost his sense of self in the time since his death, blurring his spectral image somewhat. He swirls up through the floorboards like a gust of blue smoke, gradually taking shape before my eyes. It is only when the phantom produces a smoldering cigarette from his own ectoplasm that I recognize him.

'Hello, Chaz.'

The ghost of my former lover makes a noise that sounds like a cat being drowned. The Dead cannot speak clearly – even to Pretenders – except on three days of the year: Fat Tuesday, Halloween, and the vernal equinox.

'Come to see how your murderer is getting on, I take it?'

Chaz makes a sound like a church bell played at half-speed.

'Sorry I don't have a Ouija board, or we could have a proper conversation. Is there a special occasion for tonight's haunting, or are things just boring over on your side?'

Chaz frowns and points at the scrap of paper I hold in my hand. The ghost light radiating from him is the only illumination in the room.

'What? You don't want me to call this number?'

Chaz nods his head, nearly sending it floating from his shoulders.

'You tried warning Palmer away from me last Mardi Gras. Didn't work; but I suppose you know that already. He's living in Yucatán right now. We're very happy.'

The ghost's laughter sounds like fingers raking a chalkboard.

'Yeah, big laugh, dead boy. And I'll tell you one thing, Chaz; Palmer's a damn sight better in bed than you ever were!'

Chaz makes an obscene gesture that is rendered pointless since he no longer has a body from the waist down. I laugh and clap my hands, rocking back and forth on my haunches.

'I *knew* that'd burn your ass, dead or not! Now piss off! I've got better things to do than play charades with a defunct hustler!'

Chaz yowls like a baby dropped in a vat of boiling oil and disappears in a swirl of dust and ectoplasm, leaving me alone with Judd's phone number still clenched in one fist.

Hell, I think as I reach for the cordless phone beside the futon, *if Chaz didn't want me to call the guy, then it must be the right thing to do.*

The place where we rendezvous is a twenty-four-hour establishment in the French Quarter that has, over the course of the last fifty years, been a bank, a show bar, and a porno shop before becoming a coffeehouse. We sit at a small table in the back and sip iced coffee.

Judd's hair is freshly washed and he smells of aftershave, but those are the only concessions he's made to the mating ritual. He still wears his nose and earrings and a Bongwater T-shirt that had been laundered so often the silk-screened image is starting to flake off.

Judd pokes at his iced coffee with a straw. 'If I'm not getting too personal, what was last night all about?'

I study my hands as I speak. 'Look, Judd. There's a lot about me you don't know, and I'd like to keep it that way. If you insist on poking into my past, I'm afraid I'll have to leave. It's not that I don't like you – I *do* – but I'm a very private person. And it's for a good reason.'

'Is . . . is there someone else?'

'Yes. Yes, there is.'

'A husband?'

I have to think about that one for a few seconds before answering. 'In some sense. But, no, I'm not legally married.'

Judd nods as if this explains something. It is obvious that some of what I've said is bothering him, but he is trying to play it cool. I wonder what it is like, living a life where the worst things you have to deal with are jealous lovers and hurt feelings. It seems almost idyllic from where I am.

After we finish our iced coffees, we hit the Quarter. It is after midnight, and the lower sector of Decatur Street, the portion located in the French Market, is starting to wake up. The streets outside the bars are decorated with clots of young people dressed in black leather, sequins, and recycled seventies rags. The hipsters mill about, flashing their tattoos and bumming cigarettes off one another, as they wait for something to happen.

Someone calls Judd's name and he swerves across the street towards a knot of youths lounging outside a dance bar called the Crystal Blue Persuasion. I hesitate before following him.

A young man dressed in a black duster, his shoulder-length hair braided into three pigtails and held in place by ivory beads carved in the shape of skulls, moves forward to greet Judd.

Out of habit, I scan his face for Pretender taint. Human. While the two speak, I casually examine the rest of the group loitering outside the club. Human. Human. Human. Hu—

I freeze.

The smell of *vargr* is strong, like the stink of a wet dog. It radiates from a young man with a shaved forehead, like that of an ancient samurai. The hair at the back of his head is extremely long and held in a loose ponytail, making him look like a punk mandarin. He wears a leather jacket, the sleeves of which look as if they've been chewed off at the shoulder, trailing streamers of mangled leather and lining like gristle. He has one arm draped over the shoulder of a little goth chick, her face made deathly pale by powder.

The *vargr* meets my gaze and holds it, grinning his contempt. Without realizing it, my hand closes around the switchblade.

'I'd like you to meet a friend of mine—'

Judd's hand is on my elbow, drawing my attention away from the teenaged werewolf.

'Sonja, I'd like you to meet Arlo, he's an old buddy of mine . . .'

Arlo frowns at me as if I've just emerged from under a rock, but offers his hand in deference to his friend. 'Pleased to meet you,' he mumbles.

'Yeah. Sure.'

I shoot a sidewise glance at the *vargr* twelve feet away. He is murmuring something into the punk girl's ear. She giggles and nods her head and the two break away from the rest of the group, sauntering down the street in the direction of the river.

The *vargr* pauses to give me one last look over his shoulder, his grin too wide and his teeth too big, before disappearing into the shadows with his victim.

That's right. Pretend you didn't see it. Pretend you don't know what that grinning hellhound's going to do with that girl. You can't offend lover boy here by running off to do hand-to-hand combat with a werewolf, can you?

'Shut the fuck up, damn you,' I mutter under my breath.

'You say something, Sonja?'

'Just talking to myself.'

After leaving Arlo and his friends, we head farther down Decatur. This is a part of the French Quarter that few tourists wander into after dark, populated by gay bars and less wholesome establishments. As we pass one of the seedy bars that cater to the late-night hardcore alcoholic trade, someone's mind calls my name.

A black man, his hair plaited into dreadlocks, steps from the doorway of the Monastery. He wears a black turtleneck sweater and immaculate designer jeans, a golden peace sign the size of a hood ornament slung around his neck.

'Long time no see, Blue.'

'Hello, Mal.'

The demon Malfeis smiles, exposing teeth that belong in the mouth of a shark. 'No hard feelings, I hope? I didn't want to sell you out like that, girlchick, but I was under orders from Below Stairs.'

'We'll talk about it later, Mal . . .'

Just then the demon notices Judd. 'Got yourself a new renfield, I see.'

'Shut up!' I hiss, my aura crackling like an electric halo.

Mal lifts his hands, palms outwards. 'Whoa! Didn't mean to hit a sore spot there, girly-girl.'

'Sonja? Is this guy bothering you?' Judd is hovering at my elbow. He gives Mal a suspicious glare, blind to the demon's true appearance.

'No. Everything's cool.' I turn my back on the grinning demon and try to block the sound of his laughter echoing in my mind.

'Who was that guy?'

'Judd—'

'I know! I promised I wouldn't pry into your past. But you can't expect me to just stand by and not say something—'

'Mal is a . . . business associate of mine. That's all you need to know about him, except that, no matter what, *never* ask him a question. *Never.*'

We walk on in silence for a few more minutes, then Judd takes my hand in his and squeezes it. We stop at the corner and he pulls me into his arms. His kiss is warm and probing and I feel myself begin to relax. Then he reaches for my sunglasses.

I bat his hand away, fighting the urge to snarl. 'Don't do that!'

'I just want to see your eyes.'

'No.' I pull away from him, my body rigid.

'I'm sorry—'

'I'd better leave. I had a nice time, Judd, I really did. But I have to go.'

'You'll call me, won't you?'

'I'm afraid so.'

Why don't you fuck him? He wants it bad. So do you. You can't hide that from me. The Other's voice is a nettle wedged into the folds of my brain, impossible to dislodge or ignore. I open the refrigerator and take out a bottle of whole blood, cracking its seal open as I would a beer.

Not that bottled crap again! I hate this shit! You might as well go back to drinking cats! Wouldn't you rather have something nice and fresh? Say a nice group B mugger or a group O rapist? There's still plenty of time to go trawling before the sun comes up . . . Or you could always pay a visit to lover boy.

'Shut up! I've had a bellyful of you tonight already!'

My-my! Aren't we being the touchy one? Tell me, how long do you think you can keep up the pretense of being normal? You've almost forgotten what it's like to be human yourself. Why torture yourself by pretending you're something you're not simply to win the favor of a piece of beefsteak?

'He likes me, damn it. He actually likes *me*.'

And what, exactly, are you?

'I'm not in the mood for your fuckin' mind games!'

Welcome to the fold, my dear. You're finally one of us. You're a Pretender.

I shriek and hurl the half-finished bottle of blood into the sink. I pick up the card table and smash it to the floor, jumping up and down on the scattered pieces. It is a stupid, pointless gesture, but it makes me feel better.

I keep calling him. I know it's stupid, even dangerous, to socialize with humans, but I can't help myself. There is something about him that keeps drawing me back, despite my better judgment. The only other time I've known such compulsion is when the Thirst is on me. Is this love? Or is it simply another form of hunger?

Our relationship, while charged with an undercurrent of eroticism, is essentially sexless. I want him so badly I dare not do more than kiss or hold hands. If I should lose control, there is no telling what might happen.

Judd, unlike Palmer, is not a sensitive. He is a human, blind and dumb to the miracles and terrors of the Real World, just like poor, doomed Claude Hagerty was. Rapid exposure to the world I inhabit could do immense damage.

To his credit, Judd has not pressed the sex issue overmuch. He is not happy with the arrangement, but honors my request that we 'take it slow'.

This, however, does not sit well with the Other. It constantly taunts me, goading me with obscene fantasies and suggestions concerning Judd. Or, failing to elicit a response using those tactics, it chastises me for being untrue to Palmer. I try to ignore its jibes as best I can, but I know that something, somewhere is bound to snap.

From the diaries of Sonja Blue

Kitty wiped at the tears oozing from the corners of her eyes, smearing mascara all over her cheek and the back of her hand. It made the words on the paper swim and crawl like insects, but she didn't care.

She loved him. She really, truly loved him. And maybe now, after she'd done what she had to do to save him, he'd finally believe her. Proof. He needed proof of her love. And what better proof than to rescue him from the clutches of a monster?

> *Dearest Judd,*
> *I tried to warn you about That Woman. But you are blind to what she Really Is. She is Evil Itself, a demon sent from Hell to claim your Soul! I knew her for what she truly is the moment I first saw her, and she knew I knew! Her hands and mouth drip blood! Her eyes burn with the fires of Hell! She is surrounded by a cloud of red energy. Red as blood. She means to drag you to Hell, Judd. But I won't let her. I love you too much to let that happen. I'll take care of this horrible monster, don't you worry. I've been talking to God a lot lately, and He told me how to deal with demons like her. I Love you so very, very much. I want you to Love me too. I'm doing this all for you. Please Love Me.*
> *Kitty*

Judd woke up at two in the afternoon, as usual. He worked six to midnight four days a week and had long since shifted over to a nocturnal lifestyle. After he got off work he normally headed down to the Quarter to chill with his buddies or, more recently, hang out with Sonja until four or five in the morning.

He yawned as he dumped a couple of heaping scoops of Guatemalan into the hopper of his Mr Coffee machine.

Sonja. Now there was a weird chick. Weird, but not in a schizzy, death-obsessed, art-school freshman way like Kitty. Her strangeness issued from something far deeper than bourgeois neurosis. Sonja was genuinely *out there*, wherever that might be. Something about the way she moved, the way she handled herself, suggested she was plugged into something Real. And as frustrating as her fits of mood might be, he could not bring himself to turn his back on her and walk away.

Still, it bothered him that none of his friends – not even Arlo, whom he'd known since high school – liked her. In fact, some even seemed to be *scared* of her. Funny. How could anyone be *frightened* of Sonja?

As he shuffled in the direction of the bathroom, he noticed an envelope shoved under his front door. He retrieved it, scowling at the all-too-familiar handwriting.

Kitty.

Probably another one of her damn fool love letters, alternately threatening him with castration and begging him to take her back. Lately she'd taken to leaving rambling, wigged-out messages on his answering machine, ranting about Sonja being some kind of vampire out to steal his soul. Crazy bitch. Sonja was crazy, too, but hardly predictable.

Judd tossed the envelope, unopened, into the trash can and staggered off to take a shower.

I greet the night from atop the roof of the warehouse where I make my nest. I stretch my arms wide as if to embrace the rising moon, listening with half an ear to the sound of the baying dogs along the riverbanks. Some, I know, are not dogs.

But the *vargr* are not my concern. I've tangled with a few over the years, but I prefer hunting my own kind. I find it vastly more satisfying.

The warehouse's exterior fire escape is badly rusted and groans noisily with the slightest movement, so I avoid it altogether. I crawl headfirst down the side of the building, moving like a lizard on a garden wall. Once I reach the bottom I routinely pat-check my jacket and pockets to make sure nothing has fallen out during my descent.

There is a sudden hissing sound in my head, as if someone has abruptly pumped up the volume on a radio tuned to a dead channel, and something heavy catches me between the shoulder blades, lifting me off my feet and knocking me into a row of garbage cans. I barely have time to roll out of the way before something big and silvery smashes down where my head was a second before. I cough and black blood flies from my lips; a rib has broken off and pierced my lungs again.

Kitty stands over me, clutching a three-foot-long silver crucifix like a baseball bat. Although her madness gives her strength, it is obvious the damn thing is still *heavy*. I wonder which church she managed to steal it from.

The dead-channel crackling in my head grows louder. It is the sound of homicidal rage. Shrieking incoherently, Kitty swings at me a third time. While crosses and crucifixes have no effect on me – or on any vampire, for that matter – if Kitty succeeds in landing a lucky blow and snaps my spine or cracks open my skull, I'm dead no matter what.

I roll clear and get to my feet in one swift, fluid motion. Kitty swings at me again, but this time I step inside her reach and grab the crucifix, wresting it from her. The crucifix is at least three inches thick, the cross beams as wide as a man's hand. At its center hangs a miniature Christ fashioned of gold and platinum. Kitty staggers back, staring in disbelief as I heft the heavy silver cross. She is waiting for my hands to burst into flames.

'What the hell did you think you were going to solve, clobbering me with this piece of junk?' I snarl.

Kitty's eyes are huge, the pupils swimming in madness. 'You can't have him! I won't let you take his soul!'

'Who said anything about me stealing—'

'Monster!' Kitty launches herself at me, her fingers clawing at my face. 'Monster!'

I hit her with the crucifix.

Kitty drops to the alley floor, the top of her skull resting on her left shoulder. The only things still holding her head onto her body are the muscles of her neck.

Way to go, kiddo! You just killed lover boy's bug-shit ex-girlfriend! You're batting a thousand!

'Damn.'

I toss the crucifix aside and squat next to the body. No need to check for vital signs. The girl is d-e-a-d.

What to do? I can't just toss the corpse in a dumpster. Someone is bound to find it, and once the body is identified, New Orleans Homicide will no doubt bring Judd in for questioning. Which means they'd be looking for *me*, sooner or later. And I can't have *that*.

I've got an idea, croons the Other. *Just let me handle it.*

Stealing the car is easy. It's a '76 Ford Ltd with a muffler held in place with baling wire, and a *Duke for Governor* sticker on the sagging rear bumper. Just the thing to unobtrusively dispose of a murder victim in the swamps surrounding New Orleans during the dead of night.

I take an exit off the Interstate leading out of New Orleans East. Originally it was to have connected a cookie-cutter housing development built on the very fringes of the marshlands to the rest of the world. The contractors got as far as pouring the concrete slab foundations before the recession hit. The condos were never built, but the access road remains, although there is nothing at its end but an overgrown tangle of briars and vines that has become a breeding ground for snakes and alligators.

I drive without lights. Not that I need them. I can see just fine in the dark. Having reached my destination, I cut the engine and roll to a stop. Except for the croaking of frogs and the grunting of gators, everything is quiet.

I climb out of the car and open the trunk with a length of bent coat hanger. I stand for a second, silently inventorying the collection of plastic trash bags. There are six: one for the head, one for the torso, and one apiece for each limb. I've already burned Kitty's clothing in the warehouse's furnace and disposed of her jewelry and teeth by tossing them into the river.

I gather up the bags and leave the road, heading in the direction of the bayou. I can hear things splashing in the water, some of them quite large. I pause for a second on the bank of the bayou. Something nearby hisses. I toss the bag containing Kitty's head into the murky water.

'Come and get it!'

The assembled gators splash and wrestle amongst themselves for the tender morsels like ducks fighting for scraps of stale bread.

I am tired. Very tired. After this is over I still have to drive the car I stole to a suitably disreputable urban area and set it on fire. I look down at my hands. They are streaked with blood. I absently lick them clean.

When I am finished, the Other looks through my eyes and smiles.

The Other isn't tired. Not in the least.

From the diaries of Sonja Blue

It hadn't been a very good night, as far as Judd was concerned. He'd been chewed out concerning his attitude at work, Arlo and the others treated him like he had a championship case of halitosis, and, to cap the evening, Sonja pulled a no-show. Time to pack it in.

It was four in the morning by the time he got home. He was in such a piss-poor mood he didn't even bother to turn on the lights. His answering machine, for once, didn't have one of Kitty's bizarre messages on it. Nothing from Sonja, either. He grunted as he removed his shirt. Was she mad at him? Did he say or do something the last time they were together that ticked her off? It was hard to figure out her moods, since she refused to take off those damn mirrored sunglasses. Judd wondered, not for the first time, how she could navigate in the dark so well while wearing those fuckers.

Out of the corner of his eye he saw something move. It was the curtain covering the window that faced the alley. Judd frowned as he went to close the window. Funny, he didn't remember leaving the window open . . .

She stepped out of the shadows, greeting him with a smile that displayed teeth that were too sharp. She could smell the adrenaline coursing through him as his system jerked itself into overdrive. He was about to yell for help, then he recognized her. Or thought he did.

'S-Sonja?'

'Did I scare you?' She sounded like pain given voice. She sniffed the air and her smile grew even sharper. 'Yes. Yes, I *did* scare you, didn't I?' She moved toward him, her hands making slow, hypnotic passes as she spoke. 'I *love* the smell of fear in the morning.'

'Sonja, what's wrong with your voice?'

'Wrong?' She chuckled as she unzipped her leather jacket. 'I always sound like this!'

She was on him so fast he didn't even see her move, lifting him by his belt buckle and flinging him onto the bed so hard he bounced. She grabbed his jaw in one hand, angling it back so the jugular was exposed. Judd heard the *snikt!* of a switchblade and felt a cold, sharp pressure against his throat.

'*Sonja?*'

'Do not struggle. Do not cry out. Do as I command, and maybe I'll let you live. Maybe.'

'What do you want?'

'Why, my dear, I just want to get to know you better.' She removed the sunglasses protecting her eyes. 'And vice versa.'

Judd had often begged Sonja to let him look at her eyes. Were they almond-shaped or round? Blue or brown or green? No doubt he'd always imagined them as looking human, though. Certainly he hadn't pictured them as blood-red with pupils so hugely dilated they resembled shoe buttons.

She smirked, savoring the look of disgust on Judd's face. She pressed her lips against his, thrusting his teeth apart with her tongue, and penetrated his will with one quick shove of her mind.

Judd's limbs twitched convulsively as she took control of his nervous system, then went still. She disengaged, physically, and stared down at him. He did not move. She had made sure of that. His body was locked into partial paralysis. Satisfied her control was secure, she moved the switchblade away from Judd's throat.

'I can see why she finds you attractive. You're a pretty thing . . . *very* pretty.' She reached out and pinched one of his nipples. Judd didn't flinch. Of course not. She did not give him permission to.

'But she's much too old-fashioned when it comes to sex, don't you agree? She's afraid to let herself go and walk on the wild side. She's *so* repressed.' She shrugged out of her leather jacket, allowing it to fall to the floor.

'I will explain this to you once, and once only. I *own* you. If you do as I tell you, and you please me, then you shall be rewarded. Like *this*.'

She reached into his cortex and tweaked its pleasure center. Judd shuddered as the wave of ecstasy swept over him, his hips involuntarily humping empty air.

'But if you fight me, or displease me in *any* way, then I will punish you. Like *so*.'

Judd emitted a strangled cry of pain as he was speared through the pain receptor in his head. It was as if the top of his skull had been removed and someone had dumped the contents of an ant farm on his exposed brain. His back arched until the muscles creaked. Then the pain stopped as if it had never been there at all.

'Hold me.'

Judd did as he was told, dragging himself upright and wrapping his arms around her waist. She knotted her fingers in his hair, pulling his head back so she could look into his

56

eyes. There was fear there. Fear – and something more. She liked that.

'Am I hurting you? Say yes.'

'Yes.'

She smiled, exposing her fangs, and he realized then that it was just beginning. The fear in Judd's eyes gave way to terror. And she liked that even more.

They fucked for three solid hours. She skillfully manipulated Judd's pleasure centers so he remained perpetually erect, despite exhaustion. She randomly induced orgasms, often one right after another, until they numbered in the dozens. After the seventh or eighth orgasm, Judd was shooting air. She enjoyed how he wailed in pain each time he spasmed.

As dawn began to make its way into the room, she severed her control of Judd's body. He fell away from her in mid-thrust, his eyes rolled back behind flickering lids. She dressed quickly, her attention fixed on the rising sun. Judd lay curled in a fetal position on the soiled and tangled bedclothes, his naked body shuddering and jerking as his nervous system reasserted its control.

'Parting is such sweet sorrow,' she purred, caressing his shivering flank. Judd gasped at her touch but did not pull away.

'You pleased me. This time. So I will let you live. This time.'

She lowered her head, brushing his jugular lightly with her lips. Judd squeezed his eyes shut in anticipation of the bite. But all she did was whisper: 'Get used to it, lover boy.'

When he opened his eyes again, she was gone. For the time being.

The Other takes a great deal of pleasure in telling me what it did to Judd, making sure not to leave out a single, nasty detail as it reruns the morning's exploits inside my skull.

My response to the news is to scream and run headfirst into the nearest wall. Then to continue pounding my skull against the floorboards until my glasses shatter and blood streams down my face and mats my hair. I succeed in breaking my nose and shattering both cheekbones before collapsing.

It's not enough.

'Girly-girl! Long time no see! What brings you into my little den of iniquity this time?'

The demon Malfeis sports the exterior of a flabby white male in late middle age, dressed in a loud plaid polyester leisure suit with white buck loafers. A collection of gold medallions dangle under his chins, and he holds a racing form in one hand.

I slide into the booth opposite the demon. 'I need magic, Mal.'

'Don't we all? Say, what's with the face? You can reconstruct better than that!'

I shrug, one hand straying to my swollen left cheek. The bone squelches under my fingertips and slides slightly askew. Heavy-duty facial reconstruction requires feeding for it to be done right, and I deliberately skipped my waking meal.

'You tangle with an ogre? One of those *vargr* punks?'

'Leave it be, Mal.'

Malfeis shrugs. 'Just trying to be friendly, that's all. Now, what kind of magic are you in the market for?'

'Binding and containment.'

The demon grunts and fishes out a pocket calculator. 'What are you looking to bind? Ghost? Elemental? Demon? Muse? There's a difference in the prices, you know.'

'Myself.'

'Huh?' Mal halts in mid-computation, his exterior flickering for a moment to reveal a hulking creature that resembles an orangutan with a boar's snout.

'You heard me. I wish to have myself bound and contained.'

'Sonja—'

'Name your price, damn you.'

'Don't be redundant, girlchick.'

I sigh and heft a knapsack onto the tabletop. 'I brought some of my finest acquisitions. I've got hair shaved from Ted Bundy's head just before he went to the chair, dried blood scraped from the walls of the Labianco home, a spent rifle casing from the grassy knoll, and a cedar cigar box with what's left of Rasputin's penis in it. Quality shit. I swear by its authenticity. And it's all yours, if you do this for me.'

Malfeis fidgets, drumming his talons against the table. Such close proximity to so much human suffering and evil is bringing on a jones. 'Okay. I'll do it. But I'm not going to take responsibility for anything that happens to you.'

'Did I ask you to?'

'Are you *sure* you want to go through with this, Sonja?'

'Your concern touches me, Mal. It really does.'

The demon shakes his head in disbelief. 'You really mean to go through with this, don't you?'

'I've already said so, haven't I?'

'Sonja, you realize once you're in there, there's no way you'll be able to get out, unless someone breaks the seal.'

'Maybe.'

'There's no *maybe* to it!' he retorts.

'The spell you're using is for the binding and containing of vampiric energies, right?'

'Of course. You're a vampire.'

I shrug. 'Part of me is. And I'm not letting it out to hurt anyone ever again. I'm going to kill it or die trying.'

'You're going to *starve* in there!'

'That's the whole point.'

'Whatever you say, girly-girl.'

I hug myself as I stare into the open doorway of the meat locker. It is cold and dark inside, just like my heart. 'Let's get this show on the road.'

Malfeis nods and produces a number of candles, bottles of oil, pieces of black chalk, and vials of white powder from his black gladstone bag. I swallow and step inside the meat locker, closing the heavy door behind me with a muffled thump.

From the diaries of Sonja Blue

Malfeis lighted the candles and began to chant in a deep, sonorous voice, scrawling elaborate designs on the outer walls of the locker with the black chalk. As the chanting grew faster and more impassioned, he smeared oil on the hinges and handle of the door. There was an electric crackle and the door glowed with blue fire.

Malfeis's incantation lost its resemblance to human speech as it reached its climax. He carefully poured a line of white powder, made from equal parts salt, sand, and the crushed bones of unbaptized babies, across the threshold. Then he stepped back to assess his handiwork.

To human eyes it looked like someone had scrawled graffiti all over the face of the stainless-steel locker, nothing more. But to Pretender eyes, eyes adjusted to the Real World, the door to the locker was barred shut by a tangle of darkly pulsing *veve*, the semi-sentient protective symbols of the voodoo powers. As long as the tableau remained undisturbed, the entity known as Sonja Blue would remain trapped within the chill darkness of the meat locker.

Malfeis replaced the tools of his trade in his gladstone bag. He paused as he left the warehouse, glancing over his shoulder.

'Goodbye, girly-girl. It was nice knowing you.'

'I'm looking for Mal.'

The bartender looked up from his racing form and frowned at Judd. After taking in his unwashed hair and four days' growth of beard, he nodded in the direction of the back booth.

Judd had never been inside the Monastery before. It had a reputation for being one of the more sleazy – and unsavory

– French Quarter dives, and he could see why. The booths lining the wall had once been church pews. Plaster saints in various stages of decay were on display. A Madonna, skin blackened and made leprous by age, regarded him from above the bar with flat, faded blue eyes. She held in her arms an equally scabrous Christ-child, its uplifted chubby arms ending in misshapen stumps. Hardly a place to party down big time.

He walked to the back of the bar and looked into the last booth. All he saw was a paunchy middle-aged man dressed in a bad suit smoking a cigar and reading a racing form.

'Excuse me?'

The man in the bad suit looked up at him, arching a bushy, upswept eyebrow.

'Uh, excuse me, but I'm looking for Mal.'

'You found him.'

Judd blinked, confused. 'No, I'm afraid there's been some kind of mistake. The guy I'm looking for is black, with dreadlocks . . .'

The man in the bad suit smiled. It was not a pleasant sight. 'Sit down, kid. He'll be with you in just a moment.'

Still uncertain of what he was getting himself into, Judd slid into the opposite pew.

The older man lowered his head, exposing a bald pate, and hunched his shoulders. His fingers and arms began to vibrate, the skin growing darker as if his entire body had become suddenly bruised. There was the sound of dry grass rustling under a high wind and thick, black dreadlocks emerged from his scalp, whipping about like a nest of snakes. Judd was too shocked by the transformation to do anything but stare.

Mal lifted his head and grinned at Judd, tugging at the collar of his turtleneck. 'Ah, yes. I remember you now. Sonja's renfield.'

'M-my name's not Renfield.'

Mal shrugged his indifference. 'So, what brings you here, boychick?'

'I'm looking for Sonja. I can't find her.'

'She doesn't want to be found.'

'I *have* to find her! I just *have* to! Before she does something stupid. Kills herself, maybe!'

Mal regarded the young human for a long moment. 'Tell me more.'

'Something . . . happened between us. She feels responsible for hurting me. She sent me this letter a few days ago.' Judd fished a folded envelope out of his back pocket and held it out to Mal. 'Here, you read it.'

The demon plucked the letter out of its envelope like a gourmet removing an escargot from its shell. He unfolded the paper, noting the lack of signature and the smears of blood on its edges.

Judd,

I can never be forgiven for what was done to you. I was not the one who did those things to you. Please believe that. It was her. She is the one that makes me kill and hurt people. Hurt you. I promise I'll never let her hurt anyone, ever again. Especially you. I'm going to do something I should have tried years ago, before she became so strong. So dangerous. So uncontrollable. She's sated right now. Asleep in my head. By the time she becomes aware of what I'm planning to do, it'll be too late. I'm going to kill her. I might end up killing myself in the bargain, but that's a chance I'm willing to take. I won't let her hurt anyone again, damn her. I love you, Judd. Please believe that. Don't try to find me. Escape while you can.

'She doesn't understand.' Judd was now close to tears. 'I do forgive her. I *love* her, damn it! I can't let her *die!*'

'You know what she is.' It wasn't a question.

Judd nodded. 'And I don't *care*.'

'And why have you come to me?'

'You know where she is, don't you?'

Malfeis shifted in his seat, his eyes developing reptilian slits. 'Are you asking me a question?'

Judd hesitated, recalling Sonja's warning that he should *never*, under any circumstances, ask Mal a question.

'Uh, yeah.'

Mal smiled, displaying shark's teeth. 'Before I respond to any questions put to me, you must pay the price of the answer. Is that understood, boychick?'

Judd swallowed and nodded.

'Very well. Tell me your name. All of it.'

'Michael Judd Rieser. Is that it? That's all you want? My name?'

'To know a thing's name gives one power over that thing, my sweet. Didn't they teach you that in school? Come to think of it, I guess not.'

'What about my question? Do you know where Sonja is?'

'Yes, I *do* know.' The demon scrawled an address on the back of the letter Judd had given him. 'You'll find her here. She's inside the meat locker on the ground floor.'

'*Meat locker?*'

'I wouldn't open it, if I were you.'

Judd snatched up the address and slid out of the pew. 'But I'm *not* you!'

Malfeis watched Judd hurry out of the bar with an amused grin. 'That's what *you* think, boychick.' He leaned back and closed his eyes. When he reopened them, he had shoulder-length hair pulled up in a ponytail, a ring in his nose, and four days' growth of beard.

It is cold. So very, very cold.

I am huddled in the far corner of the meat locker, my knees drawn up to my chest. My breath drifts from my mouth and nostrils in wisps before condensing and turning to frost on my face.

How long? How many days have I been in here? Three? Four? Twenty? A hundred? There is no way of telling. I no longer sleep. The Other's screams and curses keep me awake.

Let me out! Let me out of this hellhole! I've got to feed! I'm starving!

'Good.'

You stupid cunt! If I starve to death, you go with me! I'm not a damned tapeworm!

'Couldn't prove it by me.'

I'm getting out of here! I don't care what you say!

I do not fight the Other as it asserts its ascendancy over my body. The Other forces stiffened limbs to bend, levering me onto my feet. My joints crack like rotten timber as I move. The Other staggers in the direction of the door. In my weakened condition I have difficulty seeing in the pitch-black of the meat locker. I abandoned the sunglasses days ago, but as my condition worsened, so did my night vision.

The Other's groping hands close on the door's interior handle. There is a sharp crackle and a flash of blue light as the Other is thrown halfway across the locker. It screams and writhes like a cat hit by a car, holding its blistered, smoking hands away from its body. This is the twentieth time it's tried to open the door and several fingers are on the verge of gangrene.

'You're not going anywhere. Not now. Not ever!'

Fuck you! Fuck you! I'll get you for this, you human-loving cow!

'What? Are you gonna *kill* me?'

I crawl back to my place in the corner. The effort starts me coughing again, bringing up black, clotted blood. I wipe at my mouth with the sleeve of my jacket, nearly dislocating my jaw in the process.

You're falling apart. You're too weak to regenerate properly . . .

'If you hadn't pounded your head against the fuckin' wall trying to get out in the first place—'

You're the one that got us locked up in here! Don't blame me!

'I *am* blaming you. But not for that.'

It's that fucking stupid human again! You think you can punish me for that? I didn't do anything that you hadn't already fantasized about!

'You *raped* him, damn you! You almost killed him!'
I didn't, though. I could have. But I didn't.
'I *love* him!' My voice cracks, becomes a sob.
You don't love him. You love being mistaken for human. That's what you're mad about; not that I molested your precious lover boy, but that I ruined your little game of Let's Pretend!
'Shut up.'
Make me.

From the diaries of Sonja Blue

Judd checked the street number of the warehouse against the address that Mal had given him. It was one of the few remaining warehouses in the district that had not been turned into trendy yuppie condominiums. There was a small sign posted on the front door that read 'Indigo Imports', but nothing else. A heavy chain and double padlock secured the entrance, and all the ground-floor windows were barred. But there had to be *some* way of getting in and out. He rounded the side of the building and spotted the loading dock. After a few minutes of determined tugging, he succeeded in wrenching one of the sliding corrugated metal doors far enough open to slip through.

The inside of the warehouse was lit by the mid-afternoon sunlight slanting through the barred windows. The whole place smelled of dust and rat piss. The meat locker was on the ground floor, just where Mal said it would be. Its metal walls and door were covered in swirls of spray-painted graffiti. What looked like a huge line of coke marked the locker's threshold. Judd grabbed the door's handle and yanked it open. There was a faint crackling sound, like that of static electricity, and a rush of cold, foul air. He squinted into the darkness, covering his nose and breathing through his mouth to try and mask the stench.

'Sonja?'

Something moved in the deepest shadows of the freezer.

*   *   *

'J-Judd? Is that you?'

'It's me, baby. I've come to get you out of here.'

'Go away, Judd. You don't know what you're doing.'

Judd steps into the locker, his eyes adjusting to the gloom. He sees me now, crouching in the far corner with my knees drawn against my chest, my face turned to the wall.

'No, you're wrong, Sonja. I know *exactly* what I'm doing.'

'I let her hurt you, Judd. I could have stopped her, but I didn't. I let her . . . let her—' My voice grows tight and my shoulders begin to shake. 'Go away, Judd. Go away before I hurt you again!'

Judd kneels beside me. I smell like a side of beef gone bad. My hands are covered with blisters and oozing sores. Some of the fingers jut at odd angles, since I'd broken them and they healed without being properly set. I pull away at his touch, pressing myself against the wall as if I can squeeze between the cracks if I try hard enough.

'Don't look at me.'

'Sonja, you don't understand. I *love* you. I know what you are, what you're capable of, and I love you *anyway*.'

'Even if I hurt you?'

'*Especially* when you hurt me.'

I turn my head in his direction. My face looks like it has been smashed then reassembled by a well-meaning but inept plastic surgeon who only had a blurry photograph to go by. My eyes glow like those of an animal pinned in the headlights of an oncoming car.

'What?'

Judd leans closer, his eyes reflecting a hunger I know all too well. 'When you did those things to me, at first I was scared. Then, after a while, I realized I wasn't frightened anymore. I was actually getting into it. It was like the barriers between pain and pleasure, animal and human, ecstasy and horror, had been removed! I've never known anything like it before! I love you, Sonja! *All* of you!'

I reach out and caress his face with one of my charred hands. A renfield. The Other turned him into a renfield. And he doesn't even know it, the poor sap. In the space of just a few hours he had been transformed into a junkie, and now I'm his fix.

'I love you, too, Judd. Kiss me.'

I want to think I am being merciful.

I sit behind the wheel of the car for a long time, staring out into the dark on the other side of the windshield. Nothing has changed since the last time I was out here, disposing of Kitty.

I press my fingertips against my right cheek, and this time it holds. My fingers are healed and straight again, as well. I readjust my shades and open the car door and slide out from behind the wheel of the Caddy I bought off the lot, cash in hand, earlier in the evening.

Judd is in the trunk, divvied up into six garbage bags, just like Kitty. At least it was fast. My hunger was so intense, I drained him within seconds. He didn't try to fight when I buried my fangs in his throat, even though I didn't have the strength to trance him. Maybe part of him knew I was doing him a favor.

I drag the bags out of the trunk and head in the direction of the alligator calls. I have to leave New Orleans, maybe for good this time. Kitty might not have been missed, but Judd is another story. Arlo is sure to mention the missing Judd's weirdo new girlfriend to the authorities.

It is time to blow town and head for Mérida. Time to go and pay Palmer a visit and check on how he and the baby are making out.

Palmer.

Funny how I'd forgotten him. Of all my human companions, he is the only one I've come close to loving. Before Judd.

I hurl the sacks containing Judd's remains into the water and return to the car. I try not to hear the noise the gators make as they fight amongst themselves.

I climb back into the car and slam a cassette into the Caddy's tape deck. Lard's *The Last Temptation of Reid* thunders through the speakers, causing the steering wheel to vibrate under my hands. I wonder when the emptiness will go away. Or at least be replaced by pain. Anything would be preferable to the nothing inside me.

I don't see why you had to go and kill him like that. We could have used a renfield. They do come in handy, now and then. Besides, he was kind of cute . . .

'Shut up and drive.'

From the diaries of Sonja Blue

4

It was late afternoon, sliding toward evening, and Palmer was out in the courtyard, hammering together a shipping crate for a collection of hand-painted Day of the Dead masks. The masks – made of papier-mâché and painted in primary colors so bright you could still see them when you closed your eyes – were piled in a small heap nearby, grimacing blindly at the failing sun.

Palmer dropped his hammer and straightened up, massaging his lower back. He pulled a bandanna from his pocket and mopped his brow. God, he hated this part of the business. Building the crates for shipping was a relatively minor hassle. It was loading up the Land Rover and taking it into the city that was the real ball-buster. Still, the pay was pretty good, and money went a lot farther in Yucatán than it did back in the US.

Looking down, his gaze fell across the masks in their nest of excelsior. He'd bought them as part of a larger job lot from a family of artisans who'd been producing carnival decorations for over four generations. Until now, he hadn't paid that much attention to them. He shifted through the collection, studying the workmanship. Most of the masks were small, designed to cover the face of a child. All of the traditional carnival personae were represented: there were skeletons, their teeth bared in aggressive, lipless grins; what were supposed to be tigers, judging by the stripes, but looked more like jaguars, broom-straw whiskers bristling from snarling muzzles; blood-red devils with grease-pencil mustaches and shoe-polish goatees, licorice-black horns jutting from their foreheads; grinning clowns whose noses and chins met, like the ancient Punch puppets of Europe.

Yet there were less typical false faces scattered throughout: a sheep's head, the wool cunningly made from balls of cotton; a wolf, fangs bared in a predatory snarl; a rooster caught in mid-crow, its beak open and throat sac extended. Palmer chuckled to himself as he sifted through the empty masks, remembering Halloweens spent dressed as a pirate, a cowboy, a hobo, and other exotica.

Then he found the black mask.

It was at the very bottom of the pile. He frowned and picked it up, turning it over in his hands. Like the others, it was papier-mâché. Unlike the others, it was adult-sized. And, except for the eyeholes, it was without features of any kind. There were no overexaggerated human or animal characteristics, merely an oval painted black and coated with several layers of varnish, so that it shone like a scarab's carapace. There was something oddly compelling about the mask, something that made him set it aside from the others as he prepared to load them into their crate.

It was dusk by the time he finished driving the last nail into place. He tossed the hammer back into the toolbox and stepped back to appraise his handiwork. A boot heel scraped behind him. There was a figure standing in the door leading to the front of the house. Whatever had breached the security of his home could not be human, or else he would have heard – or at least felt – its thoughts long before it reached the front door.

Before Palmer could launch his psionic strike, the figure laughed dryly and stepped from the shadows.

'Hello, Bill. Did you miss me?'

'Sonja!'

She stood there looking tired, her leather jacket powdered with road dust, her mirrored shades equally grimy. In one hand she held a battered black nylon duffel bag, in the other a neatly wrapped present bound with colored twine. She smiled tightly, as if the corners of her mouth concealed fishhooks. Her head was surrounded by a blackish-red halo that strobed and pulsated like a lava lamp. The Other was very active tonight, it seemed. Palmer tried not to let his dismay taint his own aura.

He hugged her, savoring the smell of her as he pressed his face into her hair. For a moment her shoulders seemed to quiver, as if struggling to shrug off an invisible burden.

'Auntie Blue! Auntie Blue!'

Palmer and Sonja stepped apart as Lethe bounded onto the patio, grinning broadly. Dressed in a Teenage Mutant Ninja Turtle T-shirt and a pair of bright yellow stirrup pants, she could have passed for a normal child – except for her golden, pupil-less eyes. Shambling in her wake, Fido paused at the sight of Sonja. Although Palmer could rarely 'read' the seraphim's aura, he knew that it, too, was disturbed by evidence of the Other's activity.

Sonja smiled at the sight of her godchild, the stress draining from her face, and dropped down on one knee, opening her arms wide. 'C'mere and give me a hug, sweetie!'

Lethe shot into Sonja's arms like an arrow, clinging to her tightly.

'Are you staying this time, Auntie? Are you really staying for good?'

'Maybe not for good, but at least for a couple of months. Here, let me have a look at you . . . You've grown, child! Hasn't she, Bill?'

'Eighteen inches in the last six months.'

'Did you bring me something, Auntie Blue?'

Sonja laughed and ruffled Lethe's dark hair. 'Here you go, darling. I just hope you haven't gotten too big for dolls.'

'I'll never be too big for dolls! They're my babies!'

Palmer stepped forward, gently nudging Lethe in the direction of the house. 'Lethe, why don't you and Fido go play with your new doll? Auntie Blue and I have some things to talk about. And tell her thank you for the gift.'

'Okay, Daddy. Thank you, Auntie!'

Sonja watched as Lethe skipped away, Fido lumbering after her like a demented pull-toy.

'She's big, Bill. Too big for thirty months.'

'You're telling me? That's why I've been trying to get you to come home. We need to figure out what to do with her.'

It was several hours before they could be alone. First Palmer had to prepare dinner for those members of the household that actually ate food, then they had to go through the process of readying Lethe for bed. After baths and bedtime stories, it was close to midnight before he could join Sonja on the front porch. He found her curled up in the hammock, watching the night sky. She was still wearing her sunglasses.

'I brought some refreshments,' he said, holding up a bottle of tequila. 'Any room there for me?'

'Maybe,' Sonja smiled, moving so he could join her.

Palmer cracked the seal on the bottle and took a hefty swig before placing it on the floorboards of the porch. He lifted his arm and Sonja flowed into its hollow like a shadow, one cheek pressed against his breastbone. They lay there for a long moment, Palmer idly stroking her hair.

'Things are getting weird, Sonja.'

She lifted her head from his chest and gave him a quizzical look. '"Getting"? I thought they'd been there for some time now!'

'You know what I mean. This stuff with Lethe is getting out of hand – I don't know what to expect from her one day to the next! Hell, this time last year she looked like she was ready for kindergarten! Now she looks like she should be in the fourth grade!'

'Is she giving you problems?'

'No, far from it. She's a little angel. A little rambunctious at times, but she's no real trouble. But she's starting to want to go with me on my trips to the city. She's becoming curious about the outside world. We can't keep her hidden away forever, Sonja.'

'We can't risk anyone finding out about her. You know that as well as I do. If Morgan discovers where she is, there's no telling what he'd do to her. Or with her. I promised her parents I'd never let Lethe fall into that bastard's hands. Besides, the locals would probably not look kindly on a child as . . . unique . . . as Lethe.'

'I realize that, Sonja. It's just that . . . well, it's not *natural* for her to be alone like this! All she has in the way of playmates are Fido, Lefty, and me. That's hardly what I'd call a "well-rounded" play atmosphere.'

'What do you expect me to do? I know as much about Lethe's true nature as you do. Hell, you probably know more, since you're the one who actually takes care of her. As far as I can tell, she's a healthy little girl who just happens to be somewhat . . . advanced . . . for her age. There's nothing either of us can do except try and take care of her and wait to see what will happen. And as to her having playmates . . . well, Fido and Lefty will have to do for the time being. At least she isn't being raised by the lousy TV set!'

The subject was closed. Palmer knew enough not to reopen it. At least not now. He took another hit from the tequila bottle, offering it to Sonja. She shook her head.

'So . . . How was New Orleans?'

Her body tensed, like a cat preparing to leap. 'Fine. Why do you ask?'

'No reason. Just curious, that's all. That's where we first met, after all. Remember?'

'Yeah. I remember.'

'Hey, what's wrong? You're really tense, you know that? I feel like I'm cuddling an ironing board!'

'Sorry,' she muttered, pulling away from him. 'I guess I'm not ready to relax yet. It's just that I . . .' She let the sentence trail off.

'Just what? Did something happen in New Orleans?'

She turned her mirrored gaze away from him. 'I had some trouble with the Other. Bad stuff.'

'Want to tell me about it?'

Silence.

Palmer took another hit from the tequila and began to climb free of the hammock. 'I better go check on Lethe . . .'

Sonja touched his arm. 'No, you stay here. Let me do it.'

Palmer shrugged and settled back. 'Whatever. Bring me back a couple of beers, won't you?'

'Sure thing.' As Sonja entered the house she paused on the threshold, fixing Palmer with her unreadable eyes. 'Do you love me?'

Palmer looked up, slightly taken aback by the question. She rarely spoke the word 'love' with her mouth – only her mind. 'Of course I love you!' He gave a short laugh to show how silly a question it was.

She paused, as if weighing his response. 'Why?'

Palmer blinked, his smile slowly dissolving into a frown. 'I just love you, that's all.'

'Oh.' Again the pause. 'I'll be back with your beer in a few minutes.'

Palmer sat in the hammock under the starlit sky, listening to the calls of the night birds, and wondered what the hell had gone down in New Orleans.

The door to Lethe's bedroom was slightly ajar, allowing light from the hall to filter in, so Lethe wouldn't wake up in the middle of the night and be scared to find herself alone in the dark. Sonja was uncertain whether Lethe was actually scared of the dark or not, but it seemed the proper thing to do.

She stuck her head inside the door, her eyes automatically adjusting to the dim light. Lethe lay on her side, her back to the door, surrounded by a multitude of dolls. She had kicked off her bedclothes. Sonja stepped inside the room, quiet as a shadow, and stooped to retrieve the discarded covers. As she straightened up, she noticed something moving out of the corner of her eye.

Fido had shifted from its sentinel position at the foot of the bed, its eyes glowing like molten ore. Although she knew the seraphim meant her no harm, Sonja felt the hair on her scalp prickle and a low, guttural growl begin deep inside her chest.

Lethe rolled over and opened her eyes, smiling beatifically. 'Don't be afraid, Auntie Blue. Fido's just protectin' me, that's all.'

'Why should he have to protect you from me? I'd never hurt you, sweetie.'

'I know, Auntie. But the Other would. It wants to hurt me right now, doesn't it?'

Smart little fucker, isn't she?

'I would never let the Other harm you, Lethe. You know that.'

'I know, Auntie Blue. But Fido isn't so sure.'

Palmer started from a light doze as a Tecate, still dripping ice from the cooler, was pressed into his hand. He jerked awake like a science-lab frog zapped by a dry-cell battery.

'Uhn! Oh, thanks.' He tilted back the bottle for a quick slug. Sonja straddled him as he lay in the hammock. Except for her sunglasses, she was naked.

She perched atop his crotch, the moonlight outlining her body in silver and shadow. Her breasts were still as full, her stomach and thighs just as taut as he remembered. Perhaps even more so. Palmer set aside his beer and reached up with one damp hand to tweak her nipples. They were cool and hard between his fingers, like smooth little stones.

She reached down with one hand and yanked open his denim shirt as if it was made of newspaper, sending buttons flying in every direction. Lowering herself atop him, she slid her legs down his, wrapping her arms around his neck. Palmer caressed her naked hips and she moved to fill his hand, like a cat eager to be stroked. A heady rush of arousal and fear surged through him, as it always did before their lovemaking.

On a deep, instinctual level, Palmer knew the beautiful creature that fondled him was death personified; yet he trusted her not to kill him. His physical excitement came from the knowledge that his lover could, at any given moment, tear him apart like fresh bread.

The moment his fly was open, Palmer's penis leapt free. He closed his eyes as Sonja took him into her mouth, exhaling a long sigh as the curvature of her fangs glided against the head of his penis. A sane man would go limp knowing razor-sharp teeth encircled his cock. But Palmer hadn't been sane in a long while. Trembling, he pulled her head away from his crotch, gasping between his teeth as he fought to regain control.

She moved quickly, lowering herself onto him before he could protest. Palmer reached up to cup her breasts and, with a firm upward thrust of his hips, penetrated both her body and her mind. To tell the truth, he missed the mental bonding more than he missed the physical aspects of sex. He could always jerk off when she was gone, but there was no such thing as masturbatory telepathy. And without further effort, he surrendered all thought and self, all barriers dissolving with the bond.

Once again Palmer found himself in the other place he and Sonja shared during their trysts. As he moved through a gray space that was neither air nor water, he was uncertain whether he was flying or swimming. It was warm and comforting, like he imagined the womb must be. Sonja emerged from the gray, as swift and sure as a shark in its element, her features blurred by speed. She wrapped herself around Palmer, her arms and legs impossibly long and tapered. Her hair was a dark blur, trailing behind her like jet exhaust. She looked more like a nude painted by an Impressionist than a flesh-and-blood woman.

He wrapped his own limbs about her, pulling her into himself. Thoughts, feelings, perceptions jittered between them like static electricity, the inner voices growing louder and softer as they merged. This sharing of self and experience, more than anything else, was how they managed to 'catch up' with one another after so many months apart. Sonja's face floated inside his mind's eye, the features softened by release as she flowed into him and he into her.

Missed you . . .
Need you . . .
Love you . . .
Worried . . .
Gone so long . . .
Love you . . .
Judd . . .
Judd?

Sonja's eyes went hard and cold and suddenly Palmer was no longer in the warm gray place, but falling, plummeting through space as if he had stepped from the lip of a cliff into the deepest, darkest pit in the Carlsbad Cavern. It felt as if he was spiraling down, down, down into the mouth of hell itself. The transition was so sudden, he didn't even have the time or breath to scream for his life.

He hit hard, but because he was not a physical thing, there were no broken bones. He groaned and got to his feet, surveying his new surroundings. The first thing he felt was the wind, cutting into him like a flaying knife. He was in the middle of a vast arctic ice field, a dark, moon-haunted sky overhead. In the far distance he could make out the humps of vast glacier-bound mountains. As he turned around, shuddering in the frigid mind winds, he marveled at the frozen desolation surrounding him. There was nothing but an empty tract of ice, gleaming blackly in the moonlight. As far as he could tell, he was the only living thing to be seen for thousands of miles in any direction.

Sonja?

77

There was no answer to his mind call as it echoed across the frozen sea.

SONJA!

Nothing moved or waved or responded to his cry.

Exasperated, and starting to get a little scared, Palmer struck off in the direction of the full moon on the horizon. He didn't know why – it simply seemed like the thing to do. He had never gotten lost inside anyone before – at least he assumed the ice-bound tundra was Sonja's mental construct, not his own. But he was certain he would have to rely on his instincts if he wanted to get out of this mess.

The ice was smooth beneath his feet, at least ten feet thick, but he didn't have any trouble moving across the glass-like surface. He had gone a mile, possibly more, before he realized he was being followed by something below the ice.

At first it looked to be a shadow, black and amorphous beneath the thick layer of ice. For a moment Palmer experienced a surge of blind fear, recalling a nature documentary he'd once seen on PBS where a killer whale stalked a seal sunning itself on a floe, smashing its way through several feet of ice to snatch the hapless beast and drag it to its death.

Struggling to remain calm, he reminded himself that he was nowhere near the Arctic Circle and that whatever might be lurking beneath the ice, it certainly wasn't a killer whale. Marshaling his courage, he dropped to his knees, wiping at the fine layer of dry snow covering the ice with numbed hands, peering intently at the thing beneath the ice. It was probably Sonja, no doubt trying to find him.

Sonja?

Twin fires blinked on underneath the ice, glowing like embers lost from hell's furnace. Only then did Palmer realize what he'd stumbled across. He opened his mouth to scream for help, but it was too late. The Other knew he was there. And unprotected.

Arms burst through the ice floe, the skin cold and hard

and blue. The hands were those of a crone, with hooked, cracked nails. They flailed about blindly, seeking purchase on the slippery surface. The Other pulled itself out of its frozen grave, like a woman wriggling free of a girdle. The head emerged after the arms, the hair transformed into a dark sunburst by rapidly forming icicles. The eyes burned with an unending anger, and the lips seemed obscenely full, like freshly fed leeches. They pulled back into a predator's grin of anticipation, revealing shriveled black gums and the teeth of a killing thing. As demonic as the Other's features were, there was a horrible familiarity about them – like those of a loved one in a picture torn to shreds and pasted back together by inexpert hands.

Look who's come to pay me a visit!

The Other's mind voice sounded like a clogged kitchen sink trying to approximate human speech. It made Palmer ill to feel its cold, hateful venom leaking into his consciousness.

Give me a kiss, lover boy!

He smashed his fist into its face as hard as he could. Blood the color and consistency of transmission fluid flew from the Other's nostrils. It laughed – a sound that lay somewhere between a lion roaring and a toilet backing up. The Other's laugh made him hit it harder – and harder. But all it did was laugh and laugh and laugh.

Suddenly Palmer was back in his own body. He landed two more blows before he realized he was hitting Sonja.

Somehow he had gotten astride her and pinned her throat with his left hand while his right rose and fell, rose and fell. She lay underneath him, her face smeared with something sticky. Her sunglasses had fallen off, revealing eyes the color of a dying sun. In the dark, the pale ichor that passed for blood amongst her kind almost looked normal. Palmer stared at his lover's bruised and swollen face – the damage already righting itself before his stunned eyes – then at his right hand. It was still clenched in a fist. He slowly opened it, as if expecting a stinging insect to fly out.

'Oh, God. God. I'm sorry, Sonja. I don't know what happened. I was . . . I thought I was fighting . . . I must have flipped out. I didn't mean to hurt you.'

She smiled then – the slow, lazy smile of satiation – and placed a finger on his trembling lips, halting his babbled apology.

'Hush.'

'But—'

'I said hush.' She pulled him down to her, pressing his face between her breasts. He could not have escaped her embrace even if he tried.

They lay together for a long time until Palmer finally fell asleep. In his dreams he heard the groaning of approaching glaciers and the echo of inhuman laughter.

5

They had sex nearly every night after that. Sometimes more than once. But the telepathic communion they had once shared was now strained, bordering nonexistent. Sonja was always guarded during their trysts, her psionic defenses at the ready. It was as though she did not dare allow herself to relax, even at the most intimate of moments. Palmer was uncertain whether she was afraid of the Other getting out or of his getting in.

She was a blank wall as far as he was concerned – unreadable and impenetrable, shrugging off his attempts at psychic rapport. While her mental frigidity bothered him, Palmer never pressed the issue. Whatever secrets Sonja kept locked inside herself were hers and hers alone.

As the telepathic aspect of their relationship dwindled, the sadistic side grew. The first time she came to him with the whip, he threw it down. He yelled his defiance. He did not want to play that game. He refused to hurt her. Then she took off her sunglasses and looked at him with those terrible eyes mutated beyond tears, and something within him broke.

He beat her until the blood flew, stippling the walls and spotting the bare light-bulb hanging over the bed. He beat her until his arm ached and the whip fell from numbed fingers. All to meet her need. She *needed* his blows. Needed them as much as his caresses. Maybe more. Palmer did not know what sins she hoped to expiate with stinging leather kisses and roses fashioned of swollen flesh and splattered blood, nor did he want to. Some things are sacred. Even to monsters.

About a week after her arrival home, Palmer awoke in the

middle of the night to find the bed empty. His first thought was of Lethe, and his heart leapt in fear. He hurried to the child's bedroom, but Lethe was sound asleep. He felt a surge of shame. Sonja would no more harm Lethe than he would. He looked out the window at the nearby forest. No doubt she was out hunting. After all, she *was* nocturnal. He returned to his room as she crawled in through the window. She was completely nude, her mouth and belly smeared with fresh blood.

'Sonja?'

She turned like a startled cat, hissing a warning. The hairs on his testicles stood on end as he realized he was looking into the face of the Other.

The Other spoke in a gravelly, slurred baritone, sounding like a cleverly remixed version of Sonja's normal voice. 'So, lover boy's still up! Why does she keep you around, Palmer? It can't be the way you fuck!'

The Other laughed as Palmer flinched, licking the blood smearing the back of its hand like a cat cleaning itself. It enjoyed making him twitch. Palmer was still uncertain whether Sonja's vampiric alter ego was a genuinely separate identity or simply an elaborate self-delusion; her id given voice. Was his lover possessed or mad? Either way, Palmer had to be careful when dealing with the Other. It definitely lacked Sonja's patience – marginal as that might be at times – and made it clear more than once that it suffered Palmer's presence only as a 'favor' to its host.

'I want to talk to Sonja.'

'Tough titty, asshole,' the Other growled, dropping onto the bed. 'She ain't here.'

'Then I'll wait until she gets back,' Palmer said, folding his arms.

'Back off, renfield!' the Other snapped, showing its fangs in ritual display. 'I'm not in the mood!'

There was a sound from the direction of the door and the Other fell silent, something resembling fear flickering across its face. Palmer glanced over his shoulder and saw

Fido standing on the threshold, his eyes glowing in the dark. When Palmer turned his attention back to the Other, Sonja was sitting there, looking puzzled.

'Bill?' She frowned at the blood drying on her belly. She wiped her finger along the smear and tasted it, grimacing slightly. 'Don't worry, it's not human—' She glanced back up at him. 'Why are you looking at me that way?'

'You went out hunting and the Other came back.'

She shifted uncomfortably. 'Did . . . did it say anything?'

'About what?'

Her eyes flashed angrily and for a heart-stopping moment Palmer was afraid the Other had returned. 'Did it *talk*?'

'Yeah, but it didn't say much. Told me I was a lousy lay, if that's what you mean.'

'That's not true, you know that.'

'Do I?' Palmer knelt beside her on the bed, taking her hands into his. 'Sonja, what's wrong? What happened in New Orleans that you're not telling me?'

She looked at him, her dark-adapted pupils so dilated they filled her eyes. The sadness inside her pressed against him, wrapping him in stifling grayness. Her depression filled his lungs, crushing the breath from him. His heart seemed to swell then wither as the misery inside her sought to pull him down into its depths. Palmer knew that if he succumbed to the vortex, he would be lost. Marshaling all his strength, both physical and mental, he drew back and punched her as hard as he could, right in the face.

He told himself it wasn't cruelty. It was self-preservation. The gray pain retreated from his mind. In its place was a red-hot coal of anger, betrayal – arousal.

He hit her again.

And again.

And again.

His orgasm took him by surprise. He looked down at his wilting penis, blinking in confusion. He hadn't even touched himself. Sonja lay facedown on the bed, her body twisted in sheets smeared with her blood and sweat and Palmer's spent seed. She didn't seem to be breathing.

'Sonja?'

No response. His fists ached from the pounding they'd administered. His body was still trembling like a plucked guitar string.

'Sonja?'

He rolled her over. Her body was so heavy, so limp. Her face was a mess of blood, pulped cartilage and shattered bone. The walls looked as if someone had tried to clean a dirty paintbrush by flicking it dry. She still wasn't breathing. Her brain sounded like a radio tuned to an empty channel.

Bile rising in his throat, Palmer lurched to his feet and headed for the bathroom. He locked the door behind him and splashed water on his face. When he looked up, he found his reflection, haggard and drawn, staring out at him from the mirror. There was a mad gleam in the eyes – a gleam he recognized. He'd seen its like in the eyes of the humans in the service of the vampires Pangloss and Morgan. Renfields. They called them renfields.

The Other had called him a renfield.

Palmer pressed his bruised and bleeding hands against his eyes. The screech and squall of the mind-world pushed against his head, threatening to breach his barriers and inundate him with other people's fears, hopes, dreams, secrets, and sins until his individuality, his consciousness was erased.

'Stop it!' he yelled at an old lady in Poughkeepsie, who couldn't decide whether to put her cancer-ridden poodle down or not. 'Get out of my head!' he screeched at an aging businessman in Taipei, who was worried about his waning potency. 'Leave me alone!' he bellowed at a Nazi war criminal in Paraguay, who was certain he was being followed by an Israeli task force.

'Bill?'

He jerked open the bathroom door. Sonja was standing on the other side, her cheekbones already restructuring themselves, her lips deflating, the bruises covering her eyes fading from black to blue to yellow.

'You all right in there?'

He had failed her. He would always fail her. She was insatiable. How could he hope to satisfy a woman who healed within minutes? Palmer wondered if he would ever be able to fuck a woman again without trying to kill her.

As he lay beside her on the bloodstained bed, watching the dawn chase the shadows across the walls of their room, he wondered which was worse: thinking that he'd killed her, or being disappointed she was alive.

Later that day, while Palmer was building yet another shipping crate – this time for obscene pull-toys: terracotta figurines sporting enormous penises with wheels affixed to the glans – Lethe came out onto the patio to watch him. She was carrying the black mask he'd kept from the previous shipment.

'Where's Auntie Boo?'

'Auntie Boo's sleeping. You know she sleeps during the day, Lethe.'

'Not all the time.'

'You're right. Sometimes she's awake during the day. But only under special circumstances.'

Lethe held up the mask so that it covered her face. Her eyes, golden and pupil-less, shone in the empty sockets. For some reason it made Palmer's flesh creep.

'Put that thing away!'

Lethe flinched at the sharpness in his voice and Palmer inwardly cursed himself. His problems with Sonja were beginning to reflect in his attitude toward others. He opened his mouth to tell Lethe he was sorry, that he hadn't meant to bark at her like that, but she was already back inside the house.

Lefty crawled out from under a pile of excelsior and began playing with one of the pull-toys, rolling it back and forth on its wobbly hand-carved wheels. Palmer set aside his tools and massaged the back of his neck, grimacing down at his former incarnation's left hand.

'Well, I screwed the pooch that time, didn't I, Lefty? Just like last night. I should have toughed it out, ridden out the depression until I got to the heart of what's been bugging Sonja, but I was weak. I freaked and took the easy way out, because I was afraid of being alone with the Other again. It's not that I don't want to help her, it's just that she's making it so damned hard.' Palmer shook his head and grimaced in disgust. 'Jesus! I must be crazier than I thought! I'm telling a disembodied hand about my woman trouble!'

Lethe stood in the house and looked out the window facing the courtyard. Daddy was squatting down, talking to Lefty and looking sad. Lethe knew Daddy didn't want to be mean to her. She knew he was having problems – something to do with Auntie Blue. Still, Lethe's feelings were hurt. She looked down at the black mask she still held in her hands. It was turned towards her, the empty eyes and mouth staring up at her, as if awaiting an answer.

Sighing to herself, Lethe placed the mask on her stepfather's worktable, where she'd first found it. She wondered what she would do to pass the day. She was tired of playing by herself and she'd read all her books so many times she'd lost interest in them. Daddy tried hard to keep up with her needs, but at thirty months she'd long outgrown Laura Ingals, Frank L. Baum, and Robert Louis Stevenson. Even *David Copperfield* and *Huckleberry Finn* were no longer challenging.

She wished Daddy would let her go into town with him. She really wanted to see other children, other people, other places. There was the video player and its monitor, but seeing pictures of things wasn't the same thing as experiencing them. All her life, for as far back as she could remember, she had been kept away from what Daddy called 'normal people'.

Daddy and Auntie Blue agreed that 'normal people' would not understand her. She was different, and 'normal people' didn't like things that were different. They would look at her eyes and get scared. They'd want to take her away from Daddy and Auntie Blue and put her in some horrible place where they would experiment on her. The other reason Daddy refused to take her anywhere was fear of the Bad Man finding her. Lethe knew the Bad Man's real name was Morgan, and that he'd done something to hurt Auntie Blue a long time ago. She also knew that he was somehow related to her. Like a grandfather. Auntie Blue said the Bad Man killed Lethe's real mommy and daddy, back when Lethe was a little baby.

Lethe couldn't remember much of what happened back then. What memories she did have were of being hungry or cold or wet – baby stuff. If she thought about it really hard, she could dredge up a memory of someone warm and dark, who smelled like milk. When Lethe told Auntie Blue about it, she told her she was remembering her real mother, Anise. When Lethe asked if Anise was Auntie Blue's sister, she said they'd had the same father. So did Lethe's real daddy, Fell. Lethe couldn't remember *him* at all. The first time she'd been told that Daddy wasn't really her flesh-and-blood father she'd burst into tears and clutched his pant legs, terrified that she was going to be taken away. But that was back when she was a little kid and didn't know any better – twenty months ago.

But now she was growing up – faster than Daddy or even Auntie Blue could possibly realize. They only one who knew that her childhood was nearing its end was Fido. Fido talked to her at night while she was asleep. Well, he didn't real *talk*. Not with his mouth, anyway. But he didn't talk with his head, the way Daddy and Auntie Blue did at times, either. It was more like he *felt* things to her.

Fido was as important a part of her life as Daddy, even though he never did things like fix her peanut-butter and banana sandwiches or buy her toys or read Dr Seuss to her before going to bed. Fido made sure she was safe. It was his presence, more than anything else, that ensured that the Bad Man would never be able to find her. It was his job – or 'destiny', as he called it – to make sure she grew up, so she could fulfill *her* destiny. (Fido used the word 'destiny' a lot whenever he talked to her.)

Even now, as she thought of him, Fido lumbered into view. He was big and bulky and shaggy, like a Saint Bernard given human form, wrapped in filthy cast-off sweaters with newspapers stuffed in his boots. Daddy said Fido looked like a homeless person, which confused Lethe somewhat, because Fido had always lived in their house. She knew it took a lot of energy for Fido to maintain his physical form, and that he would be a lot happier if he could go around without his body slowing him down, but it was important for him to remain manifested on the physical plane, at least for as long as she required protection. Which wouldn't be much longer. Fido was kind of excited about the prospect of being able to rejoin his brother-sisters, but part of him was sad, too, because this meant Lethe was growing up and wouldn't need him anymore. Lethe tried to cheer him up and told him she'd *always* need him, but they both knew it wasn't true.

Growing up was scary, but then everything really important is kind of scary, once you think about it. Soon she wouldn't be able to turn to Daddy for help, or rely on Fido for protection. Her success or failure was totally up to her, and nobody else. Part of her cringed at the thought of so much responsibility. But, at the same time, growing up meant she would finally be free to see the world and everything in it firsthand. She could go to town, if she wanted – or anywhere else on the face of the planet. Thinking about growing up made her scared and excited all at once, mixing her up inside.

Lethe padded down the hall to the bedroom Daddy shared with Auntie Blue whenever she was home. The door was shut but not locked, so Lethe was able to get in. The room was very dark and stiflingly hot. No one human could possibly sleep in such a sweatbox, but Auntie Blue lay on the bed, covered by a sheet.

Lethe moved to the bed while Fido hung back. Auntie Blue

didn't like Fido. She said he made her nervous. What she meant was that the Other was scared of him. Lethe sent Fido to go and scare the Other away the other night because she could tell it wanted to hurt Daddy. Lethe knew Auntie Blue loved Daddy, but she sometimes had a hard time controlling the Other.

Auntie Blue lay cold, white, and silent on the bed. She wasn't wearing any clothes under the sheet. She wasn't breathing and she wasn't sweating, although the room's temperature must have been over ninety degrees. There was what looked like blood smeared on the pillowcases and sheets and the room smelled like stinky socks. Lethe looked back at Fido, who shuffled back and forth at the threshold.

'It's okay, Fido. The Other's asleep, too.'

Lethe gently brushed aside a lock of dark hair from her stepmother's forehead and kissed her brow. Sonja's skin was cool and dry under her lips.

'Bye, Auntie Blue,' she whispered. 'Thanks for helping me get born.'

Palmer decided to fix Lethe's favorite meal as a peace offering and went to her room to tell her to wash up, assuming she was either playing with her dolls or reading books to Fido.

'Lethe? Time for dinner! I made pigs-in-a-blanket – how does that sound? Lethe?'

Fido looked up from his guard post at the foot of Lethe's bed, his eyes unreadable as ever. Palmer's eyes went automatically to the bed, but there was no sign of Lethe amongst the jumble of dolls and stuffed animals. In the space where she normally slept was what looked like a sleeping bag made of semi-opaque yellow plastic.

'What the—?' Palmer stepped forward, frowning. Maybe it was something Sonja had brought back for Lethe from New Orleans . . .

As he got closer, he could tell that whatever it was, it sure as hell wasn't a sleeping bag. Almost four feet long and two feet around, the thing seemed to pulse and glow from within. And even though he could not see enough of her to make a positive identification, he knew whose small, slender body it was hanging suspended at its amber core.

'Lethe!'

Palmer lunged at the cocoon to tear it open with his bare hands and yank his daughter free, but the moment his fingers brushed the outer casing a surge of psychic energy, as painful as it was powerful, shot up his arms and into his brain, hurling him backward as if he'd tried to scale an electric fence.

As he shook his head to clear it, Fido moved to stand between him and the bed. The seraphim's arms were outspread, his chin lowered in what Palmer recognized as a protective stance.

Palmer's legs were wobblier than a newborn colt's and his nose was dripping blood, but he was unharmed. 'Damn you! Stand aside!' he snapped as he got to his feet.

Fido did not offer to move.

'She's hurt! I've got to help her!'

Fido's arms wavered for a second, then lowered.

Palmer stepped forward.

The second blast kicked him into the hall. His goatee and hair were singed. Without using his hands, Fido closed the door to Lethe's bedroom.

It took Palmer a few seconds, but he somehow managed to get to his feet. His nose was still bleeding and his ears rang as if he'd been sitting on top of an air-raid siren. He staggered down the hall, propping his shoulder against the wall to keep from falling.

Sonja was still asleep. Her skin felt strangely dry and cool under his hands, like that of a reptile.

'Sonja!'

She moved sluggishly, brushing at him with her left hand as if he was a bothersome insect intruding on her sleep. She mumbled something under her breath, then rolled over, pulling the sheet over her head. Trying not to let the panic overwhelm him, Palmer took a deep breath and stepped back from the bed, focusing himself long enough to fashion a heavy-wattage thought bolt. Then he threw it at her head.

Sonja!

The thought bolt bowed Sonja's body upward as if she'd been juiced with a car battery. Her eyes flew open and she sat up like a knife blade. The hair on her head stood on end and crackled like static on a radio. When he reached out to grab her naked shoulder she drew back and hissed at him.

'Sonja! Sonja – it's me! Something's happened!'

Sonja blinked and lifted a hand to her brow. 'Something's happened to Lethe?'

'How'd you know that?'

Sonja slid out of the bed and began pulling on her clothes. 'I had a dream she told me good-bye.'

She followed Palmer back up the hall, listening to him recount what had happened earlier. The door to Lethe's room was still closed. She tried the door; it wasn't locked.

'It's probably safe to go in. Fido would never let anything hurt Lethe, so whatever you were planning to do was probably interpreted as dangerous to her.'

'I was going to get her out of that . . . that *thing*!'

Sonja gave Palmer a hard look. 'Bill, just shut up and let me handle this, okay?'

The door opened effortlessly. Sonja stepped inside, Palmer following her. Fido still stood on guard, shuffling from one foot to the other, watching them intently with his golden eyes. Sonja held up her hands, palms outward, smiling nervously. Being in such close proximity to the seraphim was actively unpleasant – it felt as if she'd been dipped in honey and placed on top of an anthill.

'We don't want to hurt Lethe, Fido. We know you won't allow that. We're not going to touch her, Fido—'

'Like hell we aren't!'

'Shut up, Palmer! Don't mind him, Fido. He's just scared. He thinks something bad has happened, and he just wants to help Lethe.'

The seraphim continued rocking back and forth, its head wavering like that of someone suffering from Parkinson's disease.

Sonja turned back to Palmer and grabbed his arm above the elbow, squeezing it until he grimaced. 'Bill, I want you to promise me that you won't do anything stupid, like try and touch Lethe. You got off lucky the first two times, but if you try it again Fido will burn your brain like bacon in the pan, do you understand me?'

'Yeah. I don't like it, but I understand.'

Sonja turned back to Fido. 'We just want to *look* at her, that's all.'

Slowly, the seraphim moved aside, allowing them an unimpeded view of what lay on Lethe's bed. Sonja could see why Palmer had first mistaken it for a sleeping bag, since it resembled one of the mummy-case models. It was close to five feet long and three feet around, and seemed to be made from amber. It was translucent in spots and filled with a thick fluid that gave off a diffuse light, like that of a glowworm. Deep within the fluid she glimpsed what looked to be the outline of a child.

'It's grown,' Palmer muttered. 'It wasn't this big when I first found it . . . Whatever it is.'

'By the looks of it, I'd say it's a cocoon.'

'What the hell is she doing in a fuckin' *cocoon*?'

'Undergoing some sort of metamorphosis – that's what cocoons are for.'

'For the love of God, Sonja, aren't you going to *do* something? That's our little girl in there!' Palmer shouted, lunging for the bed.

Fido moved to block his path and the sound of dynamos gearing up filled the room, the vibrations causing Sonja's fangs to ache. Swearing under her breath, she grabbed Palmer and tossed him over her shoulder in a fireman's carry, slamming the door shut behind her.

She stomped into the kitchen and dropped him, unceremoniously, into one of the chairs. Palmer was livid, his anger so fierce he was choking on his words. It didn't matter – she could hear what he was thinking.

'You can think I'm a cold-blooded bitch all you want, William Palmer,' Sonja snapped. 'But I just saved you from having your brains scrambled in your skull! If Fido had let you have it, you'd be shitting in diapers and eating through tubes for the rest of your natural days!'

Palmer's face lost some of its blood. 'I . . . I realize that, Sonja. I'm sorry I thought those things about you, but surely you can't expect me to stand by and do nothing!'

'That's *exactly* what I expect you to do – and that's what you're *going* to do! Bill, you've known all along that Lethe isn't a human child. Hell, you were there when she was born.'

'Don't remind me,' he mumbled, massaging his calf. 'I still have scars from where that mutant hell-twin of hers tried to chew off my leg.'

'Lethe was born of two human vampires – creatures such as myself. But she's obviously not a vampire. I used to think she was some kind of seraphim, but now I'm not so sure. But whatever she might be, the seraphim have considered her important enough to be placed under their protection. And for all we know, this cocoon stage is perfectly natural. The fact that Fido won't let us touch her suggests that interfering with this – I dunno, call it a larval stage – would be dangerous to Lethe.'

Palmer shook his head and got up to retrieve the bottle of tequila he kept in the pantry. Sonja was surprised by how old he looked. The psychokinetic pummeling he'd taken certainly didn't help matters; his face was puffy and bruises were slowly blossoming under his eyes, as if he'd been struck by the world's biggest air hammer.

They had first met two and a half years ago, when Pangloss hired him to track her down. Not even three years, and already he was starting to age. His once-dark hair and goatee were now liberally shot with gray, and his nose was beginning to dominate his face. Palmer had changed dramatically during their time together, what with his obsession with Mayan body modification, and now he was starting to grow old. Funny that she hadn't noticed that before. Was this how it was between vampires and their human lovers? One day they're a handsome youth, the next they're old and withered? She had to struggle to remember his age. Forty-three? Forty-four? How old was that in human years?

And, without realizing it, she began to think of Judd. About his youth and his innocence and his humanity . . .

'Sonja?'

She reined in her thoughts, slamming them behind a protective wall. 'Yes, Bill?'

He was sitting there at the table, the tequila bottle at his elbow. Palmer watched her with eyes as distant and unreadable as a dead man's.

'Nothing. Nothing at all.'

6

Sonja woke up just as the sun went down. She showered immediately, making sure to wash away the previous evening's blood and semen. Then, wrapping herself in a kimono she had picked up in Tokyo, she went to check on Lethe's cocoon. She soon discovered that it was no longer resting on the child's bed but out on the patio, with Fido still standing guard.

Palmer was in the kitchen, drinking tequila. In the three days since Lethe retreated into her golden cocoon, Sonja had yet to see Palmer do anything but drink. Maybe he ate while she was asleep, but she doubted it.

'What's the deal? Why's the cocoon on the patio?'

'Dunno,' Palmer slurred, lifting the bottle to his lips. He wasn't even bothering with the rituals of salt and lime. 'Mebbe it got too big for the bed. Fucker's almost six feet long now.'

Sonja glanced out the window facing the courtyard. Palmer was right. The cocoon had grown at least another foot in length.

'All I know is that when I woke up today, it was sittin' out on the patio. Guess laughing boy there moved it while I wasn't looking.' Palmer set aside the bottle and began pawing through the pile of mail and invoices on the kitchen table. 'By the way, you got a letter . . .'

Sonja stiffened. 'A letter? Addressed to me?'

'That's what I said – here.' Palmer retrieved a business-length envelope from the pile and handed it to her. 'There's no return address, but it was mailed from the States. There's a New York City postmark.'

She took the letter, smiling grimly. He was still the private detective, even pickled in tequila. Or perhaps being this drunk made him feel more like the old Palmer, the one who had existed before he learned the truth about the things in the shadows.

The envelope was nondescript, addressed to 'Sonja Blue c/o Indigo Imports'. The address was typed, not handwritten. There was no way to tell who – or what – had tracked her down. Was it a friend or foe? The only way for her to find out was to open it.

Inside the envelope was a single sheet of paper. Sonja carefully unfolded it, frowning to herself. It was a photocopy of a news clipping from a national paper. The headline read: 'Wife of Millionaire Industrialist Suffers Stroke.'

'What's it say?' Palmer asked, one eye fixed on her as he tilted back the tequila bottle.

'My mother's in the hospital.'

'You're not really going, are you?'

Palmer watches me from the door of our bedroom as I busy myself with packing my bag. He's drunk. Sloppily so. His sense of betrayal wraps itself around me like a damp towel left to mildew in a gym locker for a few weeks. I know it should make me feel bad, but I'm getting angry with him instead. I always get mad when people try to make me feel guilty.

'Of course I'm going! What the hell does it look like?' I snap, shoving a pair of leopard-skin bikini briefs, a black lace camisole, and a Revolting Cocks T-shirt into my flight bag.

I go to the wall safe and retrieve the special strongbox I keep my various passports and credit cards in. I dump them onto the bed, rummaging through them for an appropriate alias for my trip to the States. I decide to use Anya Cyan and pocket the corresponding identification.

'But what about Lethe? You can't just leave her like this!'

'Bill, I can't do anything for her while she's like this! What the hell difference does it make if I'm here or not?'

'Sonja, please. Don't go. I need you to stay. Please.'

I turn to look at him and I'm shocked to see how quickly he's fallen apart. He hasn't shaved since Lethe went into the cocoon, nor has he bathed – or changed his clothes, for that matter. With his earplugs, tattoos, and nose piercings, he looks like a demented Humphrey Bogart from *The Treasure of the Sierra Madre*. His weakness radiates from him like carbon monoxide fumes from a busted muffler, and I turn away for fear he will sense the disgust welling inside me. I know, then, that I cannot stay in that house another hour; for it is in the vampire's nature to exploit – even destroy – those weaker than themselves.

Palmer raises a trembling hand to his face, brushing drunkenly at his tears. 'Jesus, Sonja, what's happening to us?'

Part of me hears the sorrow and confusion in his voice and wants to reach out and hold him; to pull him into my arms and comfort him as best I can. But another, darker part sees his tears and wants to smash him in the face and grind its boot in his groin. I stuff the last of my gear into the flight bag and zip it shut, all the while refusing to look at him eye to eye.

'I doubt if anything *is* happening, Bill.'

And I leave them behind, just like that.

I'm not proud of what I'm doing. I realize I'm using my mother's illness to escape an uncomfortable situation at home. Things have changed between us, and there is no use in trying to get what we had back. I've been trying to figure a way out of the situation since the day I got back. Lethe's metamorphosis merely accelerated the process, that's all. I've developed this ability over the years of being able to cut myself off from people I care about. Or thought I cared about. It's a survival mechanism, one I've been forced to evolve over the last twenty years. I don't think it's a side effect of my being a vampire. I'd like to be able to blame it on that, but I know better. Monsters don't have a lock on cruelty.

I catch the first flight for the States, flying first class as usual. I always fly first class — it guarantees a certain amount of privacy and if the stewardesses notice I don't seem to breathe while I sleep, they keep it to themselves.

I spend most of the flight from Yucatán trying to remember my mother. That's not entirely true. Shirley Thorne was never *my* mother — she was Denise's.

As I sit watching the clouds slide by my window, I try to find a memory from the life before my own. I reach back . . . back . . . back before Palmer . . . back before Chaz . . . back before Ghilardi and Pangloss . . . beyond Morgan and his horrible, blood-red kisses . . .

I am sitting on a picnic bench – Where? Backyard? Which house? The one in Connecticut? There are lots of balloons and brightly colored crepe-paper streamers and other children running around, dressed in party clothes. I'm wearing a pink dress with lots of ruffles and petticoats. I don't like the petticoats because they're itchy and make it hard for me to put my arms down to my sides. There's a man dressed like a clown walking around making Wiener dogs and bunnies out of balloons for all the children. Another man is leading a pony around in a big circle. Some of the older kids cling to its mane and wave to their moms. Or maybe they're their stepmoms. Or nannies. Everybody's wearing silly cardboard hats and carrying party-favor noisemakers. How old am I? Four? Five? And suddenly everyone's smiling and pointing behind me and I turn around and look. There is my mother, standing in the doorway that leads from the house to the backyard and she's holding a big cake with lots of pink icing and big roses made out of white marzipan. She's smiling and she looks so happy and beautiful and everyone starts singing 'Happy Birthday' and gathering around the picnic table. Someone says 'Make a wish, Denise' and I have to stand up on the seat to blow out the candles. I don't remember whether I made a wish or if it came true . . .

'Ma'am, are you all right? Did you hurt yourself?'

I look up at the stewardess, still too stunned by the weight of the memory I've unearthed to do more than grunt. 'What?'

'Ma'am, your hand.'

I glance down at my left hand. One of the 'perks' of first-class service is that your drinks are served in actual glassware, as opposed to crappy plastic cocktail cups. My fist is full of shattered glass, melting ice, and Seagrams VO.

All I can say is 'Oh.'

'Are you hurt?' the stewardess asks again, and I can tell she's trying to figure out if I'm drunk, stoned, or stupid. She can't see past the sunglasses and it's making her uneasy. I don't want her watching me the rest of the trip so I reach into her skull and plant an explanation.

'There must have been a flaw in the glass. What with the cabin pressure changes and everything – I'm just lucky I didn't get cut.'

'You're really lucky, ma'am,' she clucks, her head bobbing in agreement as she takes what's left of my drink out of my hand. 'You could have gotten a bad cut.'

'Yeah, I'm really lucky,' I mutter, moving my hand so she does not spot the gaping bloodless slice across my palm.

From the diaries of Sonja Blue

It was daylight by the time she reached her destination. Her bones ached from spending close to forty-eight hours in a cramped position. The flight from Yucatán took six hours, then she spent six hours in Los Angeles, waiting for the proper domestic carrier. She could stay active during the day, but not without it taking its toll. It made her slower, more vulnerable to the tricks and pitfalls that might come her way. Although her body craved its sleep – or rather, the regenerative coma necessary to repair any physical damage encountered over the course of the night – at least she didn't have to worry about contracting immediate and lethal skin cancer from being exposed to the sun's rays. Not yet, anyway.

She rented a car at the airport and drove into the town that, until 1969, Denise Thorne had called home. Although her first instinct was to unlock the trunk and crawl inside, she climbed in behind the wheel instead. As she drove through the suburbs into the city, she passed the Thorne Industrial Complex. It was even bigger than she – that is, Denise – remembered. She had to hand it to the old man, he always knew how to make a buck and a half.

The light poured into the car, making Sonja's skin prickle a little bit. She told herself that she wasn't used to direct sun anymore, although she kept eyeing her hands, looking for signs of quick-blooming melanomas. She'd seen a couple of vampires die of sunlight poisoning – not a pretty sight. Their skin burned and was quickly covered in blisters that swelled and swelled until they exploded. Then they simply withered away, like earthworms on a hot sidewalk. It only took a couple of minutes – five, tops – for a dead boy to bust 'n' bake.

Yep, not a pretty sight.

The clipping had said Shirley Thorne was staying at St Mary's Hospital, over on the Upper East Side. It was the same hospital where Denise had been born. She parked in the public garage attached to the hospital and made her way to the information desk. An aged nun wearing bifocals looked up at her, frowning quizzically.

'Can I be of some assistance, young lady?'

'Yes, sister. I'm looking for a relative's room. Thorne? Shirley Thorne?'

The nun scribbled down the name on a slip of paper and turned to consult a computer terminal. She clucked her tongue and shook her head and turned back to face Sonja, her bifocals making her eyes look strangely warped. 'I'm so sorry, dear, but I'm afraid Mrs Thorne isn't with us anymore.'

'She's been released?'

'She died yesterday afternoon, according to the computer.'

Sonja stared at the terminal, at the name highlighted in amber against a black screen. The cursor blinked like a stuttering firefly.

'I . . . Is there any notation on where to send memorials?'

'It says flowers should be sent to the Bester-Williamson Funeral Home.' The nun pursed her lips and offered Sonja a sympathetic smile. 'I'm dreadfully sorry, dear. Was she a close relative?'

'No. Not really.'

Sonja called the funeral home from the lobby of the hospital. The receptionist informed her that the loved one's services were scheduled for the next day, during the late afternoon. The graveside services were to be held at Rolling Lawn Cemetery. Sonja didn't have to ask where that was – it was the same graveyard Claude Hagerty was buried in. And Chaz.

After finding out all she needed to know concerning her mother's funeral, Sonja drove the rental car out to a suburban shopping mall and crawled inside the trunk to sleep away the remaining hours of daylight.

She wasn't certain what went on inside her head when she was not awake qualified as 'dreaming'. She saw things. But were they dreams, or shadows of things that had happened before or of things to come? Sometimes she found herself inside other people's dreams – or their nightmares. Or their madness.

She was walking through a dreamscape made of dripping moss and rotten lace. Sitting on a canopy bed with satin draperies coated with mildew, was a woman dressed in a white bridal gown. She seemed to be adjusting her dress. As Sonja drew closer the bride looked up, like a fawn surprised while drinking at a stream, her face almost obscured by the heavy veil. She spoke without opening her mouth. It was the voice of a five-year-old girl.

He made me dirty.

She looked down at the woman's lap, expecting to see a bouquet. Instead she saw the woman's hands – they were

101

those of an aged crone, with long, crooked nails. She clawed at her crotch with hideous witch's fingers. The material of the gown was torn away, exposing her withered thighs and her gray and wrinkled sex. It was all bloody because she'd scratched away her labia and clitoris.

When Sonja woke up, the car was in motion. She pressed her ear to the dividing wall that separated the back seat from the trunk and heard the heavy, rhythmic thump of rap music and, above that, laughter.

Males. Two of them. Adolescent from the sound of their voices and taste in music. Two kids on a joyride? She concentrated harder, tuning out the intrusive music and background noise, focusing on their conversation.

'The Chopper will pay five, mebbe six bills for this baby—'

'What about the Red? He ships cars over to the Russian black market.'

'He only takes Japanese and Euro shit. This thing's American.'

'Fuck!'

'Shit, there's no point in lettin' the Chopper get *everything*. Maybe there's something in the trunk we can take over to King Fence for a quick buck or two, huh?'

The car slid off the road onto gravel. She bounced around for a few minutes more until everything came to a stop. As she thought about it, she realized she was pretty damn hungry. She hadn't eaten in almost seventy-two hours and it was beginning to make her irritable. The car doors slammed and shoes crunched on gravel, heading back for the trunk.

'Think there's anything back there?'

'Maybe just a spare tire and some jumper cables. Then again, mebbe some cunt left her bags from Nordstrom's.'

There was a scraping sound as one of the car thieves worked at the lock with a screwdriver. Probably the same one he'd used to force the door, open the ignition cowl, and start the car. The lock gave with a loud pop and the trunk swung open. Sonja was on them in six seconds flat.

They were young. Their surprise and fear made them seem even younger. They were suburban white boys with bad haircuts, dressed in clothes four sizes too big for them. One of them had a gun stuck in the waistband of his pants. She grabbed him first, taking him to the ground hard enough to break his back. He screamed like a little girl – high and pure – as she tore into his throat.

His companion shouted something and tried to drive a six-inch screwdriver into her back. The leather jacket deflected the blow, but it was enough to make her look up from her feeding. She grinned at him, displaying her fangs, and hissed in disapproval. The kid dropped his weapon and wet himself. It took less than a second to snap his neck. Sonja finished draining the first youth, then took as much as she could handle from the second. She then kicked their emptied bodies into a nearby ditch. How thoughtful of them to pick such a nice, secluded spot for their own disposal.

The ignition was hanging from its socket, so she had to hot-wire the car to get it started. No doubt the rental company would not be pleased. Like she cared.

It was still early, by her standards – just after midnight. She decided to cruise the old hometown, too see if anything kicked a memory out of what was left of Denise Thorne. It worried Sonja, at times, that she felt so little of her previous self's pain. Denise used to be more a part of her personality, decades ago, but over the last few years her voice had grown gradually weaker until it had been drowned out by the increasingly strident Other. Maybe a visual cue would spark something inside her, generate an emotion that went with the memories in her head. Because without those flashes of sentiment, all Sonja had were dry and flavorless souvenirs of another's life; shadows of the dead rendered meaningless to her – like watching someone else's jerky, disintegrating home movies

103

without the benefit of sound or reference to the players.

She drove around and around, but so much had changed in the twenty years since Denise Thorne walked those streets that nothing seemed familiar. Suddenly the gates were in front of the headlights, throwing up striated shadows. Sonja blinked and looked around, uncertain how she'd gotten there. Had she deliberately steered the car in this direction? Or was something besides her subconscious behind her arrival? The gate was rusty and the twelve-foot brick walls that screened the estate from the road were overgrown with creeping ivy and covered with graffiti. There was a heavy chain coiled around the gate like a chrome python, secured by a padlock the size of a baby's head. A metal sign read: 'No Trespassing. Violators Will Be Prosecuted to the Full Extent of the Law.'

Sonja killed the headlights and slid out from behind the wheel of the car. She held the lock in her right hand, judging its heft; it was a beauty all right. It would even give a New York bicycle thief reason to pause. Sonja yanked on it twice and it came away in her hand, the chain unspooling at her feet. The gates to the Wheele Estate swung inward with a rusty squeal.

She walked in the direction of where the main house once stood, her boot heels crunching on the overgrown drive. Weeds and small trees poked their way through the slowly dissolving layer of bleached shells.

She scanned the area for signs of derelict habitation or teenage lovers and came up empty. This surprised her. The abandoned five-acre estate was perfect for suburban youths to hide from the apathy of their parents and practice their drinking and sex, but she couldn't pick up the faintest trace of such activity. Instead, as she neared the blackened remains of the Wheele mansion, she began to receive psychic signals similar to those she'd experienced at Ghost Trap. The place was haunted. Big time.

Sonja wrinkled her nose. Even though the place had burned to the ground five years ago, it still smelled scorched. There wasn't a lot left of the house – she'd made sure of that when she set it on fire. She'd also killed everyone in it beforehand. And a lot of people in the surrounding area, for that matter. Sonja still felt bad about that part of the massacre. But it wasn't really her fault; the Wheele bitch was the one who'd kidnapped her and kept her in that shit-hole of an insane asylum for six months. Wheele was the one who'd started it, not her. But she had finished it, by damn. Besides, the psychic shock wave she'd released that night only affected those with true darkness in their souls. At least, that's what she liked to tell herself.

There was a light moving amongst the ruins. It was a cold, unnatural luminescence, glowing greenish-white against the darkness. At first it was formless, a glob of pulsating light hovering amidst the collapsed timbers and fallen masonry of the destroyed house. The will-o'-the-wisp fluttered for a few seconds, then began to change, taking on shape and substance. It was a woman – or something that had once been a woman.

It had no eyes, no ears, no tongue; its skin hung from its phantom bones like an empty sack. Although it had arms and an upper torso, its legs ended in glowing tatters. Even though it had no eyes in its sockets, Sonja knew it could see her. And that it recognized her.

'Hello, Catherine. It's been a long time, girlfriend.'

The ghost of Catherine Wheele, erstwhile televangelist and faith healer, raised its glowing arms and howled like a damned soul. Which was only natural, since that was what it was.

'Can the spook routine, sister. It might work on teenagers looking for a place to screw and bums out for a midnight tipple, but it doesn't cut any mustard with me.'

The ghost shrieked like an owl with its tail caught in a blender and swooped towards her, fingers crooked into claws. Sonja held up her right hand and a burst of electric-blue light flew from her palm, catching the ghost in its reconstituted midsection. Catherine Wheele rolled up like a window shade, reverting to the pulsating ball of light.

'You're as ignorant dead as you were when you were alive,' Sonja sighed. 'The dead cannot physically interface with the mortal plane except on Mardi Gras, the vernal equinox, and All Hallows' Eve. And just because you're dead doesn't mean I can't kick your butt, lady.'

Catherine Wheele reassembled herself, scowling at Sonja from across the Divide. Smaller, feebler lights began to appear, floating through the night air like fireflies. One of the ghostly balls unraveled itself, taking on the appearance of Dr Wexler, the corrupt psychiatrist who first steered Shirley Thorne in Catherine Wheele's direction, then arranged to keep Sonja locked up in his sanitarium. Sonja was glad to see he was being forced to spend his afterlife in the company of his former lover. The other, lesser lights took on human forms as well, turning into the Wheelers, Catherine's private cadre; a mixture of religious fanatics, hired muscle, and stud muffins. Sonja had killed each and every one of them.

'It's nice to see you're not lonely,' she smirked, carefully searching the wanly glowing faces in search of one in particular. When she did not find it, she heaved a small sigh of relief and turned to go. But she couldn't resist one last jab. 'You know, they called it "Jonestown in America". All the stuff about your parents dying under mysterious circumstances, your late husband's fraud convictions, the graft and corruption in your church – all of that got into the papers. The Wheeles of God Ministry is gone – kaput. All your worshippers jumped ship for other, less controversial preachers. And since Waco went down, you're old news. You're trivia for atrocity buffs, nothing more. Just thought you'd like to know.'

The ghost of Catherine Wheele threw its mouth open so wide it struck its breastbone, and issued an agonized shriek that told Sonja she'd better watch her ass come Halloween.

Sonja chuckled to herself as she sauntered back to the car. Who says you have to be nice to people simply because they're dead?

*   *   *

Rolling Lawn Cemetery unlocked its gates at dawn. By that time, Sonja had been inside the grounds for a couple of hours. But before crashing in a suitable tomb, she had a couple of visits to make.

She did Chaz first.

She wasn't sorry she'd killed him. She'd felt a little guilty about it at first, but she never really felt sorry. Chaz had been a deep-down, dyed-in-the-wool bastard. He'd betrayed her, sold her out for a suitcase of money. Not that it did him any good in the end. Instead of running off to South America, like he'd always dreamed of, the idiot hung around town, frittering his fortune away on hard drugs and rough boys. It was like he was waiting for her to find him.

Just like he was waiting for her now, perched atop his gravestone.

'Hello, Chaz. You're looking well.'

Truth to tell, he looked like shit. Composed of a grayish-purple fog, his features were beginning to soften, the eyes turning into empty smudges, the nose a hint of shadow. If she hadn't known him so well, it would have been difficult for her to identify him. He was still smoking, though. He remembered enough about his former life to cling to its habits, at least.

'Judd's dead. I guess you already know that, though.'

She expected some sign of malevolent glee on his part, but he gestured dismissively with one hand, leaving trails of ghost in its wake. He remained as ambivalent in death as he had been in life.

'Why haven't you moved on? What holds you to this plane? Is it me?'

Something flickered in the smudges that were once his eyes. As Sonja looked at the tattered shadow, memories rose inside her. Memories of when they had been friends, of times when they had been lovers. She closed her eyes to ease their stinging, but she still couldn't find it in herself to feel sorry.

When she opened her eyes again, Chaz was gone.

*   *   *

Claude was nowhere to be found. For that she was relieved. His death had been an unpleasant one, and often such traumas keep the dead tethered to the mortal plane for years, even decades, after their deaths. But it seemed Claude Hagerty had managed to move on to whatever it is that awaits humans when they die. The same could not be said of all of Rolling Lawn's internees, whose after-selves flickered amidst the tombstones and vaults like phantom fireflies.

The sun would be rising soon. She went to the tomb she'd chosen as her crash space. Since the last occupant had been laid to rest two decades before, she knew she could sleep without having to worry about being discovered by a grieving family member. The memorial sconces were empty and cobwebs hung from the ceiling in delicate tatters. It smelled pleasantly of graveyard mold and dead leaves. She curled up in the darkest corner, setting her watch alarm for four o'clock. As she drifted off into what passed for sleep amongst her kind, she marveled at how little she'd thought about either Palmer or Lethe. That probably meant they were okay.

7

Palmer couldn't remember the last time he'd taken a sober breath. He couldn't remember the last time he'd shaved or changed his clothes, either. He was certain he'd been sitting at the kitchen table, naked except for a pair of khaki safari shorts, for several days, but he wasn't sure exactly how long.

He staggered over to the calendar hanging next to the stove and squinted at it. He'd gotten it from a *pharmacia* in Medina. The calendar showed a handsomely muscled Aztec warrior, garbed in brilliantly colored feathers and a skimpy loincloth, shooting a bow at the coming twilight while at his sandaled feet lay sprawled a voluptuous Aztec maiden, wrapped in a diaphanous robe and looking more like a Vargas model than a virgin priestess. Palmer was unfamiliar with the myth the picture was supposed to represent. Was the warrior defending the fallen priestess, or was he the one responsible for her death? And what the hell was he shooting at, anyway?

Thinking about the picture on the calendar made his head hurt. Palmer wobbled back to the kitchen table and sat down with an explosive sigh. It took him a few seconds to realize he'd forgot to count how many days it'd been since Lethe disappeared into the cocoon and his life went into the crapper.

He wasn't sure how long Sonja had been gone, either. He had been too drunk to cast his mind for her, but something told him he would not have been able to reach her, even if he was sober. Besides, the possibility of accidently locking minds with the Other again, no matter how distant, was enough to keep him from trying.

Palmer's gaze fell on the black mask, sitting atop a pile of unpaid bills and unfiled invoices. The empty eyes stared up at him, the lips parted as if in anticipation of a kiss – or a bite. His head continued to hurt, so he rested it on the table.

When he opened his eyes again, it was dark.

Palmer grunted and jerked upright in his chair, knocking the half-empty tequila bottle onto the floor. It shattered, spraying his bare feet and legs with liquid gold. The color of the tequila made him think of Lethe's eyes. And the cocoon.

The cocoon. Time to check the cocoon.

He lurched to his feet and turned to face the patio door. He always checked the cocoon at night. During the day it didn't seem necessary, but night was different. Strange things happened at night. Plus, he had to admit the cocoon was pretty once the sun went down. The weird glow that suffused it grew more intense, making it look like a piece of amber held in front of a flashlight. Sometimes he could see something moving inside the cocoon, as if someone was swimming around in there.

Palmer opened the door and stepped out onto the patio, expecting to be greeted by the cocoon's mellow glow. Instead, there was only darkness. The second thing he noticed was that its guardian was nowhere to be seen.

'Fido?'

He stepped forward hesitantly, looking around for some sign of the seraphim's bulky figure. Had it taken Lethe's cocoon someplace else? Then, as his eyes became more accustomed to the dark, he saw something lying on the bricks of the patio.

At first it looked like a big, deflated balloon, the kind used by weather services. It lay there, limp and forlorn, like an octopus cast upon a shore after a storm. As he moved closer, he could make out a faint, yellowish fluorescence. He knelt and poked at the empty chrysalis. It felt like a cross between a freshly shed snakeskin and a wet blanket.

Palmer's head swiveled around drunkenly. 'Lethe? Lethe, where are you, darlin'?' He struggled to get to his feet, trying his best not to black out. The adrenaline in his system was now battling the tequila for mastery, but he was too far gone to sober up fast.

'Lethe?'

The light came from above, pouring down on him as if someone had switched on a tiny sun right over his head. Palmer cringed and lifted a hand to shield his eyes. His first thought was that someone was hovering over the house in a helicopter, pointing a surveillance light down at him, like they do in Los Angeles. Then he realized that what he had thought was the sound of rotors chopping the air was his own pulse hammering away inside his ears. And then the light spoke.

Daddy.

The light lowered its wattage, became a steady glow, and Palmer saw the thing at its heart. Its form was that of a young woman, no older than sixteen or seventeen. Her hair was long enough to braid into a rope, floating free like a mantle buffeted by gentle winds. Her skin was dusky, her eyes golden without pupil or iris. Her breasts were full, her hips wide, drawing his eye to the dark triangle of hair between her thighs. She was beautiful. She was woman. Unbidden, Palmer felt his penis stir and grow heavy at the sight of the lovely, naked woman suspended above him like a vision of Venus. Or the Madonna.

'L-Lethe?'

The glowing woman smiled and when she spoke her lips did not move. Her voice was smooth as velvet, as comforting as a cool hand on a fevered brow.

My childhood is over. It is time for me to begin my work. I owe you much for keeping me safe, for giving me love and treating me as your own, for showing me what it is like to be human. I owe you all this, and that is why I shall make you the First.

'First? First what?'

Father of the coming race.

Before Palmer could ask her what *that* meant, Lethe swooped down, catching him up in her arms. He was too drunk and

111

surprised to protest, until he looked down and saw the tops of trees skimming by below his feet.

'Lethe! What the hell do you think you're—?'

He didn't finish the sentence because Lethe placed her mouth over his, her tongue darting inside his mouth. For a moment Palmer felt himself begin to respond, then he retched and tried to push her away.

'Lethe! Stop that! I'm your father!'

My father was a vampire named Fell.

'You know very well what I mean! Stop this foolishness and put me down on solid ground right this minute, young lady!'

Lethe's face filled his vision, her eyes becoming huge twin harvest moons. Palmer wanted to scream, but there was no breath inside him. The child he had cared for for the better part of three years was nowhere to be found in this strange, glowing woman.

You are the First of my Bridegrooms. The First to engage in the wedding flight. Do not fear me, William Palmer. This is your reward for your years of nurturing. You are being honored.

Palmer shuddered as he felt his penis stiffen, responding to hormonal cues older than upright posture. He kept telling himself that it wasn't happening, that he wasn't being ravaged against his will by a glowing woman as they sped across the night sky, that in fact he had passed out in a pool of his own piss in the kitchen. Even as orgasm seized his body and wadded it up like a piece of old newspaper, he kept telling himself it was just a dream, nothing more.

When he woke up, it was to find himself lying in an orchard, miles from his home. He was naked, his safari shorts lost somewhere along the way. His head throbbed with a monstrous hangover and his crotch was sticky and smelled of sex. Palmer rolled onto his stomach and began to sob, tearing at the grass with clawing hands. Then he threw up.

There was the sound of a twig snapping, and Palmer began looking around for something with which to cover himself. He froze at the sight of the young native girl, a basket of fruit balanced atop her head, staring down at him. He could tell by her diminutive stature and the shape of her eyes and cheekbones that she was one of the Lacandon, the descendants of the ancient Mayan kings who once ruled the land before the arrival of the conquistadores. The girl regarded him curiously, but did not seem to be afraid or alarmed by his nakedness.

'Are you well, señor?' she asked.

Palmer began to laugh, which made the girl look at him even more oddly. 'No. I am not well at all.' This made him laugh even harder. Then he threw up some more.

8

She'd overslept somewhat and nearly missed the funeral. She
made it just in time to see Shirley Thorne's casket lowered
to its final rest. It was made of mahogany and shone like a
burnished shield in the dying sun. A large floral tribute rested
atop, clutching it like a spider. After each of the mourners
tossed the traditional handful of sod into the grave, they
broke up and wandered towards the phalanxes of black limos,
BMWs, and Rolls-Royces.

Sonja stood at a distance, screened from view by a weeping
angel. She scanned the milling crowd, trying to spot the faces
of family and friends, but it was no use. The only person
she recognized was Jacob Thorne.

He looked considerably older than the last time she'd seen
him, five years ago. The iron will and steely resolve that had
made him a millionaire several times over had succumbed
to rust. Jacob Thorne, once the mightiest industrialist this
side of Howard Hughes, had become an old man. When
the last of the mourners shook his hand and muttered their
sympathies, Thorne did not move to join them in leaving
the cemetery. Instead, Denise's father stood by his wife's
open grave, hands clasped before him, peering down into the
hole as if he could see the future in its depths. No doubt he
did.

Sonja moved from her hiding place, gliding between the
headstones as if maneuvering across a dance floor. She knew
he was not her father. At least not the part of her that called
itself Sonja. She knew this as surely as she knew that the sun
rises in the east and sets in the west. She opened her mouth to
call his name, to say 'Mr Thorne'; but what came out was:

'Daddy?'

Jacob Thorne looked up from his wife's grave. He did not seem surprised to see her. But neither did he appear pleased. His brow furrowed and his scowl deepened.

'Somehow I knew you'd be here.'

'Mr Thorne? Is everything all right?' Thorne's chauffeur made his way towards the grave site. He was a big man with an obvious holster bulge inside his jacket.

Thorne dismissed his bodyguard with a wave of his hand. Sonja could see that it was covered with liver spots. 'It's okay, Carl. I know the young lady.'

She joined Thorne at the lip of the grave. It was very dark down there. And lonely.

'I . . . I'm sorry. Did she . . . did she suffer?'

Thorne shrugged, his shoulders looking thin and narrow in his suit. 'In her way. But that was always Shirley's prerogative – suffering. She was designed for self-martyrdom. Agonizing over Denise was the one thing that kept her going.' He looked at her, his eyes hard. 'You killed her, you know that? Whatever it was you did to her mind that night – the night she finally accepted Denise's death – that was the beginning of the end for her. She just gave up living after that.'

'Please believe me when I tell you I meant only to help her, to free her from her madness. I never intended to harm her. She . . . she was my mother.'

Thorne's pale features suddenly grew red and he began to tremble. He pulled a handkerchief out of his breast pocket and used it to blot his face. 'The hell she was! I don't know who – or what – you are, but you are not Denise!'

'No. I am not Denise anymore. But once, a long time ago. A lifetime ago . . .' Sonja bent and gathered a handful of dirt. It felt damp and rich between her fingers. It struck the lid of her mother's casket with a dull thud. 'Mr Thorne, I did not ask to come into this world. Nor did Denise ask to leave it. I did not choose to be what I am.'

Thorne looked at her again, the hardness leaking from his eyes. 'No. I guess you didn't.'

'I . . . I have memories now and again. Some are dim. Others are quite vivid. There is one of a birthday party – there were other children, a clown, a man giving pony rides . . .'

Thorne barked a laugh, sounding both surprised and pleased by the memory. 'You couldn't possibly remember that! You were only two years—' He cut himself short, his hands fisting the handkerchief into a ball. 'I mean, Denise was only two years old at the time.'

'Your wife was wearing a dress with a Peter Pan collar and a big skirt – she was so pretty. And happy. And the birthday cake was vanilla with pink icing—'

'Why are you telling me this?' Thorne's eyes gleamed with anger and tears. His voice was tight, wavering on the verge of breaking down. 'Isn't it enough I've lost my wife? Do you have to make me relive the loss of my daughter as well?'

'Mr Thorne, there is another place beyond this world. Several, actually. Every man, woman, and child holds the keys to heaven and hell within them. There are as many different paradises as there are living things. Just as there are innumerable varieties of damnation. I just want you to know that your wife is happy now.'

'That's what the minister said,' Thorne sniffed contemptuously. '"She's in a better place, Jacob. She's beyond the pain of this world." Hmph!'

'Mr Thorne, would you say that I might be something of an authority on the supernatural?'

Thorne looked at her oddly, as if it had never occurred to him that a vampire might actually be evidence of there being something beyond the worm and the tomb and the winding sheet.

'Mr Thorne, your wife *is* at peace. You see, heaven means different things to everyone. And, for your wife, heaven was an afternoon in 1955, celebrating the birthday of her only child.'

Thorne nodded his head. 'Yes . . . yes, I could see where it would be. I . . . I— Oh, God—'

Tears began to run down his cheeks. No doubt they were the first real ones he'd shed since his wife died. His shoulders shook so violently he looked like he was about to topple headlong into the open grave. 'Dear God, Denise—'

He reached for her with his trembling, old man's hand, but she was already gone.

9

By the time she got back everything had turned to shit. She could smell it the moment she got off the plane in Cozumel. The psychic stench a dead relationship gives off is a lot like that of days-old fish mixed with vomit and a garnish of dirty diapers.

The closer she drew to Mérida, the more powerful the reek became. She had no idea what had happened during her absence, but it had not been good.

The house was empty when she arrived, the front door unlocked. She scanned for signs of life and came up empty. The kitchen table was covered with unpaid bills, unopened mail, and empty tequila bottles. Lots of tequila bottles. Sonja went out onto the patio, searching for signs of Lethe's cocoon, but all she found was something that looked like pieces of snake molt, made brittle and black from exposure to the sun.

'Lethe?' Sonja called out, half expecting her stepdaughter to come rushing from some hiding place, giggling in delight at having tricked her. There was no answer.

'Lethe?'

Silence.

She went back into the house and headed for the nursery. She stared at the plush stuffed animals and coyly smiling rag dolls that lined the shelves and filled every corner of the room. Something behind her eyes began to pulse and ache. She could hear Shirley Thorne's voice singing 'Happy Birthday to You'.

Sonja waded into the sea of stuffed toys, tossing them aside as she searched for her child. Panic and confusion and self-loathing rose in her gut. How could she have been so stupid? How could she have walked off and left the child? Was this how Shirley Thorne felt when she received the news that her daughter had disappeared? No wonder the poor woman retreated into madness.

'Lethe, this isn't funny anymore! Come out where I can see you!' Failing to get any response with her voice, Sonja called with her mind.

Lethe!

'Lethe doesn't live here anymore.'

Palmer stood slumped in the doorway, arms folded across his chest, watching with unreadable eyes. He looked rough, but he was wearing clean clothes and was freshly shaven. Nor was he drunk. The odor of dead love came off him in waves.

He'd come up behind her without Sonja picking him up on radar. Which meant either she'd been really out of it, or he was screening himself. Probably both.

Bill?

She stepped towards him and he drew back, hugging his elbows as if he was afraid she was going to try and touch him.

'Talk with your mouth,' he rasped. 'I don't want you in my head.'

'What do you mean she doesn't live here anymore? Where the hell is she?'

Palmer laughed, only it sounded more like a hiccup. He hugged himself tighter. 'I don't know where she is. Nor do I want to.'

'What the—? Bill, we're talking about Lethe here! She's only three years old! Where the hell could she go?'

Palmer shrugged and laughed that weird laugh again.

'Palmer, damn it, what's wrong with you? Where's Lethe? She couldn't have just flown away!'

Palmer's laughter now had the edge of hysteria to it. He guffawed until he couldn't catch his breath and dropped to his knees, doubling over to cradle his heaving stomach. Sonja reached down to touch him but he recoiled from her, shaking his head frantically as he forced himself to speak between bursts of giggling.

'Don't . . . touch . . . me.'

'Palmer, what the fuck is going on? For the love of God, straighten up, man!' She grabbed his elbow, helping him back to his feet. He snarled and lashed out at her with his mind. Had she been a normal human, he might have succeeded in crippling her, but Sonja was far from human. Palmer's attack was the same as that of an angry child, hammering at the legs of his mother with chubby fists. And mother had had enough of it.

She pinned him to the floor with her mind as easily as she might mount a butterfly on a piece of velvet. He lay at her feet, his muscles twitching and jerking as he tried, in vain, to regain control of his body.

'I don't want to play rough, Palmer, but you're leaving me no choice. Now stand up.'

Palmer's arms and legs moved jerkily as he obeyed her commands. The look in his eyes was black and ugly. Sonja looked away, but there was no way she could shield herself from his hate. It was thick and viscous and burned like boiling tar.

She led Palmer's body out of Lethe's bedroom into his own, where she made him sit on the bed. She positioned herself opposite him and withdrew her control. Palmer's shoulders sagged and for a moment Sonja was afraid he was going to pass out on her, but then he straightened his back and took a deep breath.

'Okay, tell me what happened here.'

Palmer glared at her, then glanced in the direction of the patio. 'She – she came out.'

'When?'

He shrugged. 'I . . . I don't know. A couple of days after you left. I was too drunk to remember exactly when.'

'What happened when Lethe came out of the cocoon? What did she look like?'

Palmer's eyes suddenly went distant, as if he was seeing something inside himself. 'Beautiful. She was beautiful. She was older than when she went in – she was maybe sixteen or seventeen. But she was beautiful. And she . . . and she . . . she was on fire.'

'On fire. Like the pyrotics?'

Palmer shook his head violently. 'No! Not like burning on fire – she was glowing, you know? Like in the pictures of the Virgin Mary.'

'Palmer, what did Lethe say to you? What did she do?'

Palmer took a deep breath and his gaze fell to his hands, which were battling with one another like dueling tarantulas. 'She . . . she thanked me for taking care of her, for protecting her when she needed it, and she said I was . . . I was going to be the first.'

'The first? The first what?'

'Bridegroom.' Palmer's lower lip began to tremble and he looked up at Sonja. There was anger and confusion and hurt in his eyes, and for a moment she was once again standing by her mother's grave, staring into the face of her father.

'Bridegroom? Palmer, what did she mean by that?'

'I don't know. All I know is that she . . . she made me do it. I wouldn't have done it on my own, you know that, don't you? You know I would never have done something like that—'

'Done what? What did Lethe make you do, Palmer?'

'Fuck her.'

Sonja sat there for a moment, letting what Palmer had said sink in. She didn't know if she was shocked or not. After all, Palmer hadn't actually sired Lethe. But, then again, what difference did that make? He'd been a daddy to her in every other way. As much as he'd professed to detest children, Palmer had proven himself to be a championship father.

God, no wonder he was in such a state. The human animal came with a lot of behavioral hard-wiring – some of it biological, some of it societal. The incest taboo was one of the few that might be both.

Sonja walked over to the window and stared out at the jungle-covered hills.

Forget Palmer. He's meat. Look at him, if you don't believe me: his circuits are blown, whispered the Other. *You knew it'd come some day, sooner or later. It happens to all renfields, eventually.*

Sonja closed her eyes and dug her fingernails into her palms until the blood came.

'Palmer, what happened then? After . . . after Lethe fucked you?'

'She flew away.'

She sighed and turned back to face Palmer. He was still seated on the corner of the bed, staring down at his hands as his fingers battled one another. What had she gotten herself into? She comes home to try and patch up her family, only to find her stepchild has raped its father and flown off to who knows where, leaving behind a severely traumatized victim of incest.

'Bill?'

'Yes, Sonja?'

'You're going to go to sleep for a little while. When you wake up, you won't remember anything about Lethe. You won't remember her living with us. You won't remember taking care of her. You won't remember anything. It will be as if she never existed.'

'But—'

'Go to sleep, Bill.'

She was out hunting, tracking a wild pig through the dense jungle undergrowth. She brought it down with her bare hands. It squealed angrily and tried to slash her with its tusks. It struggled hard, like all things do when they know their lives are at stake. Just before she sank her fangs into its jugular, the pig released twin streams of shit and piss in a last-ditch bid for freedom. Or maybe it was simply that scared.

It was well past midnight by the time she returned to the house. She climbed in through the bedroom window, expecting to find Palmer where she'd left him; sprawled, fully clothed, across the bed. Instead, the bed was empty, Palmer gone. She searched the other rooms. Palmer was nowhere to be found in the house.

She stepped outside and cast her mind into the dark, searching for the hum and buzz of thought that had become so familiar to her in the last three years. At first she picked up nothing; then, as she intensified her scan, she found traces of him. He had constructed an elaborate system of telepathic baffles in order to shield himself. But why? She had edited Lethe from his mind. His trauma should have vanished along with his memories. So why was he still trying to keep her from speaking to him mind to mind?

Sonja found a path at the bottom of the property, leading into the jungle. She recognized it as the trail that led to a Mayan ruin on a nearby hill. She'd only been there once, but she knew Palmer visited it often. Quite often, if the condition of the path was anything to go by.

She followed the trail to the top of the hill, where a vine-covered jumble of stone that had once been an ancient observatory sat lumped against the night sky. Palmer was seated on a mammoth block carved to resemble a snarling jaguar. He was not alone.

The woman with him was young, little more than a girl. She was from one of the native tribes, the ones Palmer called the Lacandon. She was short, with long black hair that hung down between her shoulders like a curtain. They sat side by side, turned towards one another. Palmer held her hand in his and they spoke in a language she did not recognize. Not that she needed to recognize the words to know what they were saying. It was perfectly clear they spoke as lovers.

See? See what your precious little lover boy is doing? The Other's voice was sharp, sweet, and nasty, like honeyed razor blades. *This is what happens when you let your renfields run free. It happened with Chaz, now it's happening with Palmer. In the end, they betray you. They'll always betray you.*

Palmer lowered his head, bringing his face close to the girl's. Sonja could imagine the heat of his breath on the girl's cheek, the smell of him filling her senses, the taste of his lips. She clenched her fists and ground her teeth together. The anger building inside her was thick and hot, like boiling wax. Her head ached and her forebrain felt as if it had been stung by a swarm of wasps. The Other's voice was loud, giggling like a harpy.

You have to put them on a short leash. That's how to keep them in line. That's how Pangloss and Morgan and all the others keep their renfields loyal. You've got to scrape every vestige of free will out of them, hollow them out like a fuckin' jack-o'-lantern. You have to turn them into slaves. Believe me, that's the only way. And they deserve it. They even like it.

'How cozy.'

Palmer jumped up at the sound of her voice, automatically shielding the girl with his body. Sonja felt first a twinge of pain, then anger, at seeing this.

'Sonja!'

She emerged from the darkness like blood from a wound, the jungle moonlight dappling her leather jacket. She paused, leaning against the pockmarked limestone of the ruin like a tough lounging under a street lamp. The girl gasped and crossed herself. Obviously Palmer had told her about his live-in girlfriend.

'So, this is your back-door woman, huh?' She jerked her head at the cowering girl. 'Does she know you're fresh from my bed? Can she smell me on you, like I can smell *her*?' The last few words came out as a growl as she showed her fangs. The girl cried out and her nails bit into Palmer's naked upper arm.

'Leave her be, Sonja. Concha's innocent. If you've got to punish someone, punish me.'

'You love her.' It wasn't a question.

Palmer glanced down into Concha's dark brown eyes, now bright with fear, and nodded. 'Yes, I do.'

When she finally spoke, her voice was very still. She could tell this scared Palmer more than anything else.

'I could kill her, you know. I could kill her and make it so you wouldn't even know she had ever existed. It would be as easy for me as wiping a chalkboard clean. Easier.'

'Don't you think I know that?'

'Do you?' She laughed, taking a step forward. It would have been so easy for her to reach into his head and flip the switch, releasing the memories she had hidden from him only hours before. Part of her wanted to see the look on his girlfriend's face when the memories came back, washing over him like a tidal wave, smashing his ego into kindling. That would be fun. She could do it over and over again, wiping his memories of Lethe, then restoring them, so every time he experienced the pain it would be fresh and raw, as though it had never happened before. Maybe she would do that with his girlfriend's murder. Make him forget her, then force him to relive her death over and over . . .

Sonja halted, swaying slightly like a drunkard brought up short. Her gaze was fixed on Concha, who returned her stare like a sparrow entranced by a snake.

'Don't do it, Sonja. Don't make me try and kill you.'

Her laughter was as hollow as old bone. 'Try is all you *could* do. You're no match for me, Palmer.'

'I know that. There's no way I could hope to defeat you. But I'd try.'

She grunted and came closer, peering down at the cowering girl pressed tightly to Palmer's side. Palmer was watching her face, trying to decide if he was dealing with Sonja or the Other. Concha moaned slightly and gripped Palmer even tighter than before.

'Why this one? What's so special about this particular female?' Sonja sniffed.

'Concha found me naked and sick in the jungle miles from here . . . I don't know how I got there, or why I was there, but she nursed me back to health. She helped me get home. She was there for me when I needed someone.'

'But she's not like you!'

'She's human. I need human, Sonja.'

'You know what I mean! She's not a sensitive. You can never commune with her on the same plane as you and I do.'

'We don't have that anymore, Sonja. You know that as well as I do. You shut yourself away from me the moment you got back from New Orleans. I tried to reach out to you, to try and understand whatever it was you were going through, but it was no use. It's as if you can't be satisfied unless I'm as miserable as you are!'

'Palmer – Bill – you don't understand! I didn't want you to be hurt, that's all. I didn't want you to see me as a monster—'

'It's a little late for that, don't you think?'

'Don't do this to me, Bill. Don't make me beg. I need you.'

'You don't need me. You don't need anyone.'

'That's not true.'

'Isn't it? Sonja, if I stay with you, I'm in danger of losing my soul. I'll end up just like one of Morgan's renfields. Is that what you want for me? Is it?'

Don't bother answering the jerk, just reach into his head and snap his will off at the faucet, hissed the Other. *By the way, I liked the bit about killing his girlfriend and making him forget her, then relive her death whenever you feel like a chuckle. Not bad. Not bad at all. You're getting the hang of this stuff, girlfriend.*

Sonja balled her fists and looked down at her boots. 'No. Of course not.'

The Other hissed and spat obscenities no one else could hear.

'Then give me my freedom.'

She jerked her head up, moonlight flaring across the mirrored lenses of her glasses. 'You've always had it!'

'Have I?'

Sonja opened her mouth as if to answer, then turned her back on Palmer and his lover.

'Go.'

Her voice felt tight and sharp, like a piano-wire garrote had been slipped around her throat. She could hear Palmer shift his weight, trying to decide whether to stay or flee.

'Sonja—' There was a hesitancy in his voice.

'I said *go*! Before I change my mind!'

Palmer grabbed Concha by the hand and hurried from the ruins into the surrounding jungle. Just before he disappeared into the tangled shadows, he turned and called out to her with his mind one last time.

I did love you.

Then he was gone.

Sonja tossed her head back and shrieked like a cornered jaguar. Yowling obscenities, she kicked and pummeled the ancient limestone ruins, obliterating friezes depicting the rule of Mayan wizard-kings a thousand years dead. With a yell that swelled her throat like a bull ape's, she bashed her shoulder against the remaining wall until it collapsed in an explosion of yellowish-white powder.

When it was over, she stood in the middle of her handiwork, trembling like a winded stallion, her face and clothes limned with the dust of centuries.

I loved you too, she thought.

But there was no one there to hear her.

When she got back to the house Sonja was too tired to hate or even feel sorry for herself. The house seemed horribly empty. Lethe was gone. Now Palmer was, too. Within the span of a few days, the little nest she'd built for her family had turned into a tomb.

A featureless black papier-mâché mask sat atop a small pile of mail heaped on the kitchen table. As she picked up the mask, a thick business envelope slid off the heap and fell onto the floor. She noticed, with a rush of excitement, that it was addressed to Sonja Blue.

Inside the envelope were several clippings from the New York City/Triborough papers, the oldest dating back six months, the most recent clipping dated two weeks previously. Most of them were brief, taciturn accounts of the deaths of nameless prostitutes, none of the columns garnering more than an inch. As she placed them on the table where she could read them, she immediately noticed the one item that linked them: 'the deceased was found dressed in a black leather jacket, wearing mirrored sunglasses.'

Sonja picked up the envelope and searched for a letter. Nothing. The postmark told her it had been mailed in New York City from the Cooper Postal Station. The West Village. Already the gears were engaged, the wheels in her head turning. Palmer and Lethe might no longer be a part of her life.

But there was still Morgan.

10

London, England:

Mavis Bannister was a charwoman. Oh, they had a fancy
name for it nowadays – 'maintenance engineer', she thought
it was. Just like they had a fancy name for the women's
toilet: 'the ladies' lounge'. But, in essence, her job was to
swab down the loos at Farquier & Sons.

Farquier & Sons was one of the more prestigious depart-
ment stores in London. It began by catering to the carriage
trade over a century ago. The store's reputation rested on a
royal commission it had landed during the Edwardian era and
had yet to be updated – something involving spats. In any
case, its clientele included movie stars and rock musicians,
not to mention stockbrokers and MPs. Still, if anyone was to
ask Mavis, she would tell them that the rich and famous treat
public lavatories just like the hoi polloi. You'd be surprised
how many couldn't bother to flush.

Still, mopping the jakes of the overprivileged had its definite
perks. Like the time she found a pair of mink-lined gloves left
next to the sink. Or the time she found close to twenty quid
lying on the floor next to the second stall – no doubt it fell
out of some rich twit's pocketbook. Most of them were so
well off they'd never notice it was gone, or, if they did, would
assume they'd dropped it while getting in or out of a taxi, not
while they were taking a squat in a public bog.

Mavis wasn't really thinking about anything much that
day except whether to warm up a tin of stew when she got
home or pop for some takeout vindaloo, as she wheeled her
mop and bucket into the ladies' lounge. It was towards the

end of the business day and time for the third of the four
scheduled daily cleanings. Farquier & Sons prided itself on
the cleanliness of its 'lounges'.

At first she thought she was hearing things. It sounded like
a baby crying, only muffled. No doubt a child was crying out
on the floor. Then she realized that the sound was coming
from the litter bin next to the sinks.

Mavis flipped back the little metal hood and stared down
into the cylinder. There, nestled amidst wadded-up brown
paper towels and discarded tampons was a newborn infant,
wrapped in a swaddling of newspaper, just like an order of
fish and chips. The baby stopped crying and looked up at
Mavis with eyes the color of marigolds and smiled at her.

'Merciful God!' Mavis gasped. 'You poor thing!' She set
aside her mop and bucket and removed the top of the litter
bin, reaching in to retrieve the child. There was a sound from
behind her as the Home Secretary's wife entered the ladies'
lounge.

'Go and get the shopwalker!' Mavis barked.

The Home Secretary's wife looked first startled, then
indignant, that she was being ordered about by a simple
charwoman. 'I *beg* your pardon—?' she began to huff.

'I said, go and fetch the shopwalker! Someone's gone an'
left a baby in the bleedin' litter bin!'

The Home Secretary's wife blinked, her face going blank
for a moment. 'Oh. Oh dear. Of course. I'll go and find
him.'

Mavis chuckled to herself, taking a moment's pleasure in the
role reversal, then looked down at the baby she held cradled
in her arms. It had been a long time since she'd held a child
that small. The baby's dark hair was still damp with birth
fluids and his skin was smeared with tacky blood. It was
a boy and apparently healthy, although the umbilical cord
looked like it had been chewed off. Whoever the mother was,
she must have given birth in one of the stalls. Mavis opened
each and every one of the doors, looking for signs of blood

and placenta. To her surprise, the toilets and the floors were spotless. But that was impossible . . .

The shopwalker, an elderly man with a neatly clipped salt-and-pepper mustache, opened the door to the ladies' lounge and peered in, mustache twitching. 'What's all this nonsense about there being a baby left in here? And have you gone mad? That was the Home Secretary's wife you yelled at!'

Mavis held up the baby, still wrapped in its receiving blanket of newsprint. 'You call this nonsense, sir?'

The shopwalker's eyes widened at the sight of the child. 'Good Lord!'

'Did you see a pregnant woman come in here in the last ten or fifteen minutes? The poor thing can't be more than five minutes old himself!'

The shopwalker looked genuinely perplexed. 'I don't understand! There hasn't been a woman in such a condition on this floor since noon! I could swear it! I'm sure I would have noticed . . .'

'So where'd this poor tad come from, eh?' Mavis sighed, running her work-roughened hand against the baby's cheek. 'His mum must have been in the store. Surely the fairies didn't leave him. Too bad he can't tell us who he belongs to.'

The nameless son of William Palmer yawned, waved his chubby little fists in the air, and smacked his toothless gums, wondering all the while when he was going to be fed.

Heilongjiang Province, the People's Republic of China:

The madman's name was Sun Wang Zuocai, and he had spent the last thirty-three of his seventy-seven years locked away in a private sanitarium in the frozen climes of Heilongjiang Province in the People's Republic of China. There are many such sanitariums scattered throughout Communist China where those considered bent on 'criminal insanity against the State' and deemed impossible to reeducate have been banished. What made this particular sanitarium different from the others was that Sun Wang Zuocai was its only inmate.

None of the six staff members assigned to watch over him could understand what was so important – or dangerous – about the old man that he had to be kept in isolated confinement and dosed with the most potent of psychoactive drugs.

Thin to the point of being emaciated, his arms and legs withered from decades spent strapped into a straitjacket and manacled to his bed, with a long beard and mustache the color of fresh snow, and a piercing gaze that seemed to look through both time and space, Sun Wang Zuocai looked more like a crazed wizard from the Beijing opera than a senile mental patient. And that, more or less, was the truth. Although no one save a select handful of Party leaders knew of his existence, at one time Sun Wang Zuocai had served as mystic adviser to Chairman Mao.

Wang Zuocai was born in 1917 in Zhejiang Province, a place renowned for its scenic beauty. His father was a wealthy man, heir to a sizable tea plantation and silkworm concern that stretched back three centuries. His mother, however, was of even nobler stock. Her family was descended from a long line of wise men and sorcerers who had advised the emperors since the days of the Ch'in Dynasty. By the time he was five years old, Wang Zuocai's talent as an oracle was already making itself known. But then the Japanese came and things became bad for his family. His parents hoped that he would someday become a member of General Chiang Kai-shek's retinue, but Wang Zuocai's second sight told him that the future lay with Mao Zedong. So, at the age of eighteen, he joined the Chinese Communist Party and found himself on the Long March.

During those hard, torturous years, on the run from both the Nationalists and the occupying Japanese, Wang Zuocai came to be one of Mao's most trusted – and secret – personal advisers. At first his precognitive abilities were limited to a few minutes and those who were physically present, but as time progressed, so did his power to see into the future.

Mao relied on Wang Zuocai's talents a great deal, but he had to be exceptionally careful in screening the exact nature of his confidant's ability. If his Soviet advisers got wind of Wang Zuocai, they would either dismiss Mao as a fool or try to steal Wang for their own uses. It would not help matters amongst his fellow workers if it was discovered he was using the services of an oracle, a habit associated with the Imperial dynasties. Sun Wang Zuocai was one of the most powerful and influential members of the CCP, yet no one knew who he was. And so it went for twenty-two years.

Until 1958.

Before 1958, there had been the First Five-Year Plan, which emphasized rapid industrial development and expansion. Iron and steel, electric power, heavy engineering, and other sophisticated, highly capital-intensive plants were pushed at the expense of agriculture, which, up until then, had occupied more than eighty percent of the population.

Now Mao proposed the introduction of the Second Five-Year Plan, which he called the Great Leap Forward. The Great Leap Forward called for the abolition of private plots and the formation of communes, and the increase of agricultural output through greater cooperation and physical effort. The Chairman called his oracle to him and told him of his plans and asked what great future Wang Zuocai foresaw for China.

What Wang Zuocai saw was crop failure and famine, leading to the starvation of millions and, eventually, to the dissolution of diplomatic ties between China and the Russians and Mao being forced to retire as chairman of the republic. Mao, already growing accustomed to being worshiped as the wisest of men, took exception with Wang Zuocai's prophecy and denounced him as a reactionary. The very next day, Wang Zuocai was arrested as he left his house and taken to a 'reeducation facility' in Jiangxi Province.

He spent most of his time in solitary confinement, endless tape loops quoting the wisdom of the Chairman haranguing him from hidden speakers day and night. The only time he saw other people was when the guards came in to beat him. Malnourished and forced to sleep on lice-ridden straw, denied anything to read except the writings of the Chairman, Wang Zuocai's talent began feeding on itself, growing stronger and wilder. Soon he was able to predict the guards' arrival to the minute, even though he had no way of keeping time.

On one occasion, as he was being beaten, he looked up into the face of one of his guards and said: 'Your wife is being untrue behind your back. She takes the village Party official into her bed the moment you leave the house. He is with her now.' The guard called him a liar and struck him with his rifle, breaking Wang's jaw. Two days later, the guard caught his wife in bed with the village Party official and shot them both, then turned the rifle on himself. Wang Zuocai had seen that part, too, which is why he'd told the guard in the first place.

By 1961 the Great Leap Forward had proven itself to be a disaster. Uncounted millions had starved to death in the outlying provinces, and the Soviets had left in disgust, taking their blueprints with them. Mao, chastised, retired as chairman of the republic, if not the Party. Not long after his resignation, Mao ordered Wang Zuocai's release from prison and had his old adviser brought back to the Forbidden City. But he quickly discovered that the Sun Wang Zuocai who stood before him was not the man he used to know.

Although Wang Zuocai was only forty-four, his ordeal had turned his hair white and cost him most of his teeth. But what Mao found most discomforting were his eyes – they seemed to see into a disturbing distance. Occasionally Wang Zuocai would grimace or shake his head or smirk at something only he could see. After offering his former confidant some rice wine, Mao asked him what it was he saw. Wang Zuocai said he saw many things, but at that moment he was watching the assassination of the Americans' most recent president.

He then went on to forecast, in no real order, the fall of Saigon, the death of a black musician, and Nixon standing on the Great Wall.

Mao did not know if the oracle was, indeed, seeing the future or if he'd gone mad. When Wang Zuocai veered from forecasting the future into claiming to have knowledge of non-human races dwelling unseen amongst humanity, and accusing Mao's own wife, Jiang Qing, of having the head of a vixen, Mao decided Wang Zuocai was indeed insane. As much as it saddened him to realize that he had been instrumental in destroying his friend's mind, part of him couldn't help sigh in relief. That bit about Nixon and the Great Wall had really had him worried for a moment . . .

So Sun Wang Zuocai was bundled off to the frozen frontiers of Heilongjiang Province, to be tended by nurses and doctors better suited to the treating of farm animals, for the rest of his natural life. Which, it proved, had been considerably longer than Mao's. In the years since his initial commitment, he'd only had one visitor – Deng Xiaoping. He'd asked Wang Zuocai two questions, then never returned. However, Deng did order that Wang be kept in a straitjacket round the clock from that day forward. Now, after fifteen years, he was to receive his second – and final – visitor.

She poured herself through the reinforced window, her skin glowing like light shining through a glass of plum wine. Wang Zuocai watched silently as she moved toward his bed, her feet skimming the cold bare tiles. Everything in Heilongjiang was cold. The winters were fierce and harsh, lasting up to eight months. For someone such as himself, born and bred in the warmer southern climes, nothing was ever warm enough. But that was about to change.

The glowing woman smiled down at him, radiating a heat that sank through his wrinkled skin and into his ancient bones. How long had it been since he'd last known a woman? Thirty-six years? It had been the better part of a decade since he'd been able to masturbate.

The woman gestured with her hands and the canvas strait-jacket that had been Wang Zuocai's one article of clothing since 1979 disintegrated as if made from tissue paper. Freed at last, Wang Zuocai's member rose to greet its liberator. Smiling demurely, the woman climbed onto the bed and straddled the old oracle.

Sun Wang Zuocai had foreseen this night encounter the day he went before Mao and spoke of the American president and of Lady Mao being one of the *kitsune*. He knew that Mao would dismiss him as mad, but that was the only way to ensure that he would survive the coming years of turmoil, with its Cultural Revolution and Gang of Four and Tiananmen Square. It was the only way to make sure that he somehow managed to live to see the arrival of a beautiful glowing woman, who would make him the father of a new and wondrous race.

It didn't take him long. After all the planning, all the waiting, everything was happening so fast. As his celestial lover pulled herself off him, Sun Wang Zuocai felt something in his chest fold in on itself. Fast. Everything was happening so fast – first the mating, now his death. Even as his seed quickened in her womb, Wang Zuocai's life came to its end. Of course, he had already known it was going to happen.

Part 2

When the Dead Die

Death is not the greatest of evils; it is worse to want to die, and not be able to.

Sophocles, *Electra*

The fever called 'Living'
Is conquered at last.

Edgar Allan Poe, 'For Annie'

11

As she stepped out of the limo in front of the Chelsea Hotel the first thing she saw was a homeless person pissing in a doorway. She smiled and tossed the driver an extra twenty.

Hell, it's New York.

The limo pulled back into the traffic and she shouldered her one piece of luggage – a black nylon duffel bag – and strode towards the entrance of the hotel, just in case she was being watched. She did a turn in the revolving door and was back on the streets within seconds, her hair five inches longer and the color of raw honey.

She kept a nest in Tribeca, a stone's throw from City Hall. There were a couple of holding companies and realty agencies involved in collecting rents and maintaining the property, but essentially she owned the building. She'd bought it several years ago with some of the proceeds from Ghilardi's estate.

She dodged into the subway entrance on Eighth Avenue, dropping her vision into the Pretender spectrum, scanning for signs of the inhuman amongst the commuting hordes. In any major city there were numerous shadow races hidden amongst the bread-and-butter featherless bipeds, and New York was certainly no exception.

It was five-thirty – well into the rush hour – and the subway platform swarmed with the Pretending kind of a dozen different cultures, each having followed its traditional prey group to the New World in search of a better life. A *naga* wearing the skin of an elderly Pakistani gentleman flared his cobra's hood at her in ritual warning, then went back to peruse its newspaper. A *garuda*, cloaked in the disguise of a lowly busboy, clattered its bill nervously as it fed itself unshelled sunflower seeds. It kept exchanging glances with the *naga*. Their respective species were ancestral enemies, but having to maintain the appearance of humans – and catch a train – forced the necessity of coexistence. At least for the moment.

An ogre, its misshapen limbs hidden by homeboy fashion, slouched against one of the support beams. A succubus, dressed in the body of a young woman, smiled seductively at an older man in a London Fog raincoat carrying a briefcase, who was fumbling for a light for her cigarette. She doubted he could see the succubus's cyclopean eye or the mane of living, writhing worms she sported in place of hair.

Suddenly the platform was full of the smell of ozone and filth and the A train came thundering out of the tunnel. It screeched to a halt and the doors opened. Inside she found a *vargr* dressed as an investment banker, and a thickset, clay-eyed golem serving as an escort for an extremely old Hasidic man who, according to her peripheral mind scan, was carrying a fortune in diamonds on his person.

She rode the train to the World Trade Center, then made her way to the surface. The first thing she saw as she exited the glass and steel megalith was the seventeenth-century churchyard across the street. Twilight had mellowed into dusk while she was underground, and, amazing as it might seem in such an urban landscape, a handful of fireflies danced between the leaning tombstones.

Her nest was located on Chambers Street off West Broadway. The building was six storeys tall, identical to those flanking it. The first three floors housed various businesses – a karate school, a photographer's studio, an accounting firm – while the top two floors were left vacant.

It was after six o'clock and all of the businesses were closed for the day. The elevator was old, with a collapsible gate and a control switch that looked like something from an old-fashioned ocean liner. She stopped the elevator on the fifth floor and rolled back the protective gate so she could unlock the outer barrier. She made a mental note to be careful not to trigger the booby traps she'd installed.

The entrance barrier rolled back with a rusty squeal, and she squeezed her eyes shut and grimaced, but nothing happened. She stepped out of the elevator into the foyer. A double-barreled shotgun and a loaded crossbow, rigged with fishing line and lead counterweights, were pointed at the elevator.

She unlocked the door to the fifth-floor loft and entered into total darkness. Not that it mattered. She could read the *New York Times* in the deepest pit in Carlsbad Cavern without straining her eyes. The loft had the dusty, close smell that sealed rooms often get. As it was, her nest was actually on the sixth floor. The fifth was empty of anything except booby traps. She liked keeping as much space between herself and whatever might be looking for her as possible.

One of the first things she had the renovators do when she bought the building a decade ago was alter the interior staircases. The original staircases had been sealed after the fifth floor and a second staircase installed that bypassed the fifth and sixth floors on its way to the roof, thus ensuring her privacy. But, this *was* New York City, after all, so she placed a few booby traps in her private stairwell just to be on the safe side.

She unlocked the door that led to the roof after disarming the spear gun aimed at gut level. The moment she opened the door, she knew that one of the traps had been sprung.

She found what was left of the would-be burglar on the landing between the roof and the sixth floor. He'd triggered the deadfall, sending a cinder block secured by a rope into the middle of his face. He had probably been young, although it was hard to tell with most of his features pulped. He'd been lying there at least a month or two, and he'd decayed to the point where she couldn't tell if he was black, white, latino, or asian. In any case, he was dead.

Sonja dragged the body down to the sixth floor and unlocked the door to the loft, careful not to trigger the old box-spring mattress studded with bayonets hinged to the ceiling just inside the threshold. The sixth floor was sectioned into three large areas centered around a long hallway. The one closest to the entrance was a fully outfitted workroom with a carpenter's bench and a huge array of power tools. Not to mention a large glass-lined metal tub.

With the help of a few well-chosen power tools, it took her less than ten minutes to reduce her unwanted guest to component parts. She tossed the limbs and viscera into the glass-lined tub and opened one of the industrial-sized hydrocholoric acid bottles she kept in a special cabinet. The solution was meant to process metal, but it was also handy in turning troublesome dead bodies into soup.

Satisfied that her erstwhile intruder was liquefying nicely, Sonja shucked her protective gloves and apron and headed down the hall to the room set aside as living space. At a thousand square feet, it was larger than most New York apartments. A kitchenette, complete with microwave, dishwasher, gas range, refrigerator, and breakfast bar took up one corner. There was an inch or more of dust on every surface and a shriveled orange the size of a walnut in the fridge. What had once been a walk-in closet was now a bathroom, with shower and toilet, and a loft bed occupied the exposed brick wall. Thick Persian carpets covered the floor, and the ceiling was decorated with drooping falls of mosquito netting, giving the space the feel of a bedouin's tent. A couple of starkly chic halogen lamps, a free-standing antique wardrobe, and an oversized leather chair set in front of a projection television screen were the only other pieces of furniture.

Sonja opened the wardrobe and the smell of cedar filled the room. Inside were hung several expensive silk suits sealed in protective plastic wrappers, along with half a dozen matching black silk shirts. Four pairs of Italian shoes littered the floor of the wardrobe. Chaz's stuff. He'd had a taste for the expensive things in life. Not necessarily good, mind you, just expensive. She bundled the suits together and dumped them in the tub with the melting burglar, then went back into the living area and stripped naked.

She hadn't realized she was still a blonde until she looked down at her crotch in the shower. She closed her eyes and, when she reopened them, the last of the yellow was being replaced by black. Her hair was still long, though. Since it was impossible for her to shorten her hair the same way she forced its growth, she elected to jettison it. She ran her fingers through her hair and all twelve inches dropped to the floor of the shower. By the time she'd stepped out to towel herself dry, her scalp was already bristling with fresh growth.

If I am going to find a clue as to where to locate Morgan, it will be in the traditional hunting grounds of the urban vampire – the nightclub. I hit the first one around midnight. The interior is designed to resemble a church, with stained-glass windows and a disc jockey spinning CDs in the pulpit. The waitresses are dressed as nuns, except that they wear miniskirts, high heels, and fishnet stockings. There are a lot of lasers and loud music, but the faces that stare back at me through the dance floor fog are painfully human. I leave before one o'clock.

The second club is a cavernous space filled with taxidermy exhibits liberated from defunct roadside attractions. A cougar, frozen in mid-leap, reaches out for a startled mountain goat. A grizzly bear, its fur somewhat moth-eaten, towers over the main bar, as if warding off imprudent drinkers. The head of a gigantic water buffalo, its nose worn down by club patrons stroking it for luck, peers off into space, no doubt eyeing the ghost of the Great White Hunter who plugged it decades ago.

As I wind my way through the club-goers, I get the distinct feeling I'm being watched – and not just by the glass eyes of the dead animals on the wall. I duck through a beaded curtain into one of the orgy alcoves off the main floor. The walls are painted with fluorescent paint and lit by black light-tubes. A king-size mattress on a carpeted dais dominates the middle of the room. A couple of queens tricked out in Mary Tyler

Moore drag, wearing six-inch platform shoes, are sitting on the bed, smoking a joint. They look at me quizzically, then return to their previous conversation.

'So what did you tell Donny?'

'Just that she should go ahead and get *big* ones. I mean, if she's planning on dancing to pay for the operation, she ought to give them what they want . . .'

I grab my shadow before he even clears the curtain, slamming him against the wall. I have my forearm pinned against his windpipe and my switchblade a millimeter from his right eye.

'Tell me why you're following me, or I'll put it out,' I hiss.

The drag queens gather up their purses and exit the alcove as quickly as their platform heels can carry them.

My shadow smiles slow and wide, opening his hands to show me they are empty. 'No need to get hostile, milady. I mean you no harm.'

I step back and let him go, but I do not put away the knife. My shadow is a man of slight build, about five foot seven. His hair, which he wears in a medusa's coil of tightly woven dreadlocks, is gray, but it is hard to guess his age. There are ceramic beads, pieces of metal, and what look like knucklebones braided into his locks. He wears a loose-fitting black overcoat that reaches almost to his ankles, tight-fitting black leather pants, a black velvet dress shirt with a ruffled dickey, and Doc Martens that lace up to his knees. Although his hands are finely manicured, he sports pimp spoons on both ring fingers; his nails are so long they curl inward. He smiles easily at me, but his pale blue eyes watch me intently, like a cat trying to calculate the best way to evade the jaws of a dog.

'Why were you following me?'

'It's my job to follow . . . those such as you.' His right hand dips into the breast pocket of his overcoat and retrieves a printed invitation. 'My . . . employers . . . are discreet and very . . . discriminating . . . as to who they allow into their establishment. Their clientele 'tis most select, indeed.' He hands me the card with a flourish. 'Tell them Jen sent you, milady.' And with that he slips from the alcove, pausing only long enough to look over his shoulder to make sure I'm not about to plunge my switchblade into his back.

I study the invitation, frowning slightly. In appearance it looks no different than any of the thousands of invites and announcements handed out on the New York party circuit every night. The picture on the front is of a naked female torso. The nipples are pierced and connected by a fine filigreed chain, the labia infibulated. A surgical steel ring winks from the model's navel. On the back is printed, in Gothic script: 'The Black Grotto at No Exit: W.14th at 10th Avenue. Open to the Trade.'

There is something odd about the texture of the ink used to print the card – and something familiar about it, as well. I sniff it, then taste it with the tip of my tongue. Human blood has been mixed with the ink. Quite a bit of it, too.

I step out of the alcove just as the two drag queens are coming back with the bouncer. I slip into the murk of the dance floor and I'm out the door in seconds. No matter. I already know which nightclub I'm going to hit next.

The doorman at the No Exit is dressed in black leather chaps, a suede jockstrap, and a leather and chrome-studded slave harness. He scowls at me and lifts his hand to block my path.

'Seventy-five dollars t'get in.'

'Jen sent me,' I reply, holding up my invitation so he can see it.

The doorman jerks back his hand as if I'd scalded him, eyes widening. 'I'm sorry, milady! I . . . I didn't realize! Welcome to No Exit. You'll want the second door on the right after the ladies' room, in back of the main hall.'

I breeze past him into a cinder-block antechamber filled with gym lockers. I pass through a doorway hung with black velvet curtains and find myself headed down a concrete corridor lit by lurid red spots that make everything seem awash in blood. Fifty feet later there is a heavy vault door. I turn the handle and the door hisses open on pneumatic pistons. The sound of the Cure amplified beyond human endurance pours into the confines of the corridor.

The main hall of No Exit is large enough to park a jet. The cinder-block and poured-concrete floor motif is continued, accompanied by standard disco fog and laser light displays. There is a long bar made from cinder-blocks and glass bricks occupying most of the west wall, with a handful of tables and booths nearby. There is an elevated stage on the north wall, with a set of stocks, a flogging post, and a rack of whips and chains.

Close to a hundred people, all in various stages of undress, wander the floor. Some have black leather masks over their heads, some wear harnesses, and one patron walks around with a chrome bit in his mouth, the reins held by a pudgy woman stuffed into a Merry Widow corset. All of them, to my surprise, are human.

I make my way to the back of the club. The ladies' room is a toilet placed in the middle of a waist-high corral of cinder-blocks. The door I was instructed to find is guarded by a monstrously huge specimen wearing leather pants, a muscle shirt, and a zippered leather face mask. Try as it might, the hood cannot conceal the fact that the bouncer is an ogre.

'Jen sent me,' I say, flashing the invitation.

The ogre grunts something and stands aside, swiping a magnetic key through the computer lock that secures the door. I glimpse a stairway leading to the basement. Once I'm inside, the ogre closes the door behind me, leaving me to whatever fate I've walked into.

I hear music – not disco or techno or rave, but the strains of Mozart – as I climb down the stairs. At the bottom is yet another secured door, this one guarded by an ogre too misshapen to ever be mistaken for human, with or without a bondage mask. His single brow furrows and he rubs his lower left-hand tusk as he studies the invitation I hand him. In his huge, gnarled hand it looks like a playing card.

'Jen sent me,' I explain.

The ogre makes a snorting noise like that of a warthog and unlocks the final door with a key the size of a tire iron. 'Have a good night,' it oinks.

The interior of the club is dark, lit by low-wattage rose-colored bulbs so the human attendants don't trip and fall as they work the room. There is a lot of black velvet drapery, antique statuary and Victorian furniture in evidence. But the first thing that catches my notice upon entering are the people hanging from the ceiling. Some are men, some are women, some are children. Almost every major ethnic group seems to be represented. They are all naked and suspended by piano wire from hooks fixed in their flesh. Some are wrapped in barbed wire. Some have been flayed, peeled to expose the muscles that lurk beneath their skin. All of them are alive.

Something warm and wet strikes my hand. It's blood. I look up to see a partially skinned young man suspended directly overhead. The skin on his legs and feet has been carefully pared away, leaving only the bone. He smiles down at me like a medieval martyr, his eyes going in and out of focus as he speaks.

'Welcome to the Black Grotto, milady.'

The other human chandeliers take up his greeting, their voices slurred and dreamy.

This is my kind of place, purrs the Other.

I'm too distracted by the chorus of flayed cherubs to try and squash the Other's voice, so I lick the blood from my hand and move on. A woman encased completely in black latex, except for her throat, her arms stuffed into a single glove and bound behind her back, walks up to me, accompanied by the whir of a chain being paid out. I notice her dog collar is attached to a spool of stainless-steel chain set into the wall. Her exposed jugular is outfitted with a phlebotomist's shunt.

A slender young man dressed in lollipop panties and a starched pinafore steps forward, holding a solid-gold serving tray. On the tray are a syringe and a Baccarat crystal wineglass. I stare at the syringe, then back at the shunt set in the woman's neck. I cannot see her face – it is obscured by a leather bondage mask, the mouth zippered shut from the outside. Her eyes are wet and gleam like a trapped animal's.

I shake my head and turn away, both disgusted and excited by the display around me. In one corner of the room is a string quartet, playing Mozart's Symphony No. 40 in G Minor. Upon closer examination I can see that their eyelids are sewn shut and their mouths filled with ball gags.

There is a scream from elsewhere in the room and a naked boy no older than ten runs out from a curtained booth, blood streaming from the wound in his neck. A vampire dressed in the cassock and collar of a priest darts after him, hissing angrily. One of the attendants grabs the frightened boy by the hair and slams him against the wall, dazing the child. As I move forward to intervene, the priest-vampire slaps the attendant so hard the blow snaps his neck. The naked, bleeding boy, sniffling and knuckling his teary eyes, runs forward to embrace the vampire. The priest coos endearments and strokes the boy's hair, all the while leading him back to the curtained booth. The string ensemble switches from Mozart to the Kronos Quartet's arrangement of 'Purple Haze'. An ogre shambles out of the shadows and picks up the body of the dead attendant as if it weighs no more than a suitcase, tossing it over one stooped shoulder.

'I see you decided to come check out the scene.'

Jen is standing off to one side, watching me with a twist of a smile on his lips. He has his left arm draped over the narrow shoulders of a naked girl who looks to be about six or seven. The girl's eyes are heavily painted, like those of an Egyptian priestess, and her hairless labia are sewn shut.

Jen's smile disappears and he jerks his head in the direction of one of the curtained alcoves. 'My employers would speak with you, milady.'

'Your employers? And who might they be?'

Jen lifts the heavy velvet curtain at the mouth of the alcove and gestures for me to enter. 'Their most Serene Majesties Baron Luxor and the Lady Nuit.'

The names sound familiar, although I cannot place them. They are Nobles, that much is certain. In the twenty years I've spent in search of Morgan, I've only come across one other vampire of power – Pangloss, Morgan's own vampiric sire. Most of the bloodsuckers I've dealt with are exceptionally minor league, many no more than brain-dead revenants. Now I'm being brought before not one, but two Nobles. I make sure my switchblade is at the ready before entering.

Inside the audience chamber is an antique love seat on which is seated a male vampire, naked except for a black leather pouch, garter belt, black silk stockings, and matching patent-leather pumps. His hair, shaped to resemble a shaggy Beatles cut, frames a long face that has neither eyebrows nor lashes. The vampire's flesh is so pale it seems translucent, like that of a finely polished opal. A human male wrapped in a full bodysuit of latex lies curled at the vampire's feet like an adoring hound. I shift my vision into the Pretender spectrum in order the gauge the vampire lord's aura. It is a powerful one, surging and bubbling around his head like boiling sugar.

'You are Baron Luxor?'

The Noble's lips pull up in the approximation of a smile. 'And you are the Blue Woman?'

'I am Sonja Blue, if that's what you mean.'

Luxor sits up slowly, his eyes never leaving me. No doubt he's assessing me as well. 'We ordered Jen to keep an eye out for you. The old man told us you'd be coming sooner or later.'

'The old man?'

'Pangloss.' Luxor stands up, wobbling slightly on four-inch heels. 'He was the one who told us about you – that you were the one who marked Morgan, the one who devoured his chimera—'

'You keep saying "we", but I only see one of you. Where is this Lady Nuit Jen mentioned?'

Luxor smiles and turns to face me, flashing a brief glimpse of fang. 'Oh, she is here. She is *always* here.'

Suddenly Luxor's opalescent flesh starts to twitch and ripple, as the muscles underneath begin to dance. The vampire lord's waist seems to draw in on itself, as if cinched by an invisible hand. The muscles lining his chest slowly ripen and swell, blossoming into small, but serviceable, breasts. The leather pouch covering Luxor's sex begins to deflate as he retracts his testes. The bones in his face squelch and groan as they mold themselves into softer, more feminine aspects. A thick nest of coppery curls sprouts from his scalp, spilling down to cover his shoulders. I have to admit I'm impressed. Such tightly controlled shape-shifting is not easy, even amongst Nobles.

Lady Nuit claps her hands and the latex-coated slave jumps up and scurries off into the shadows, returning a moment later with a silk kimono decorated with butterflies. She stands there, arms outstretched, and allows him to dress her.

'Why were you looking for me?'

'We were told you were a creature of great power. A creature of . . . purpose. And that you would see the Lord of the Morning Star dead.'

'What's that got to do with you?'

Lady Nuit produces a syringe and sticks it into a shunt that juts out of the latex slave's elbow. As she speaks, she draws quarter of a pint of blood and decants it into a champagne flute. 'Morgan has been our enemy for centuries. Our broodlings have clashed and struggled with one another since the days of the Bourbon kings. Countless renfields have died in our service protecting us from his attacks on our person. We would see him dead forever.'

'So?'

Lady Nuit pauses to sniff the blood she's just drained, then sips it. She smiles appreciatively and motions for me to help myself. 'Exquisite! Please, do try some. It's from my private stock, as you can see.'

It had been a couple of days since I last fed – and on animal blood, not human. I can feel my palms begin to sweat and itch as I eye the latex slave. 'N-no thank you.'

Lady Nuit studies me, rolling the champagne flute between her palms thoughtfully. 'Ah, yes . . . Pangloss told us you had a peculiar attachment to humans. But you have tasted their blood, have you not?'

'Yes.'

'Then why are you hesitating? All the humans you have seen here tonight came here of their own free will. They *begged* us to use them in such a fashion. The world is full of those who seek their own destruction. They are drawn to our kind, like moths to the flame. You know that, my dear.'

'Even the children?'

'Runaways, each and every one of them, fleeing parents and guardians far more inhumane than ourselves. They asked us for refuge, and we provide it.'

'I don't believe you.' I focus my attention on the latex slave crouched at Nuit's feet. There are control threads the color of raw veins sprouting from his cowled head, leading back to Nuit/Luxor. With a single swipe of my mind, I sever the leash binding master to slave.

The latex slave jumps to his feet and begins screaming. He pulls off the mask shrouding his head, revealing himself to be an older man with gray hair and the look of a prosperous banker. Still shrieking, he claws at the shunt stuck in the crook of his arm, his eyes bulging out of their sockets like ping-pong balls.

'How *dare* you!' shrieks Lady Nuit, her bone-white cheeks marred by unbecoming raspberry blotches. She must be *really* pissed to get that much blood pushed into one area. 'How dare you break my leash?!?'

The latex slave's body snaps like a whip as Nuit shoves her will back into him. He collapses on the floor, his lips foaming and limbs twitching spasmodically. There is a ripe, unpleasantly organic smell as he shits his suit.

Nuit spins to face me, her eyes flashing red, fangs bared in ritual challenge. She is so flustered she's lost control of her physical nature and her features are sliding back towards those of Luxor. I briefly glimpse the vampire for what it truly is – a walking cadaver with skin the color of tallow, its withered flesh stretched taut over desiccated muscle – then the illusion is once more in place.

'I'll take your heart out for that, stripling,' Luxor snarls, reaching for me with fingers capped by six-inch-long talons.

'I don't think so,' I reply, the blade of my switchblade leaping out from my fist.

Luxor's eyes flare with fear at the sight of the silver blade and he draws back his hand as if he realized he was about to stick it in a hornet's nest. 'Put it away! Put that horrid thing away!' he hisses.

'What's the matter, your ladyship? Didn't Pangloss tell you about my little toy? The one I used to mark both Morgan *and* him?'

Luxor doesn't take his eyes away from the blade. He stares at it the way a cobra follows the motions of a fakir's flute. 'Silver,' he mumbles. '*Sssilver.*'

I start backing away from Luxor and out of the alcove, ready to fight my way out, if need be.

'So, you hate Morgan and want me to get him out of your way, is that it? Funny, Pangloss came to me with a similar proposal three years ago. Since you two – or should I say three? – are such good friends, I'm surprised he didn't tell you. You fuckin' Nobles are all the same – too afraid to get your own hands dirty! I couldn't care less about how you feel about Morgan. Oh, I'm going to kill him all right. But I'm going to do it for *me*, not some gender-bending bloodsucker! Oh, and Luxor? Once I've done him, I'm coming back for you. *Both* of you.'

I know I'm being followed. I felt my 'fan club' stalking me long before I left the West Village. And, from what I can sense of its mind, it isn't human. One of Luxor's by-blows, no doubt, sent to keep an eye on me and find out where I'm dossing down. Well, it's going to discover that I don't like being watched – the hard way.

I pretend I don't notice him, making sure to screen my thoughts, just in case the dead boy on my tail actually has some esper muscle. I saunter along the streets, leading him in the direction of Alphabet City, my hands stuffed in the pockets of my leather jacket, whistling a tune between my teeth. I stop in front of a store on First Avenue and study an artfully arranged display of Day of the Dead figurines. A papier-mâché and pipe-cleaner skeleton dressed as a surgeon opens up a skeleton patient; a skeleton groom marries a skeleton bride, while a skeleton beautician washes the bare skull of a skeleton patron. I smile, charmed by such naïve, and practical, interpretations of the After.

Even though it is going on four a.m., there are still people on the streets. I pass a handful of party-goers standing outside one of the Korean delis, clutching thirty-ouncers to their chests as they try to figure out where to head to next. A severely drunken man with a Jersey accent is bellowing into a nearby pay phone at the top of his lungs.

'Fuck you! Fuck-fuck-fuck!'

He tries to slam the receiver into the cradle, but misses. This makes him so angry he uses the receiver to beat the pay phone's protective metal shell.

'Fuck! Fuck! Fuck!'

The party-goers back away, uncertain how to handle their companion's slide into alcoholic rage. The pay phone abuser then tries to throw the receiver at a passing cab, but it doesn't go very far. However, the momentum of his swing throws him into me as I walk by. The sound he makes as I casually slam him back into the phone is meaty, like that of a dog struck by a speeding car. He stops shouting 'fuck'. The party-goers, their eyes suddenly wide and sober, clear the sidewalk as I pass.

I feel my shadow hesitate. The unconscious drunk is tempting, especially since his companions for the evening have abruptly abandoned him to whatever fate might come his way. I don't want it to think I'm paying attention, so I keep walking towards First and Houston.

The entrance to the F train stop is in the middle of an asphalt wasteland that claims to be a recreation area. A narrow strip sandwiched between Houston and First Street, it boasts a neglected swingset, a tiny handball court, a couple of fiberglass chickens set on oversized springs for toddlers to ride to nowhere, and a basketball court without a net. Or a backboard. The rest of the area is painfully bare – except for when the homeless and the street hustlers set up their pathetic thieves' market on the weekends. But it is way too late for anyone to be interested in playing b-ball or picking over other people's rubbish. The early morning emptiness gives the area genuine urban menace.

I head down the stairs leading to the subway, switching from low to high gear. When I mingle with humans on their level, I often feel as if I'm moving underwater, like a thoroughbred horse racing with a handicap. But every so often, when no one is looking, I shed all pretense and move between the doors of human perception.

I flit past the token booth, pausing for a fraction of a heartbeat, staring into the bulletproof cage at the bored Transit Authority worker inside. To my eyes she is moving even slower than in real time, if that's possible, her index finger frozen as she pages through a copy of *People*. If she senses me at all, it is as a brief shudder of gooseflesh, nothing more.

No alarm is raised as I vault over the turnstiles and dash towards the uptown platform. I glide down the stairs, keeping to the shadows between the thick red columns that hold the crumbling roof aloft.

A bare concrete platform runs the length of Houston from First to Second Avenues, broken only by a single wooden bench and a center-post inlaid with red and white tiles. The platform is empty except for a bum, forced to sleep upright on the bench because of the wooden dividers that split the bench into individual seats. There's a puddle of vomit between the bum's busted-out army boots. If I was a human, I would no doubt be nervous about waiting for a train in such a station.

I climb up one of the red columns and squat amongst the cross-beams, surprising a rat in its nest. It squeals at me and shows its teeth. I grab the animal and snap its neck in one clean motion, silencing its complaints. Satisfied, I peer down between my boots for my shadow's arrival. I don't have long to wait.

It is a male. Looks to be thirty-something. Dressed non-descript, but respectable. A banker, maybe. Perhaps some variety of accountant. Something very unobtrusive, but not worthy of contempt. That is what vampires strive for in their camouflage – at least that's true of the majority. Only the older and more powerful ones flaunt their differences and risk drawing attention to themselves.

The vampire, like myself, is operating on high gear, which means he's practically invisible to the human eye. If the bum comes to or another passenger walks onto the platform, all they will see is a blur at the corner of their eye. Perhaps, if they are particularly astute, they might feel anxious and be in a hurry to leave.

I watch, amused, as my shadow flits back and forth along the platform, snarling in frustration at my apparent disappear-ance. It seems Luxor has sent one of his duller drones. I wait until the vampire is almost directly under me before dropping down. I tap him on the shoulder as I land, causing him to spin around in confusion. I'm pleased by the fear and surprise on his face. It's been a *long* time since anything last got the drop on him.

'Lookin' for me, dead boy?'

I catch him with a left to the jaw and the corpse just *takes* it! His lower jaw swings free like a busted gate as I plow into him, punching his gut hard enough to lift him off the ground a foot or two.

The edge is off the surprise, however, and the dead boy shrieks and claws at me, catching the side of my face and slicing it open to the bone. The mask of Marvin Milquetoast, boy executive, crumbles and I find myself tangling with a gaunt, red-eyed, noseless ghoul with three-inch fingernails and breath that could knock a buzzard off a shit wagon at ten paces.

We hit the ground, spitting and clawing at one another like a couple of wildcats in heat. Luxor's drone is strong – I'll give it that – but it lacks stamina. It's used to battening on hapless commuters and frightened street people, nothing more. It sure as hell isn't used to having a real fight on its hands.

I straddle the dead boy's chest, wrap my hands around its milk-white throat, and begin to hammer its skull into the concrete. I know I should take out my switchblade and do the deed and leave the rotting excuse for a bloodsucker's head on his master's doorstep as a warning, but I stay my hand. I want to kill the wretched piece of shit, but I want to do it *slow*.

'Freeze, punk!'

There is a gun pressed against the side of my head. I look up and find myself staring into the business end of a Glock, held by the bum that had, until a moment or two before, been unconscious on the bench. The bum, dressed in reeking rags stuffed full of newspaper, holds up a badge in a battered leather wallet. Great, just my luck! I was so preoccupied with the vampire, I hadn't bothered to check to see if the bum was real.

I let go of the dead boy and stand up slow. The muzzle of the Glock is barely an inch from my head. I could probably take the cop, but I don't want to chance it. A bullet in the head's fatal, vampire or not.

The cop grabs me by the scruff of my jacket and throws me up against the nearest column. 'Okay, you! Hands up where I can see 'em! Keep those fingers spread out or I'll fuckin' break 'em, unnerstand!?'

Keeping one hand on my shoulder, he turns back to look at my opponent. 'Are you all right, sir? I've got backup on the way – do you need an ambulance?'

I hear the approaching sirens already echoing in the subway tunnels, like the screams of banshees rushing to a feast. So can the dead boy, and it's making him nervous. His assignment has turned out bad. Bad enough that his master would no doubt do something very unpleasant to him. Something worse than being dead.

'Sir, can you answer me? Do you need assistance?'

The dead boy moves towards him and the undercover cop gets his first good look at the so-called 'victim'. The sight of the vampire's dislocated lower jaw and his gore-smeared skull makes the cop shift his weight uncomfortably.

'Uh, sir?'

The vampire's on him in less time than it takes to swallow. The cop screams as the dead boy sinks his fangs into his throat, somehow managing to squeeze off a couple of rounds into his attacker's midsection. The Glock punches huge, ugly wounds in the vampire's front and out his back, but it doesn't seem to faze him.

I grab the bloodsucker by the top of his head, peeling him off his victim like a leech. The undercover cop's lost a substantial amount of blood, but he's far from drained. He clutches his wounded throat, horror and confusion in his eyes, as I hold the vampire in a hammerlock. The beast spits and screams and claws at the air like a bobcat with a hot wire up its ass.

'Get the hell outta here!' I snarl. *'Now!'*

The cop doesn't wait to be told twice.

The sirens are almost on top of us. I've long since grown weary of the game. It's time to play hardball.

'Shut the fuck up!' I hiss at the struggling vampire. When it refuses to quiet down, I slam its head into the nearest column hard enough to make something squirt out of its ears.

'I *was* going to kick your ass and send you whimpering back to your liege like a whipped dog. But then you had to go and get cute and try and wipe the cop! That was stupid, dead boy! Very, *very* stupid!' I emphasize just *how* stupid by repeatedly banging his head against the column.

There's a sudden rumbling and the platform begins to vibrate below my feet. The tunnel fills with a hot, gritty wind that smells of piss and electricity. I grin in anticipation. A noise from the upper level draws my attention away from the approaching F train.

A couple of uniformed Transit Authority cops thunder down the stairs to the platform, guns drawn, eyes bugging with adrenaline and fear. The one in front nearly steps on the wounded undercover officer, who got as far as the foot of the stairs before collapsing from blood loss.

The second uniformed TA cop, a painfully young Hispanic who looks more afraid than an armed man should, moves toward me.

The train drowns out his words, but it's not hard to read his lips.

'Transit Police! Halt or I'll shoot!'

So I hurl the vampire in front of the F train.

I see the conductor's face in the window at the front of the train. I see the look of horror in his eyes as he realizes what is happening. The train's going very, very fast, even for late at night. No doubt he's already been alerted to the trouble on the Second Avenue platform and has been ordered not to stop. The Other finds his anguish quite amusing. And appetizing.

The train keeps going, rumbling by like a great steel dragon. The wind from its passing musses my hair and forces me to step back in deference to its blind, automotive power.

Clack-clack-rumble – brief glimpses of bleary, frightened faces peering out from the safety of the individual cars – and the F train's gone, headed for the Broadway/Lafayette stop four blocks away.

The young Transit Authority cop, momentarily frozen by the passing of the train, still has his gun trained on me. I stand at the edge of the platform, hands upraised, smiling pleasantly. The cop's partner, an older Oriental man, circles me from the side, his gun pointed directly at my head. I smell the fear radiating from them. It's thick and pungent, like that of a pot roast ready to come out of the oven. The Other's growing agitated. It wants to feed.

'Morning, officer.'

'You fuckin' crazy bitch!'

'I beg your pardon?'

'You threw him off the platform! You killed that man in cold blood!'

'I beg to differ on both counts, officer. I didn't kill him – and he wasn't a man.'

'What?'

'Look for yourself.'

Without really wanting to, the younger cop glances down onto the track – and what he sees causes him to scream.

'Jesus, Diaz!' snaps the older cop. He's patting me down while trying to keep one eye on his partner. 'You've seen suicides chewed up by trains before! Get a hold of yourself!'

The younger cop doesn't seem to hear him. Instead, he begins to empty his gun at something below the level of the platform.

The older cop loses what little patience he started out with. 'Diaz! Cut the crap!' He has his cuffs out and is securing one of the bracelets to my left wrist. 'We don't have time for bullshit like this!'

'Neither do I,' I sigh, slipping free of the older cop's hold and ramming my elbow into the middle of his face. He falls like a bag of suet.

The younger cop's exhausted his clip, but he keeps on firing anyway. His face is rigid with terror as he backs away from the platform. The vampire – or what's left of it – has finally succeeded in dragging itself off the tracks.

The train has cut him in two as neatly as a magician's saw, chopping him off at the waist. The viscera dangling from his ruined torso look like party streamers dipped in transmission fluid. Eyes glowing with an inhuman hate, he lifts his truncated torso on his arms, using clawed hands as feet.

I relieve the unconscious cop of his gun, shaking my head in amazement. 'Buddy, you just don't know when to call it quits, do you?'

The vampire swings his right arm forward, then his left, dragging a length of intestine behind him like a gory bridal train.

'Any last words, butt-munch?'

The vampire bares his fangs at me and hisses.

The policeman's gun takes off the top of his head, dropping the vampire as effectively as it would any garden-variety criminal. The younger cop stares at me for a second, his face the color of new cheese. I smile at him. His eyes get even bigger and he runs for the stairs.

There are more sirens up top. The flashing lights from arriving cop cars and ambulances leak through the cracks in the ceiling. I hear the thunder of city-issued shoe leather on pavement. Within seconds the platform will be swarming with police. It's time for me to kiss this scene good-bye.

I toss the cop's gun off the platform like I would a spent wad of chewing gum and shift back into high gear. I speed up the platform, in the direction of the Second Avenue exits, away from the arriving cops. Because the Second Avenue exits are near the Sara Delano Roosevelt Park, a favorite spot for the neighborhood derelicts, the gateways are kept chained shut from nine in the evening until six in the morning. Not that I care. I push against the gates and the chain shatters, sending the lock flying.

I ghost up the stairs on the Chrystie Street side of the intersection, gliding over an elderly black man sitting in a pool of his own waste, a bottle of malt liquor clutched to his chest like a beloved child. He starts awake, flailing at the air with a grimy claw.

'Awgeddofmutherfuckerdontocuhmahshitsparequatah?'

His voice joins the inchoate roar of the city, and it echoes in my ears as I race through the shadows, along with the screams of police sirens fading into the coming dawn.

From the diaries of Sonja Blue

12

Anhwei Province, the People's Republic of China:

Qi You Wu and his wife, Mei Li, were simple workers who lived in a two-room house on the outskirts of the town of Pangpu. Both Qi You and Mei Li liked to think of themselves as 'modern'. They had married out of love, not family obligation, having met while working side by side on the assembly line at the tractor factory. Being modern young workers, Qi You and Mei Li understood the importance of population control to their country and the Party. When Mei Li became pregnant earlier that year, they had signed a document declaring that upon the birth of their child they would both undergo sterilization procedures. They would be rewarded for their selflessness by being given special consideration for promotion at work and recognized by the local Party officials as dedicated workers.

Mei Li had been a little apprehensive at first – what if their baby was a girl? Even though she was modern, it was hard to ignore centuries of ingrained Chinese culture. Boy children have always been far more valuable than girl children. To have many sons is the definition of Chinese luck and happiness. She worried and worried about what might happen if the baby was a daughter. However, when she was finally brought to the midwife's station, she delivered a boy, whom they named Qui En. Three days later, Mei Li and her husband underwent the sterilization procedures they'd agreed to. But now, two weeks later, Mei Li was beginning to wonder if they had not made the biggest mistake of their lives.

The Wu house was a concrete box with a red tile roof, identical to the hundreds of other low-ranking industrial workers' homes lining Pang-pu's streets. The two rooms consisted of a combination kitchen and living area, and a smaller sleeping room. The house was drafty in the winter and hot in the summer and the Wus shared a communal toilet with the household next door. Mei Li and Qi You dreamed of someday making good and moving to more spacious and pleasant surroundings. But for now, Mei Li had been forced to keep the baby's cradle next to the oil stove that provided them with heat and food. It was close to midnight and Mei Li was still sitting next to the stove, watching her baby and worrying.

'Mei Li, when are you coming to bed?' Qi You was standing in the door to their bedroom, his hair tousled and eyes puffy. 'You have to be at the factory the same time as I do – how can you make your quota if you don't get any sleep? The line supervisor is sure to notice—'

'Something is wrong with Qui En. He wouldn't take his bottle.'

'It's probably just a cold. All the babies at the crèche have colds.'

Mei Li frowned and leaned forward, fussing with the blanket around the baby's feet. 'I should not have placed him in the crèche so soon. He's so little—'

'Mei Li, we've already discussed this. We agreed that leaving Qui En at the daycare center was the only logical answer. Your mother lives too far away and we cannot afford for you to stay home with the baby—'

'You are right, Qi You. I know you're speaking the truth. But I still can't help but worry. He's our only child. The only one we'll ever have.'

Qi You smiled despite his weariness and kissed the top of his wife's head. 'It is good that you worry for your son. It means you are a good mother. I worry, too. But I will be even more worried if I do not get my promotion.'

Mei Li held her husband's hand tightly for a long moment, her eyes never leaving the cradle. 'Go and get some sleep. I'll join you in a little while. I won't be up much longer, I promise.'

Qi You sighed and went back to bed alone, while Mei Li remained perched on a stool beside the stove, rocking her son's cradle and singing lullabies. She could hear her husband snoring in the other room. The sound reminded her just how tired she was. Suddenly her eyelids grew heavy and her head began to nod. Within ten minutes of his mother falling asleep, Qui En stopped breathing.

A golden light filled the front windows of the Wu house and the door opened inward, as if unlatched by a phantom hand. Standing on the threshold was a naked woman with long hair that fluttered about as if blown by gentle winds. In her arms was a baby boy with dark hair and Oriental eyes. The stranger hovered beside the sleeping woman for a moment, then took the body of little Qui En from the cradle, leaving the living baby in its place. Then, as quickly and silently as she arrived, the glowing woman floated out the door.

Mei Li awoke with a start, blinking in confusion. She must have fallen asleep. She looked into the cradle to check on Qui En and was both surprised and relieved to find that whatever had been bothering her son had passed. Qui En gurgled happily, waving his little hands at her as if in greeting.

13

New York City:

Two voices on a telephone line:
  'She's here.'
  'Are you sure it's her?'
  'I'm positive. It's her, of that you can be certain.'
  'Good. I knew she'd come once she got the clippings. But be careful. She's deadlier by far than any other you've ever crossed, my boy.'
  'I know. That's why she fascinates me so.'

Something's in the room.
  It wasn't even a thought. More a feeling. A sensation picked up by slumbering sensory apparatus and fed into an unconscious mind. Is it the real thing or merely a dream of intrusion?
  Wake up, you stupid bitch! the Other shrieked, answering the reality–dream issue once and for all. *We've got company!*
  Sonja came off the loft bed in three seconds flat, fangs extended, hair bristling like a cat's back. There was no time for her to wonder how they managed to find her. No time to try and figure out how they got past the booby traps. She hit the ground in a low crouch, hissing a warning at the intruder seated in the leather easy chair.
  'No need for such theatrics, milady,' Jen purred. There was no fear in his eyes. Caution, yes – but no fear. 'I intend you no harm.'
  'If that's the case, what are you doing here?'
  'My employers wanted to know where you're keeping your nest. They told me to assign a shadow to you. I'm sure you

167

remember him. However, you needn't fear me. I won't tell them that I know where you spend your daylight hours.'

'What are you getting at, renfield?'

Jen's spine stiffened and indignation flickered in his eyes. 'I am *not* a renfield.'

'You couldn't prove it by me. You're a human working for vampires – that makes you a renfield in *my* book. Theirs, too, I'd say.'

This seemed to make him bridle even more. 'I am my own man, damn you! I work for Luxor and Nuit because it suits my needs, not because they've got a slave collar snapped around my mind!'

'All the more reason for me not to trust you. At least renfields don't have much control in what they do. After all, they're addicts. You ... you, on the other hand ... you're one of their bellwethers. You lure your fellow humans to their doom to benefit your vampiric partners and line your own pockets!'

The pale blue of Jen's eyes seemed to intensify as he glowered at Sonja. 'I am not a renfield, nor am I a bellwether. I am like you.'

'You are *nothing* like me!'

'Perhaps. Perhaps not. But you're wrong about my species. I am not human. I am *dhampire*.'

Sonja turned to stare at him. '*Dhampire*? I've heard rumours of such things – the supposed by-product of vampire–human matings.'

Jen smoothed his braided coils like Medusa calming her snakes. 'There are very few of my kind in this world. As I said, I am *dhampire*. My mother was human—'

'And your father a vampire? Impossible! Vampires are dead things, their sperm inert. They may very well be capable of erection, even ejaculation, but they are incapable of reproducing.'

'I am very well aware of the procreative failings of the living dead,' Jen sniffed. 'If you would allow me to continue, I'll explain. My biological father was human enough, although I have no clue as to his identity. Not that it matters. My mother was a streetwalker. Whitechapel, in fact. No doubt my father was a drunken sot with tuppence in his pocket and a hard-on in his pants. She was only fourteen when she had me, mind you. However, shortly after becoming pregnant, my mother fell in with a certain gentleman of Noble mien, if you understand me.

'She was his favorite for a couple of months, until she began to show her condition. Such things are anathema to vampires – they are forever frozen in time, changeless and unchanging. The withering and dying of their human consorts is one thing – entropy, after all, is the vampire's handmaiden – but the creation of new life! Ah, that reminds them that they are, indeed, outside the chain of nature. They pretend to have disdain for how humans reproduce, but they are secretly envious and jealous to the point of mania.

'As I said, my mother's lover may have cast her aside, but it was too late. I was already affected by the venom he released into her each time he fed from her. When I was born my mother placed me in a foundling home and went in search of similar lovers. I was always . . . strange. Underweight, anemic, and of a morbid turn, my life was made a living hell by my warders and fellow inmates. Then, when I was eight years old, my mother reappeared and took me to live with her.

'Over the years my mother developed into a courtesan for those of Noble make. She'd become quite wealthy and bought a fashionable house in London, which she turned into a salon of sorts, where she entertained her clients. She even had a few lovers outside the vampire race – the occasional *vargr* prince, *kitsune* diplomat, or ogre businessman. Compared to the brutality and indifference of the foundling home, it seemed perfectly normal to me.

'It wasn't until I was twelve years old that I realized that I was far from human. While I lay curled deep within my mother's womb, her lover's tainted seed had worked its way into my system. While I was hardly a vampire, I could walk the streets of London and actually *see* the Pretenders for what they were. I also benefited from heightened senses and an intuition for what those around me truly desired. In no time I was serving as my mother's pimp, searching the streets and back alleys for eager clients.

'But, by far, my surrogate father's most lasting contribution was in the realm of longevity. How old do you think I am?'

'I don't know.' Sonja shrugged. 'Forty? Forty-five?'

'I'll be one hundred and twenty-seven come next June!' he cackled, clapping his hands. 'Bet you didn't guess *that*, milady.'

'You're right on that count. But it still doesn't answer why you're here, and why I shouldn't kill you where you sit.'

Jen held up one hand, begging her indulgence. 'My employers are just that – employers. They are not my liege and lady. I came of age in the very breast of monstrosity, if you will. I feel no kinship for humans – yet, nor do I consider myself a vampire. I am a nation unto myself. A member of a solitary race. I serve many masters, yet I am slave to none. And I am not here to see Luxor's petty blood vendetta carried out. I am here on behalf of one known to you, one who considers himself more friend than foe.'

'Pangloss.'

Jen grunted as he pushed himself out of the easy chair. 'Most astute. He sent me instead of one of his servitors because of your predilection for slaying vampires on sight. I am to bring you to him.'

Sonja shook her head and folded her arms over her chest. 'I have no interest in seeing Pangloss again. I've had my fill of his mind games and trickery. You can tell him what I told Luxor – if he wants Morgan dead, tough. I don't subcontract.'

'You misunderstand. Pangloss doesn't give a rat's ass about Morgan. Not anymore, that is. He wants to see you for other, more personal reasons.'

'Such as?'
'He's dying.'

Pangloss's lair was located on the top three floors of a tony apartment building in Gramercy Park. The doorman scowled at Sonja when they first entered the building. However, when he saw Jen his eyes glazed and his face went slack.

'Pangloss has him conditioned,' Jen stage-whispered into her ear as they hurried into the elevators. 'Whenever he sees me or one of the doctor's servants, he goes into a fugue state. Doesn't remember who came in or when. Otherwise, he's a tough doorman to sneak by unannounced.'

The elevator let them out at the penthouse. A renfield dressed in pale green surgeon's scrubs, his hair under a sterile disposable paper cap, greeted them.

'Thank goodness you brought her! We were afraid you weren't going to make it in time! He's getting worse!'

'The old bastard's managed to continue for over fifteen hundred years,' Jen sneered. 'I'm sure he can hold out for another hour or two.'

The renfield's eyes hardened and Sonja could tell he wanted to say – or do – something to Jen, but was afraid to. If Pangloss was, indeed, dying, then his renfields would soon find themselves stuck for a fix – and protection.

Jen watched the indignant servant storm off, then whispered behind his hand: 'Renfields! They're all such drama queens!'

Sonja was led into a large, handsomely appointed living room. A sliding glass door opened onto a patio that boasted a killer view of the city. The Chrysler Building glowed in the night like an art deco syringe. There was an old man seated in a wheelchair in front of a large television, watching a program with the volume turned down. The old man turned his head toward them and smiled, revealing blackened gums and fangs the color of antique ivory.

'Hello, my child. So good of you to come.'

Nancy A. Collins

Sonja was shocked by Pangloss's debilitation. The last time she'd seen him – three years ago – he'd looked as when she first met him, back in 1975. He'd seemed a healthy, vigorous, and virile man in his early fifties, with only a touch of gray in his hair. The creature that sat in the wheelchair, however, looked more like late-era Howard Hughes than classic Cary Grant.

Although he was rapidly going bald, what little hair Pangloss still possessed was the color of a soiled sheet and hung almost to the middle of his back. His frame was wasted and his limbs twisted and infirm. She noticed he had the persistent wobble of a Parkinson's patient. His hands and feet were wrinkled and looked more like the claws of a vulture. He was swaddled in a white terry-cloth bathrobe and an adult diaper. When Luxor had referred to Pangloss as 'the old man' she'd been puzzled by his choice of words. Now she understood.

'How have the mighty fallen, eh?' gasped the old vampire. 'I can tell you're surprised – I don't need to use telepathy to know that.'

'Jen said you were dying, but I really didn't believe him.' Sonja moved closer, circling the thing in the wheelchair, trying to find the flaw in the disguise that would tell her it was all a trick. She couldn't find one.

Pangloss smirked and nodded his head. Sonja couldn't tell if it was in understanding or from a body tremor. 'Jen *is* a terrible liar. And he always tells the truth. You'd be wise to remember that, my dear.' He fixed his eyes on the *dhampire* and for a fleeting second some of the old, self-assured Pangloss came back. 'You've done what was asked of you, boy. My renfields have your pay voucher ready. Go now. I would speak with my granddaughter alone.'

Jen sauntered out of the room, pausing long enough to give Sonja a wink before closing the door.

'You must forgive the boy,' Pangloss wheezed. 'His mother indulged him overmuch out of guilt for placing him amongst strangers the first few years of his life. He fancies himself

172

a *dhampire*. He is more than a little mad because of it, but is better at handling it than the renfields. He rents himself out to humans as well as vampires, did he tell you that? His pain threshold is immense, and he can withstand tremendous amounts of physical punishment without undue side effects. He rents himself out to humans with a taste for others' pain.'

'I've been there,' Sonja muttered.

'But enough about my half-bastard,' Pangloss grimaced. 'Oh, yes, I am the one responsible for his being like he is. Did he not tell you? The two of you are related, as our kind understand such things. I suspect you want to know why I sent you those news clippings.'

'I know why you sent them – you wanted me to know where Morgan is so I can kill him and you can claim the glory and come off looking big with your bloodsuckin' buddies.'

Pangloss's laughter was somewhere between a chuckle and a choke that made him double over. For a second she was afraid he was going to cough up a lung. 'My dear child, you have every reason to be suspicious of me; I've certainly done nothing to earn your trust in the past. But I am a changed man – or should I say vampire? The Pangloss you see before you is as different on the inside as he is on the outside.'

He motioned feebly with one hand in the direction of the window. 'Could you do me a favor, my dear? Could you push me over to the window? I would look at the night one last time.'

Sonja grasped the handles of the wheelchair and pushed him towards the sliding glass door. She was surprised at how little he seemed to weigh.

'I know this is going to sound stupid,' she said. 'But how can you be dying? I mean, you're already dead.'

'A good question. And not at all foolish. There are those who think that vampires – we who were first known as the *enkidu* – are immortal things. And, by human lights, we are. There are vampires who have continued for thousands of years. I myself have walked this earth since the fifth century AD, before Clovis embraced the Christian god. But all things have their spans, even the living dead.

'Oh, the dead can be destroyed – of that you're well aware. We can be killed by damaging our brains or spinal cords; we can be burned to death; decapitated; or die from exposure to the sun or silver. However, we are impervious to the host of illnesses that thin the human herds, and age no longer affects us once we are resurrected. We are immune to all diseases except one – the Ennui.'

'You mean you're dying from *boredom*?'

'Wretched, isn't it? But then, this is the fate that awaits all vampires, once they have amassed the power and knowledge to move beyond the night-to-night concerns of keeping oneself fed. What are brood wars but games of chess using animated game pawns? Why do we tamper in human affairs, if not to keep things interesting? Once we have indulged our appetite, what is left for us? We have spent so much time and energy maintaining the semblance of life, we are loath to admit that there is no reason behind any of it, beyond our inborn need to continue our existence.

'In each vampire's span there comes a time when the ceaseless scheming, plotting, and manipulation loses its attraction. When that happens, we begin to question our motives; we begin to doubt whether our needs truly are as important as we once imagined them to be. That is when the Ennui sets in and we begin to die. That is what happened to me. I can trace the beginning of my fall to Rome, when you marked me with your knife. The wound you dealt me never truly healed . . .'

He opened his robe and pointed to the long, jagged scar in the middle of his chest. There were dozens, even hundreds of pale, almost invisible scars covering his body, ghostly souvenirs of past battles. Although Sonja knew the wound he pointed to was nearly twenty years old, it still looked fresh. It was also the only part of him that looked genuinely alive.

'I have suffered far more grievous injuries in my existence. However, unlike the others, this one has refused to be dismissed. When I look at it I am reminded of how close I came to dying at your hand – and for what? I found myself musing over mortality and what, if anything, I have done in fifteen hundred years of walking this planet.

'I have known great men, both in the field of power and in the arts. I sat in the court of Charlemagne and watched it fall apart upon his death. I kept council with popes and bishops and cardinals of every stripe. I watched the plagues sweep through the cities of Europe. I saw London burn three times. I saw countries rise, kings fall, religions be born. Da Vinci, Botticelli, Bosch, Voltaire, Defoe, Molière – they all knew me, in my various guises. Yet, I had no real hand in anything that happened. I can claim no influence, except for when I used my manipulative powers to destroy a marriage or weaken a friendship. My role has never been creative, only that of a parasite, feeding off human society's veins.'

Pangloss's head was trembling so violently she was afraid it was going to snap off and land in his lap. 'They dismiss me, you know. The other Nobles. They always have. Because I never took a title like "baron" or "count" or "duke". I called myself Doctor. I knew better than to lay claim to royalty. Once you do, they're on you like leeches, trying to bring you down. I didn't continue for fifteen hundred years out of dumb luck. They also think me a fool for not feeding on the stronger emotions – I preferred the petty jealousies and intrigues of artistic clichés and intellectual movements to the horror of concentration camps and reeducation centers.

'That idiot Luxor even had the audacity to insult me last time we met! No doubt he was hoping to provoke me into declaring a brood war, seeing how weak I had become. Luxor is such a coward! And Nuit's no better! I've grown so weary of it all, Sonja. What is the point of continuing if I must spend the remainder of my days dealing with jackanapes such as Luxor? I am so tired of it all . . . so very tired.'

'But, I still don't understand. If you have, as you say, lost interest in playing the game, then why did you send for me?'

Pangloss's lower lip trembled and Sonja was shocked to realize how much, at that moment, he reminded her of Jacob Thorne.

'Because I'm scared, Sonja. I'm scared of dying by myself. I want you to be with me when it happens.'

She didn't know why she did it, but Sonja agreed to escort Pangloss to the necropolis.

There were several necropoli scattered throughout the great cities – and several of the once great. They were sacred ground to all Pretenders, no matter their breed. Sonja knew New York possessed one such place, although she had no idea where it was located.

'It's accessible only through tunnels connected to the old subway system,' Pangloss explained. 'There is an access point in the basement of this apartment building. We start from there.'

It was clear from the way Pangloss's servants behaved that none of them liked the idea of their master heading for the Elephant's Graveyard. They were all very agitated and kept talking amongst themselves, eyeing Sonja cautiously. Sonja had never liked renfields. While they served a purpose, she'd never understood why vampires elected to surround themselves with servants who were nothing more than junkies. Renfields were addicted to vampires. They had an uncanny knack for tracking down the undead. Not to mention a taste for their own destruction. Almost all of them were sensitives of one sort or another, and all were heavily dependent on their masters for whatever it was that kept them going, be it drugs, sex, pain – or the semblance of sanity.

But now, watching them flutter about their dying master like moths around a fading light, Sonja finally began to understand. Vampires spent their existence doing nothing but taking from others – be it blood or the psychic energies of the living. Vampires were needful things. But with their renfields they could experience, in a flawed fashion, what it was like to be needed.

'Please, master, I beg you to rethink what you're about to do,' whispered the renfield who had greeted Sonja and Jen when they first exited the elevator, his voice made hoarse by unshed tears.

'There's no putting it off,' Pangloss replied, levering himself out of his wheelchair. 'I've gone too far to turn back now.' He took a feeble step forward and nearly fell. Sonja reached out and grabbed his elbow, steadying him as best she could.

'But, master, what of us? What will become of us once you're gone?'

'You'll be free to make your own ways in the world, just as you have been all along,' Pangloss sighed. 'Come, Sonja, it's time to go.'

There were two basements to the apartment building. The first one was clean and well lit and had recycling bins and a set of coin-operated washer-dryers for the tenants. The second basement was dark and damp and smelled of age and rat piss and could only be reached by a special elevator in the penthouse.

Sonja held Pangloss's elbow, helping him along as they wound their way through stacks of moldering newspapers and steamer trunks dating from the last century. He pointed at a narrow, low-set iron door. There were strange runes chiseled into the lintel, written in the brain-twisting script of the Pretender tongue. Pangloss produced a key from the pocket of his robe and handed it to her.

Sonja fitted the key into the door and gave it a turn. The door swung open with a squeal, displacing enough cobwebs to rig a schooner. There was a smell of old earth and stale water and in the distance Sonja heard the rumble of subway cars. Pangloss's long, unkept nails bit into the flesh of her upper arm, but he said nothing.

The tunnel that connected Pangloss's basement to the city's underground labyrinth of service tunnels and subway tracks was indeed old. Shored with rotting timbers and lined with mammoth slabs of natural stone, it reminded Sonja of how the men who'd laid the foundations for the Brooklyn Bridge had labored hundreds of feet underwater, in little more than crude airlocks.

The entire tunnel suddenly shuddered and dirt and loose mortar drifted down from the decaying ceiling onto their heads. By her reckoning, they were directly under the Number Six line. Pangloss pointed at a set of stone steps, worn from the tread of countless feet, that led upward. The staircase was so tight and steep Sonja had to place Pangloss ahead of her and walk immediately behind him, her hands bracing his back and hips in case he lost his balance and fell. It was a slow, torturous climb, but finally they came to another old-fashioned iron door. Pangloss opened it, and they stepped out into what turned out to be the main lobby of Grand Central Station.

If anyone noticed them leaving what looked to be a locked janitor's closet, they didn't show it. Pangloss shuffled across the main concourse, leaning on Sonja for support. In the time since they had left his lair, he'd aged even more. His back was now completely bowed, his head dropped between his shoulders like a turtle's. Sonja was sure someone would notice them; no doubt one of the depot's employees would insist on providing a wheelchair for such an infirm old man. Then she realized that although people were looking right at them, no one saw them; they were walking between the cracks in human perception. Without her being aware of it, Pangloss had cast a glamour about them. Although the old vampire's body might be decaying, it seemed his psychic abilities were as strong – if not stronger – as ever.

As they made their way onto one of the lower platforms, Pangloss suddenly teetered and collapsed onto one knee. No one seemed to notice. Sonja helped Pangloss back onto his feet, but she could tell his kneecap had dissolved.

'I'm afraid . . . you'll have to carry me . . . from here on,' he rasped. 'I wanted to go to my death on my own two feet, but I fear I've left it too late.'

Sonja scooped him up into her arms. He weighed about as much as a bag of dead leaves. She was afraid to tighten her grip on him, for fear he would crumble in her hands like chalk.

Pangloss pointed to one of the tunnels and Sonja stepped off the platform onto the tracks below. The interior of the tunnel was lit by the occasional industrial-strength light-bulb set into the brakeman alcoves that lined the walls. The vaulted brick roof was black from decades of soot, and graffiti smeared the walls. There was a rumbling from behind her and Sonja quickly side-stepped into one of the alcoves, watching the Amtrack train's lighted windows flash past. An old woman with cat's-eye glasses gaped at them for a quarter of a heart-beat, then was gone.

After a few more yards, they came to what looked like a service tunnel. Pangloss motioned for Sonja to enter it. There were spent rubbers and broken syringes littering the ground, along with empty Thunderbird bottles. Pangloss reached out and pressed a brick in the wall. There was the sound of stone grating on stone and the side of the wall opened.

'Hurry,' Pangloss whispered. 'These tunnels are rife with homeless humans and other such detritus. They must not see the entrance – and live to tell of it.'

Sonja slipped through the opening and the door pivoted back into place. They were standing at the head of yet another set of ancient stone stairs corkscrewing into the earth. There was no light in the antechamber, nor was there any evidence of there ever having been any. Still, Sonja's dark-adapted eyes could see perfectly well in the inky blackness as they descended the stairs.

Pangloss plucked at his robe with long, yellowed talons, his voice as thin and fragile as a cobweb. 'Did . . . did I ever tell you how much I loved him.'

'Loved who?'

'Morgan.'

Sonja tensed at the mention of her Maker's name, the muscles going rigid in her arms. 'I believe you mentioned it, the last time we met.'

'I loved him so very, very much – more than any of the others. I'd had scores of lovers before him, and hundreds since, but he was the only one I loved as an equal. The only one I loved enough to make like myself. So we could be together forever. But he betrayed me, in the end. He left me to go off on his own. He said I was not an ambitious enough partner for his tastes. He planned great things for himself. He dreamed of raising a vampire army, loyal only to him, so that he might be the first of our kind to step from the shadows and rule the world of man.' Pangloss giggled, his body shivering with the effort. 'Well, we know where his "great plans" got him, don't we, my dear? That's what he gets for trying to use science to meet his ends! Science is a human thing. Whenever the Pretending kind try to use it, it turns in our hands, like an angry serpent. We are things outside nature, beyond reason – perhaps it senses we are not its true master.'

'Science isn't a force unto itself, like the weather or magic,' Sonja explained. 'It's just . . . well, it's just *science*.'

'That is what you think. But you're wrong. There are a lot of things that are wrong.' Pangloss's voice had taken on the vague, querulous tone of the senile. 'Did I tell you I loved him? Loved him better than any of the rest?'

'Yes. Yes, you did.'

'I forgive him. I forgive him for leaving me. For betraying me. I hated him for a long, long time – longer than I loved him, actually. I hated him for at least five centuries. I've never hated anything or anyone that long. But I forgive him, now. It's easier to forgive than hate. It doesn't use up quite as much energy. You should learn from that, child.'

'I'm not the forgiving kind.'

'Why are you carrying me, then?' Pangloss's eyes were no longer cloudy but clear and sharp, waiting for her reply. Just as quickly his gaze grew vague and his voice resumed its old man's timbre. 'Whatever happened to that nice Palmer fellow? Are you two still together?'

'No. No, we split up.'

'That's a shame. You looked so nice together.'

Finally, after what seemed like a small eternity, they reached the bottom of the stairs. Spanning outward, as far as the eye could see in every direction, was a mammoth underground labyrinth, the walls of the maze carved from the living rock itself. At the mouth of the necropolis was a huge iron gate, guarded by a pair of ogres, their flesh the translucent white of cave-born lizards. As Sonja moved forward, the bigger of the two – he stood nearly twelve feet tall – swiveled his wide, flat head in her direction. The eyes were blind lumps of jelly the color of oatmeal, but his hearing and sense of smell were quite keen.

'Who go there?' he rumbled.

'I am Pangloss of the *enkidu*. I have come here to die.'

The ogre sniffed the air and frowned. 'You not alone. Who woman?'

'She is Sonja Blue, also of the *enkidu*. She is my companion.'

The ogre held a brief conference with his fellow guard – a mere stripling at seven feet – then unlocked the gate, swinging it open as easily as a screen door. 'Very well. Good journey, *enkidu*.'

'Thank you, friend ogre,' Pangloss replied.

The interior of the necropolis reminded Sonja of the catacombs of Rome, with its narrow stone corridors and burial niches. However, some of the niches in the labyrinth were large enough to accommodate giants, while others were only big enough for a child. All of the niches closest to the entrance were occupied. As they trudged through the maze, she stared at the collection of dead ogres, *nagas, kitsune, larvae* and other Pretender species.

Pangloss motioned for her to stop as they walked by the corpse of what had once been a woman, dressed in the rotting remains of Edwardian finery. Her face was that of an unwrapped mummy, the hair long since dissolved into dust. Pangloss stared at the dead vampiress for a long moment before speaking. His voice was dry and rasped in his throat.

'I always wondered what had become of her. It never occurred to me that she was dead.'

'Did you know her?'

'In her time.'

After wandering the labyrinth for what felt like a day and a night, they finally found an empty niche. Sonja carefully eased Pangloss into his final resting place, not terribly sure what to do next. The elder vampire stretched out on the narrow stone ledge. He sighed and smiled as if he was resting on the softest mattress in the world.

'This will do just fine,' he said.

'Are you sure you're comfortable?'

'I am. But you don't seem to be.'

'I guess I'm just not used to the idea of natural death. Not only for vampires, but for *anyone*. It's not something I've experienced that much of.'

'Does it frighten you?'

'Not really. I just feel . . . awkward, I guess. What does dying feel like to you? Does it hurt?'

'Of course there is pain. But I have known greater pain than this. No, what I feel isn't physical, it comes from somewhere besides the body. I feel both empty and ready to explode. It's as if, after century upon century of taking the life-force of others, without ever giving in return, I am full to the brim. That's the funny thing about all this – even as my body wastes away from the Ennui, my psychic energies have yet to weaken. I simply have no interest in using them. It's as if I am feeding on myself, just as I once fed on others.'

Pangloss reached out and took Sonja's hand in his own. His skin felt dry and flaky, like that shed by a snake. There was fear in his eyes, and sadness. 'I'm afraid of what it will be like, Sonja. I'm afraid of what's beyond. I know what it's like to be dead. But what is there beyond unlife? What happens when the dead die? I know that humans seem to have all kinds of options as to what happens to them in the After – but what about us? Do we go to heaven? Or do we go to hell? Or do we simply not go anywhere at all?'

'I don't know, Pangloss. I honestly don't.'

Pangloss tightened his grip on her hand and motioned for Sonja to draw closer. 'You have done me a great service, Sonja. Greater than I deserve. As payment for your kindness, I will tell you something of great value.' Pangloss smiled at Sonja, his eyes rolled up so far in his head all she could see were bloodless veins. 'He loves you, did you know that? He loves you like the moth loves the flame, like the mongoose adores the cobra. He—' Pangloss's voice trembled, then broke. 'I'm so sorry, so sorry. It's all been for nothing, hasn't it? All the pain, all the death, all the intrigue – it means nothing.'

To Sonja's amazement, actual tears leaked from the corners of Pangloss's eyes. The old vampire reached up and touched the wetness running down his face, looking confused. 'What . . . what's this?'

'They're tears,' Sonja whispered. 'You're crying, Pangloss. You're actually crying.'

'At last,' Pangloss rasped. Then he died.

Within seconds, Pangloss's body seemed to cave in upon itself, as if someone had deflated a balloon. A burst of light the color of raw electricity shot out of the niche, zipping past Sonja's right ear, making the hair on her scalp tighten. She was so startled she stumbled backward and landed on her ass. A ball of St Elmo's fire bounced back and forth amongst the walls of the labyrinth like a demented pinball, then, with a crackle of static, it shot straight up and disappeared.

It took her a minute to realize she was still holding Pangloss's hand – it had snapped off at the wrist. Before she could react, it crumbled into chalk.

She resurfaced from the catacombs in Central Park. Dawn was creeping over the skyscrapers and she felt like she'd been pulled through a knothole feetfirst. She still wasn't sure what it all meant. As she strode through the park, she espied a home-less person rummaging through one of the garbage cans in search of half-eaten pretzels and aluminium cans. It looked like every other homeless person on the streets of the city, dressed in castoffs scavenged from a dozen dumpsters, its shoes stuffed full of newspapers, a dirty stocking cap pulled over hair that hadn't been washed in weeks, if not months. However, as Sonja drew closer, it looked up from what it was doing and fixed her with pupil-less eyes the color of gold. Seraphim.

Sonja paused and returned its stare. There was something familiar about this particular specimen, although she couldn't put her finger on it. It couldn't be its appearance, since they all looked more or less alike. No, the sense of recognition was on a far more intangible level. Then she noticed how the seraphim's head seemed to bob like a balloon on a string.

Pangloss.

Of course.

So *that's* where they came from! She should have figured it out for herself when Morgan's tampering with the vampire life cycle produced a baby seraphim instead of an infant bloodsucker! After centuries of feeding on the misery of others, those vampires who could no longer bring themselves to feed on the living became seraphim. It kind of balanced out, once she thought about it.

After all, what is an angel but a demon yet to fall?

14

The Great Victoria Desert, Australia:

It was a toss-up as to which was hotter, the sun under which
he walked or the ground on which he walked. His skin hung
in peeling tatters from his bare shoulders, pinker than boiled
shrimp. His back felt as if he'd lain down on a white-hot barby
grill, producing blisters the size of walnuts. How long had he
been on walkabout? Three days? Four? How long could a man
walk naked in the Northern Territory of Australia before dying
of exposure and thirst? Two days? Three?

A month ago his name was Charlie Gower. He worked as a
commercial artist in Canberra, designing logos for tinned meat
and flavored chips. Then the advertising firm he worked for
landed a state-sponsored job. Charlie wasn't too sure what the
campaign was about – some kind of anniversary of something
– but he was supposed to draw on ancient aboriginal designs
for the campaign. So he found himself checking out books on
tjurunga, the sacred object art of the aborigines. Charlie had
never paid too much attention to native art before – being
Australian, he spent most of his time in art school studying the
Old Masters of Europe and the painters of English landscapes
out of national insecurity. But the minute he laid eyes on the
sinuous primitivism of the ancient Koori, as the aborigines called
themselves before there were Australians to tell them otherwise,
something changed inside Charlie Gower.

Fascinated by the artwork of these primitive nomadic tribes,
Charlie began to look into the history of the peoples themselves
– something rarely, if ever, mentioned in his schooling. And, to
his surprise, he discovered he had aborigine blood in him.

His great-great-grandfather, Jebediah Gower of London, had been arrested for stealing a coat and sent to Australia to serve his queen and country as convict labor. He'd been fifteen years old at the time of his arrest. He worked his way to freedom by the age of twenty-one and took an aborigine girl to wife. All Charlie could find out about her was that she had been of the Wurunjerri and Jebediah had renamed her Hannah. When he asked Grandfather Gower about Jebediah and Hannah, the old man had been scandalized by the suggestion that his ancestors had been anything but good, upstanding white folk.

'Where'd you get this rubbish about your great-great bein' a convict and that he married an abo?' Grandfather Gower demanded, all but spitting his false teeth out in disgust. 'Jebediah Gower came over as a guard! And Hannah was white as you an' me!'

'I found it in the public record, Grandfather. They've got it all on microfiche now.'

'Rubbish! Absolute rubbish!'

Charlie really didn't know what he expected to hear from his grandpa. Grandfather Gower's generation had been raised to be ashamed of its convict and aborigine heritage, and his parents' generation wasn't much better. His mother, a devout Christian, was exceptionally concerned over his interest in pagan art, fearing for his immortal soul. As far as Charlie was concerned, they were all overreacting. He had simply discovered a new hobby, one that allowed him a freedom of expression denied him by the commercial strictures of his job.

Charlie read of how the Koori called the time before the birth of man the Dreamtime. At the dawn of time, beings of great power shaped the land and filled it with all the plants and animals that would ever be. After the beings of power died, they transformed their physical bodies into the stars and the rainbows and the mountains and their spirits withdrew from the earth into the spiritual realm, where they dreamed the world. However, the Dreaming things retained their power over the physical realm, which they would continue to release as long as humans followed the Great and Secret Plan. But it was only through dreams that the living could commune with the spiritual realm of the making gods and gain strength from them. All of this was well and good, if you were an anthropology major, but Charlie didn't really think that much about it. Until that night, when he found himself in the Dreaming.

In his dream he was walking naked through a strange and hostile land, both beautiful and frightening in its inhospitality to man. As he walked under the beating sun he saw the Great Snakes Ungunel, Wanambi, and Aranda rise from their watery hiding places and stretch themselves until they filled the sky with their writhing, endless bodies. Mudungkala, the old blind woman who was mother to all mankind, crawled from the middle of the earth, clutching the three babies that were the first human beings to her withered breasts, and scolded him for being so slow.

'You best hurry up, Djabo, if you would be father to the new race.'

'My name isn't Djabo, it's Charlie. Charlie Gower.'

'Maybe that is the name you wear in the land of the white men,' Mudungkala told him. 'But in the Dreaming you are Djabo. And it's best not to keep your bride waiting, no matter what your name.' The old woman pointed in the direction of the horizon. Charlie saw a beautiful woman in place of the sun, shining like she held a thousand stars in her belly. The Dream Woman opened her eyes and pinned Charlie with their golden stare. Then she spoke his name:

Djabo.

Her voice echoed in his head for several days as he tried to focus his attention on an advert for a beer company. He was supposed to be drawing a kangaroo with a six-pack of beer in its pouch in place of a joey. After he'd finished drawing the kangaroo, the clients told him they wanted the kangaroo to be wearing a bush hat because that would somehow 'masculinize' the kangaroo and then no one could accuse them of encouraging pregnant mothers to drink beer. As the client's PR representative droned on about kanga-roos with hats being more masculine than kangaroos without hats, Charlie Gower heard somebody call his name. Not his white name. His Dreaming name.

Djabo.

Charlie's eyes widened as they darted around the conference room, but he couldn't see anyone.

Djabo. It's time to go walkabout, the Dreamtime voice said. And the voice was right. It *was* time to go walkabout.

Without saying a word, Charlie stood up from his chair and began taking off his tie. Everyone in the room fell silent and stared at him as if he'd just sawed off his right leg.

'Gower! What's the meaning of this?' his boss blustered.

Charlie did not respond, instead he marched out of the conference room and headed for the elevator. He left his jacket lying on the street outside the office building he had worked in since graduating from university.

That was what? Three? Four days ago?

He'd walked along the highways until they turned into roads. Then he walked along the roads until they became trails. Then he walked along the trails until they became paths. And now he was climbing Ayers Rock, one of the biggest bloody rocks on the face of the earth.

Not that he'd done it all on his own. He'd had some help along the way, such as the elderly full-blooded Bindubi who had let him ride in the back of his beat-up old Land Rover for a hundred miles, and the shape-shifting *mura-mura* who, upon seeing how close to starvation and death from dehydration he was, came dancing out of the shimmering heat with a length of cooked 'roo tail and an emu egg full of water. Sometimes the *mura-mura* looked like aborigines, sometimes they looked like kangaroo-headed humans, other times they looked like they had dingo heads. In any case, they'd proven fairly friendly.

He clawed his way up Ayers Rock like an insect, scraping the tips of his fingers away on its rough, red surface. All con-scious thought, all identity besides that of Djabo, continued to flake away with his burnt and peeling hide. And finally, after struggling for the better part of a day and a night, he finally made the summit and lay on his back, his face turned toward the sun, his arms and legs splayed to embrace the universe.

As he stared up at the punishing sky with the last of his scorched vision, he saw a piece of the sun break off and fall from the heavens. As the piece of sun got closer, he could make out arms and legs and a head. He smiled then, for he recognized the Dream Woman and knew he was not dreaming. The Dream Woman scooped him up in her golden arms and bore him into the sky, where she wrapped his scorched flesh in soft clouds and coaxed the honey of life from his loins with only the slightest movement of her own.

When Charlie Gower woke up, he found himself being tended to by a tribe of Ngaanatjara, several hundred miles south of Ayers Rock. His skin was darker than a beetlenut, and there was what looked like tribal scarring on his face and belly. He wasn't sure if he'd done that to himself or if the Dream Woman was responsible. The first day he was in the Ngaanatjara camp he wondered how he was going to get back home to Canberra. On the second day he wondered if he still had a job, or if someone else was drawing hats on beer-packing kangaroos. On the third day he said to hell with it and declared Charlie Gower dead. From now on there was only Djabo, picture-maker and sorcerer to the Ngaanatjara. And that's who he remained for the rest of his life.

15

She's here.

Lords of the Outer Dark preserve me, she's here.

One of my operatives saw her the other day, prowling the streets of Chinatown, asking questions about Wretched Fly. Clever girl. Very clever. Seek out the master by tracing his servant. It will only be a matter of a day or two — if not hours — before she connects Wretched Fly with Kepa Hudie. Then my years of rehearsal will be behind me, and I will find myself faced with the real thing.

The question is: am I ready? Am I ready to cast aside my proxies and step inside the tiger's cage? Why do I even ask myself such a question? Am I not Morgan, Lord of the Morning Star? In the past I would no more ponder such things than I would walk unprotected in daylight. But that was before our last meeting. She did more than permanently mark me — that alone was insult enough — she took something from me as well. As we battled on the psychic combat field, in the Place Between Places, she absorbed a part of me shaped in the form of a chimera. By doing that, she gained a certain control over me. She made me love her.

It is not fair that I should find love now. I have prided myself on loving no one and nothing in seven hundred and fifty-three years. Love makes fools even of the shrewdest player — witness how it led Pangloss to the tragic mistake of making me his equal. I certainly never loved the loathsome old

pervert, either as a human or as a vampire. Either
I tolerated his attentions or else I would undergo
the gelder's knife and sing as one of the castrati
in Celestine IV's papal choir.

I have heard from reliable sources that Pangloss
is dead, or close enough to it. The old fool finally
succumbed to the Ennui. Good for him.

I have walked throughout my existence without fear
of wounds, or capture, or slavery, for I have worn
death as my armor. Nothing living could move my
heart or stir me to more than the basest appetite.
But now I find myself gazing into the eyes of Medusa,
reflected back at me by my own shield, and I find
myself smitten. It is not fair that I have found
love, for I do not want it and it will destroy me
if I give it half a chance.

She's here. She's finally, really here.

I can hardly wait.

> *From the journals of Sir Morgan,*
> *Lord of the Morning Star*

Chinatown had proven a hard nut to crack, even for one such as
herself. All Asian communities are fiercely cliquish, but none
more so than New York's. *Low faan*, be they Anglo, black, or
Hispanic, stick out like sore thumbs in its overcrowded streets.
She could use her telepathic abilities only so far – most human
minds were not designed to withstand intrusive scans. If she
wasn't careful, their consciousness could very well crumble
like an elaborate sugar confection, rendering them useless,
both to her and themselves. Still, there were those who would
always provide information – for a price.

There was nothing to distinguish the front of the Yankee-
China Drugstore from any of the others on the block. The windows of the old herb pharmacy were so dusty most passersby

would automatically assume it was no longer in business. They would be wrong.

A little bell over the threshold rang as she entered the shop. The inside was dark and dusty, although she could make out the original fixtures dating from the middle of the last century. A twenty-foot-long gilded screen of chrysanthemums and grinning lions blocked the view into the back of the store. A couple of faded paper lanterns hung from the pressed-tin ceiling. A long wooden counter with glass windows displayed mass-produced ceramic Buddhas and Mah-Jongg sets and even cheaper tea sets with poorly woven wicker handles. Everything was coated by a fine patina of dust.

A young Chinese man dressed in gray sweats stepped out from behind the screen that blocked access to the rest of the store. He looked hesitant, obviously unprepared for a *low faan* entering the establishment.

'I'm looking for Hu Tong of the *Junren Mao.*'

The young man shook his head vigorously. 'No here. No one that name here. You got wrong place maybe yes.'

'Don't hand me that crap,' Sonja snapped back in Cantonese. 'Hu Tong has been operating out of this store for one hundred and thirty-six years, give or take a year. Now go tell him he's got a customer!'

'Go back to work, Pei Lu,' purred a deep masculine voice from behind the screen. 'I shall see to our customer myself.'

Hu Tong, chieftain of the *Junren Mao*, stepped out from behind the gilded screen and fixed Sonja with his eyes of lambent green. It was hard to decide which was more impressive, his formal mandarin dress, complete with elaborately embroidered dragon robe and peacock-feather tassel, or the fact that he had the head of a tiger.

'Greetings, Hu Tong, it has been a long time since last we met.'

Hu Tong bowed his head slightly, his hands remaining tucked inside the sleeves of his *p'u-fu* jacket. 'As humans estimate such things, it has indeed been many years. Six, is it not?'

'I am in dire need of information, Hu Tong.'

'Of course. Why else would you come to the chieftain of the Cat Soldiers? Certainly not to drink tea and gossip.'

'I'm looking for a man. A Chinese human. Late forties. He's missing his right eye. His name is Wretched Fly. He's a psychic – and a powerful one, at that. He is a renfield in the service of a vampire called Morgan.'

Hu Tong removed his hands from his sleeves and picked up an abacus from behind the counter. His nails were over four inches long and tipped by protective gold sheaths that kept them from growing crooked. 'I see. And how do you propose paying for such information, provided it is mine to give?'

Sonja produced a bundle wrapped in plain brown paper and twine. A wax seal the color of old blood, bearing the imperial mark of the Ch'ing Dynasty, was affixed to the top of the package. Hu Tong's ears moved toward the front of his head.

'This is the *yen hop* of Fu-Lin, first of the Manchurian emperors. It is yours.'

Hu Tong's claws tore through the paper and twine as easily as they would tissue paper, exposing a black lacquer box, the lid inset with mother-of-pearl and fine jade in the shape of a peacock. With trembling fingers, he carefully placed the opium box's contents on the counter. The pipe was made of ivory with silver filigree and a golden mouthpiece. The bowl for the opium was made of gold, as were the dipping needle and the scissors for cutting the bricks into pills. Hu Tong regained his composure and bowed to show his appreciation.

'You honor me greatly, my friend. I am not certain, but I believe that the man you seek is of the *Bot Fun Guey*, the White Powder Ghosts. The Ghosts are a gang that deals largely in heroin and human cargo. Until recently, they were relatively small and of no consequence, compared to the *On Leong* and *Hip Sing* tongs. But in the last year they've suddenly grown quite powerful in Chinatown. They've branched out into smuggling humans into this country and gambling. They are known to be quite vicious in their dealings with others and their leader, Kepa Hudie, is said to be a sorcerer. He is missing his right eye and wears a patch embroidered with a luck dragon.'

Sonja smiled and returned Hu Tong's bow. 'I thank you, Hu Tong. Perhaps some day soon we can sit and drink tea and gossip. But as of now I have much to do.'

'Be careful, Sonja. The White Powder Ghosts are indeed fierce enemies.'

'So am I.'

Wretched Fly sat with his back to a wall full of sharks and sipped a cup of fragrant tea. He chose the Black Lotus Restaurant as his headquarters because of the wall-length saltwater fish tank filled with dog sharks, blowfish, rays, jellyfish, and other colorful, if far from pleasant, denizens of the deep. It helped his reputation as a *kiu ling*, a tong big shot, to be seen in such impressive surroundings.

In the last year he'd turned the White Powder Ghosts from a gang of scruffy drug runners into a force to be reckoned with in Chinatown – and soon Taipei and Hong Kong.

Wretched Fly caught a glimpse of his reflection in the tank's glassy wall. Dressed in an exquisitely tailored sharkskin suit, equally expensive Italian shoes, his dark hair slicked back and his right eye covered by an embroidered black velvet patch, he looked like a boss right out of a Hong Kong gangster flick, an impression he worked hard to maintain. He also worked to sustain the fear – never spoken to his face or even aloud – that he was a black sorcerer.

Oh, that part was true enough, in its way. Wretched Fly – or Kepa Hudei, as he was known to the citizens of Chinatown – possessed powers beyond those of most men. He was descended from a long line of psychics born, or so family legend had it, of a tryst between a peasant girl and a Shaolin master. His family had served the Chinese emperors from the days of

Chu I-Chun of the Ming Dynasty until the death of the dowager empress at the turn of the twentieth century.

Wretched Fly's forefathers had deliberately interbred, cultivating some of the finest psionic talents to be found in human stock. Unlike most sensitives, those of Wretched Fly's house were known for their comparative emotional and mental stability. Whether this had to do with genetics or the rigorous physical and mental training based on the teachings of that long-ago monk, not even Wretched Fly himself could say.

In any case, the minds of his fellowmen were as transparent to him as the shark wall of the Black Lotus – and filled with similar beasts. He could look at a man and know his hopes, his dreams, his plans, his schemes, even his deepest fears and darkest sins. And, if he did not like what he saw within the heads of those around him, he could reach out and crush them without lifting a finger. He'd done it twice – first to his thuggish predecessor, then again to a lieutenant he'd discovered working a deal with the Chinese Freemasons to overthrow him. Each time his victim collapsed to the floor, hemorrhaging from the eyes, ears, and nose.

Of course, no one knew the truth behind the fiction of Kepa Hudei, not even the sweet-faced little wife he'd taken earlier that month. No one knew his true name, or that the feared crime lord served a master far more powerful than the Triad bosses in Hong Kong. Wretched Fly had set himself up as a big shot in the underworld of Chinatown on orders from his one true master – Sir Morgan, Lord of the Morning Star.

Wretched Fly had been a servant of the vampire Noble for fifteen years, ever since Sir Morgan won him from his previous owner, a mandarin vampire named Shou Xi. Wretched Fly was completely and utterly devoted to his master. There was nothing he would not do for him – nothing he had *not* done. He had even lost his eye in the service of his liege lord.

If his master decreed that he should take control of a struggling gang and turn it into one of the most feared and powerful crime cartels in the city, then he would do so. His master found the combination of emotions generated by the smuggling of human cargo into the country most exhilarating. On the one hand there was the excitement and anticipation of arriving in the fabled 'land of gold'. On the other there was the disillusionment the new arrivals felt once they realized they were indentured to their smugglers for thirty thousand dollars, and were to be used as slave labor in restaurants and sweatshops scattered throughout the city. Their despair at ever earning their freedom was compounded by a paralyzing fear of the tongs. Morgan found this emotional mélange – especially the curdled hope – to be quite exquisite. After all, vampires did not exist off blood alone. The more sophisticated ones, such as Wretched Fly's master, required a psychic buffet in order to keep themselves in power.

Wretched Fly eyed the main dining room of the Black Lotus, automatically scanning everyone present as he did so. It was early evening, but the restaurant had yet to see any business. Not that it mattered. Wretched Fly paid the owner a handsome sum to make sure the place was open whenever he had a craving for steamed mussels in oyster sauce. Which was almost daily. The restaurant was on the top floor of a business tower on the edge of Chinatown, a stone's throw from the Tombs, and the only way in or out was via the elevator that faced the main dining room. Wretched Fly always made sure he was facing the elevator.

This afternoon the only people in the restaurant besides the owner, his wife, and the kitchen staff were Wretched Fly's bodyguards, Bing Yan and Zhong Ming. Both were young, energetic, stupid, and sadistic. No doubt they would go far in the gang. No one was thinking anything dangerous to him. And, as was the case with his bodyguards, some were not even thinking at all. Good. That suited Wretched Fly just fine.

Then the elevator doors pinged open and a cloud of hate as thick as a swarm of angry hornets boiled into the room.

Sonja Blue stepped out of the elevator into the main dining room of the Black Lotus Restaurant. Despite the intensity of the hatred radiating from her, her physical manner was quite nonchalant, almost insulting. Her hands were in the pockets of her leather jacket, her shoulders slumped. The owner of the restaurant, dressed in a suit and bow tie, stepped forward, smiling nervously and clutching a menu as if it was a shield.

'Yes? One for dinner? Smoking?'

Sonja shook her head and pointed at Wretched Fly. 'No thanks. I'm here to see that man sitting over there.'

The owner's smile faltered and his eyes flickered in the direction of Wretched Fly.

'That not possible.'

Sonja slid past the owner as if he didn't exist. Bing Yan and Zhong Ming moved to block her path. They were dressed in cheaper, less fashionable versions of their headman's suit, which did little to disguise the bulges made by their shoulder holsters. Bing Yan wore wraparound sunglasses, while Zhong Ming chewed an ivory toothpick.

'You go now. This not your place,' said Bing Yan, who was the more proficient in English. 'You stay, you get hurt maybe yes.'

Sonja stroked her chin and nodded to herself, as if weighing the wisdom of the thug's words. 'You know, you've got a point there, buddy.' She began to turn, as if she'd thought better of her actions. Bing Yan and Zhong Ming exchanged knowing smirks.

Sonja's fist caught Zhong Ming in the side of the head, sending the ivory toothpick in his mouth flying across the room, accompanied by a shower of teeth and blood. Bing Yan caught a spray of his friend's blood in the face and cried out in alarm and disgust, wiping at his eyes with one hand while going for his gun with the other. To his surprise, his holster was empty. Then he saw his gun in the hand of the strange woman.

'Lost something, laughing boy?' Sonja asked as she slammed the butt of the gun directly between Bing Yan's eyebrows, dropping him like an ox.

The owner's wife came out from behind the register, screaming hoarsely into her hands, her eyes starting from her head. The owner held her by the shoulders, his eyes fixed on Sonja. He was too frightened to be anything but concerned for his wife.

'Get out of here!' she told them. They stared at her, their English destroyed by their terror. She repeated herself, this time in Cantonese, and they bolted into the kitchen.

Zhong Ming was still crawling on the floor, spitting up pieces of molar and bicuspid like they were Mah-Jongg tiles. As Sonja moved towards Wretched Fly's table he clawed frantically at his shoulder holster. The steel tip of Sonja's right boot caught him in the side, lifting him off the carpet and filling his lungs with broken ribs.

Wretched Fly did not stand to greet her, but nodded his head in acknowledgment. 'So, we meet again, halfling.'

'I see you remember me.'

'One does not forget being maimed,' he said, lifting a hand to caress the velvet of his eyepatch.

'You know why I'm here, Wretched Fly.'

'I will not tell you where he is, even if he demanded it himself. But, please, be seated, Ms Blue.' He gestured to the chair opposite him.

Sonja sat down, never taking her eyes off him. 'You would disobey him? You have changed, haven't you?'

'My loyalty is without end. It is because of this that I would keep you from him.'

'You must not have much faith in your master's power if you fear a "halfling" such as myself.'

Wretched Fly's remaining eye flashed angrily. 'You wounded my master. You ruined that which was without flaw. But I must share the blame, for if I had succeeded in killing you that night in San Francisco, my master would never have been harmed. My punishment for failing was being blinded.'

'Let's get to it, then.'

Wretched Fly placed his hands, palms downward, against the table. Sonja did the same. And the battle began.

She was standing in the middle of a Chinese watercolor, the kind found on calendars. In the distance were hazy mountains, green blobs against a pale blue sky. There was the suggestion of a waterfall, the artful representation of bamboo – but none of it was real. It was a clever approximation of place, nothing more than stage dressing. Sonja knew that they were in the no man's land known as the Place Between Places, the limbo where all psychic battles were fought.

There was the sound of silk banners snapping in a high wind and something hurtled down out of the painted sky, knocking her to her knees. There was pain and Sonja stared at the hole ripped in the right sleeve of her leather jacket, and at the blood welling up from the deep scratches scoring her flesh. Although she was not physically harmed, she knew only too well that wounds dealt and suffered during psychic combat were all too real, in their own way.

She looked up into the sky and saw her attacker framed against the sun, fluttering like a kite. The storm dragon grinned down at her, thunderclouds pouring from its flared nostrils, making it look like it had a mustache. Its razor-sharp talons glistened with her blood.

The storm dragon spoke to her then, and its voice was that of Wretched Fly.

You are strong, halfling. I will give you that. But you lack finesse. You are like a child, destroying what it does not like. In this world, I am the one who is to be feared – not you!

As if to prove the point, the storm dragon went into a power-dive, extending its claws like landing gear. Sonja tried to run, but it was no use – the dragon was too fast. It caught her from behind, snatching her up like a hawk would a rabbit.

Wretched Fly's imago tightened its grip, sending talons deep into her belly and back. Sonja kicked and hammered her fists against the dragon's claws, coughing blood as she cursed Wretched Fly at the top of her lungs.

It ends now. You have caused my master much trouble, halfling. With you dead, Morgan will be as he once was. His love will be mine, and mine alone, as is my right.

Sonja opened her mouth and Wretched Fly wondered if she was begging for mercy. He hoped so. He would like it if she begged. But as her mouth continued to stretch, growing wider than it ever could in the world of flesh, he glimpsed three pairs of eyes staring at him from inside her. A three-headed tiger with the tail of a scorpion leapt from the vampire's mouth, its heads roaring in angry unison.

While Wretched Fly was expecting trickery, he was unprepared for the horrible rush of recognition that came when he saw the chimera. Although it had been vomited up by the halfling, the beast was Morgan's. It was more than a familiar of the vampire lord, it was an actual piece of him. And Wretched Fly had been conditioned from birth never to raise his hand against his master, no matter what the situation.

Sparks flew from the chimera's multiple mouths and its roar was that of swords striking shields. Wretched Fly screamed as the chimera's venomous tail delivered several stings to his dragon body in rapid succession. The storm dragon flickered, became transparent, revealing Wretched Fly coiled within its belly. The chimera pounced on the cowering psychic, sinking its fangs deep into his neck and worrying him as a farm cat would a field mouse.

When it was finished, the chimera returned to Sonja and rubbed its left head against her thigh, purring like a bus left in low gear. Sonja stroked its middle head and wiped the blood from the right head's muzzle.

'Good kitties.'

*　　*　　*

When she opened her eyes she found Wretched Fly lying facedown on the table, blood seeping from his ears, nose, and remaining eye. Wretched Fly had been a worthy opponent. She couldn't deny him that. And he had, indeed, proven himself loyal to his master. She still had no clue as to Morgan's whereabouts in the city. Then she noticed that all the fish in the wall tank were dead or dying as well. She watched a two-foot-long dog shark thrash out its final agonies then go still, drifting in the captive current. She pushed back her chair and stood on wobbly feet, scanning the room.

The owner stood framed in the door of the kitchen, watching her the way she imagined the first mammals must have watched the tyrannosaurs as they thundered by. He eased out from behind the swinging door that led to the kitchen, staring in horrified silence at the bodies littering his dining room. When he turned to look at Sonja, she fixed his mind in place as neatly as she would a butterfly with a hat pin.

'The *On Leong* did this,' she told him in Cantonese. 'Retaliation against the *Bot Fun Guey* for muscling in on their territory.'

The owner nodded his head, his voice sounding as if it was coming from miles away. 'Tong war. Such things happen all the time.' He blinked and shook his head to clear it. Horrible. So horrible. He hurried back into the kitchen to check on his wife and his cooks, who were hiding near the freezer unit. He needed to call 911 and report what had happened, but first he had to calm down his wife, who was babbling about a demon woman with mirrors for eyes. His wife was not used to the ways of the Americans yet. It wouldn't do to have her babbling about demons while the police were investigating a gang hit.

16

Jen sat astride one of the lions guarding the central branch of the New York Public Library on Fifth Avenue, grinning like a demented bareback rider. It was close to midnight and the library had long since closed its doors.

'I got your message, Jen. What do you want?'

'I heard about Wretched Fly. Impressive, milady. Truly impressive.'

'So?'

Jen mock-pouted and leaned forward, resting his chin atop the lion's chiseled mane. 'My, you *are* unsociable. You really must brush up on your small talk, milady. A little chitchat now and again never hurts. Besides, I meant what I said. I'm genuinely impressed. I always found Wretched Fly a particularly loathsome specimen – always pretending he was better than the other renfields because he could control his telepathy without the benefit of drugs.'

'Is there some point to this? Or did you summon me here simply to praise my disposal of a one-eyed psychic?'

Jen sighed and reached into his overcoat and pulled out a single, long-stemmed black rose and a sealed envelope and tossed them at her feet. 'I was told to deliver these to you.'

'Is this Luxor's doing?'

'I have more than one employer – when it suits my needs,' Jen replied, and without further comment jumped off the back of the lion and into the surrounding night.

Sonja bent down to retrieve the rose and the envelope. On closer inspection, she saw that the stem of the rose was made from braided strands of barbed wire, and that the petals were fashioned of black velvet. The wax seal on the envelope bore the symbol of Fenris swallowing the moon. Inside was a folded piece of parchment on which was written in a spidery hand: 'Meet me at the Cherub Room.'

The Cherub Room was a trendy nightspot just off Columbus Circle that catered to the bridge and tunnel crowd that poured into the city each weekend in hopes of rubbing elbows with the rich and famous or, failing that, experiencing what would pass for decadence in Hackensack.

The overall décor was that of leopard skin, pink vinyl, gold paint, and winged babies. And lots of 'em. Pudgy little dead babies everywhere: shouldering cornucopia with speakers hidden inside them, cuddling bunnies, holding aloft mirrors, peeing champagne into silver basins. Gilded baby dolls outfitted with cardboard wings hung from the ceiling. The overall feeling was not unlike that of being sealed alive inside a box of Valentine's Day chocolates.

The club was crowded and the music cranked up loud enough to render normal conversation impossible. Suspended over the dance floor were a couple of dancer cages, where young women and men dressed in silver lamé thongs and tinfoil halos gyrated to the techno beat.

Sonja was uncertain why Morgan would have chosen this place, of all the clubs in Manhattan, for their rendezvous. Unless he was afraid of what she might do to him without witnesses.

She felt him the minute he entered the room. It was a strange sensation, as if someone had thrown a switch and completed a circuit, bringing long-dormant machinery humming to life. The hair on the back of her neck prickled and her lungs felt suddenly heavy, as if the oxygen in the room had been miraculously transformed into mercury. The space between them was charged with the energy that exists between Maker and Made, Creator and Creation. It was as if they were two powerful magnets, both pulling and pushing against one another. Sonja scanned the room and found him standing in the far corner beside an oversized papier-mâché Cupid armed with an actual bow and arrow.

Although she knew she had marked him during their last confrontation, her mental image of Morgan was still that of the smiling, debonair bon vivant who had first swept Denise Thorne off her feet, twenty-five years earlier. She was shocked to see the full extent of his wounding. The left side of his face was pulled into a permanent sneer, the eye as gray and sightless as a baked fish's. Where once his hair had been dark, now there was a shock of white starting from his left temple. He wore an expensive and exquisitely tailored suit, which somehow glamorized his scars, turning mutilation into a fashion statement.

She waited for the expected surge of hate to fill her, but in its place was something else. She had hurt him. Humbled him. The snip of a girl he had tossed away like so much trash had left her mark on him, repaying him for dismissing her so callously. There was no rage inside her, only a grim sense of satisfaction and something that felt almost like – pity?

The thumping of the disco and the flashing of the lights, the smell of sickly sweet mixed drinks reminded her of the night she'd first met him. The night a naïve young heiress made the mistake of getting a little too drunk and allowing herself to be separated from her friends, then made the mistake of getting into a car with a strange man. She'd gone to the bar for a taste of the forbidden fruit of adulthood, only to find herself swept away on the wings of storybook romance.

She'd known the clumsy kisses of school friends, but Morgan was something else entirely. What he promised was true romance, the kind every woman dreams of. She was the ash-pail princess and he the noble knight. When Morgan looked at her she felt so beautiful, so special. And it had nothing to do with her daddy's millions, since he was rich himself. He loved her. Just her, and nothing else.

When he promised to treat her to a night unlike any

other, she'd eagerly accompanied him into the back of his chauffeured Rolls. Where he raped her and drank her blood and threw her, naked and dying, onto the streets of London.

Sonja began moving in his direction, wondering with each step when the hate that had been her constant companion, her motivating force, for the entirety of her existence, would boil forth, filling her guts with its familiar heat.

Morgan stiffened as she drew near, his leer belying the caution in his remaining eye. He nodded slightly, acknowledging her presence.

'I'm glad you're here.'

Sonja felt the chimera – the part of Morgan's self she had absorbed years ago – shift inside her head. It sensed its old master. It was as if there were thousands of ants crawling over her skin. She had to fight to keep from twitching and shaking like a junkie in need of a fix. Being so close to Morgan made her muscles vibrate like the cables on a suspension bridge in a high wind.

As if in response to this threat, the hate finally made its appearance, circling her brow like a crown of thorns, the weight of it digging through her skull and into her brain.

Kill him, whispered the Other, its voice urgent. *Kill him now and get it over with.*

Sonja was amazed to feel the fear surging through her vampiric half. She wiped at the cold sweat beading her upper lip. 'I'm going to kill you, Morgan.'

'You'll try. But not here.' He gestured to the dance floor. 'It's far too crowded to be discreet.'

Screw discreet, nail him now. Nail him before he tries to call the chimera back.

'Why do you insist on fighting me, child?' Morgan's voice was mellifluous, the tone as soothing as a cool hand on a fevered brow.

'You know damn well why.'

'You still consider your condition a curse? I gave you immortality, freedom from the ravages of old age and disease!'

'I didn't ask to be made into one of you. I didn't ask for any of this—'

Morgan arched an upswept brow. 'Didn't you? There are those humans our kind hunt down as prey – and there are those who seek us out. You know that as well as I do, child. You responded eagerly to your seduction. I used no beguilement, no mind control.'

'You can't blame me! You can't blame me for what happened!' she hissed.

Morgan's smile tried to be charming, but the scars twisted it into something else. 'I'm not blaming *you*, child. After all, you are not the girl who followed me into the London night, are you? You are not Denise Thorne, but a creature of my seed, shaped in my image, born within her dead flesh.'

'She never died.'

'Then where is she now?'

Sonja blinked, uncertain of how to answer. That was a question she herself had been at a loss to understand.

Stop playing word games and kill him! The Other's voice was close to hysterical. *He's playing with you, trying to lull you off guard! He's trying to throw a glamour over you!*

Morgan reached into his breast pocket and produced a small jeweler's case. 'I realize now that what I did was wrong, horribly wrong. I don't mean turning you. That I do not regret. However, I was a fool to throw such an exquisite thing as you away. I must have been indeed deluded not to recognize you for what you are—' He held the case out to her, flicking it open with his thumb. Lying on the red velvet interior was a crucifix made of sterling silver, fashioned to look like thorns. 'Please, I want you to take this as a token of my shame – of my idiocy. What I did in London was a cruel and thoughtless thing – I tossed you aside. I left you to find your way in a cold and trackless waste, where there are no paths and no road signs. I was your sire and I turned my back on you. You have every right to hate me for bringing you into the world without pity. But I want to try and change that, my child.'

Nancy A. Collins

Sonja stared at the crucifix and the length of black velvet
ribbon that held it. Morgan's voice was thick and sweet in her
ears, like honey dripping from the comb.

'What happened between Denise Thorne and myself does
not concern us, my pet. Let us begin our time together anew.
You have avenged your outrage by marking me. Our scores
are settled, wouldn't you agree?'

Sonja reached out as if in a trance, her fingertips brushing
the outside of the case.

Don't take it! Don't take anything he offers you!

She blinked rapidly, as if coming out of a trance, and
drew back her hand. There was a look of displeasure on
Morgan's face that he could not hide.

'What are you trying to pull?'

'Pull? I don't understand what you're getting at.' Morgan's
good eye suddenly dropped its pretense at civility and began
darting about. His shoulders tensed and he stood a little
straighter, his body language that of a man who has suddenly
realized he's in trouble.

'We have company, I fear.'

Sonja followed his stare, scanning the room as she did. To
her surprise, she spotted half a dozen undead making their
way across the dance floor towards them. To the eyes of
the humans nightclubbing it up, the intruders looked perfectly normal. No one seemed to notice their rotting flesh and
decaying features, in any case.

'They're Luxor's brats,' Morgan snarled. 'That accursed
half-bastard of Pangloss's must have told him I'd be here,
but I never thought the hermaphrodite so bold!'

Sonja found herself standing shoulder to shoulder with
Morgan, facing the approaching vampires. Part of her still
wanted to slay Morgan and get it over with, but this sudden
change in her game plan was forcing her to rethink her
priorities.

'Maybe he thinks we've formed a truce, that we're teaming
up against him?' she muttered.

Morgan nodded. 'That makes sense. Luxor is nothing if not insecure.'

The assembled vampires seemed to shudder, as if the air surrounding them had winked. They were shifting into over-drive. Sonja shifted as well, preparing to meet her attackers on their level. Fighting in high gear used up a lot of energy, but it was the only way she could hope to get out of the situation with her head still attached to her shoulders.

The frantically dancing nightclubbers seemed to freeze in mid-step, like the images on a videotape placed on pause. The strobes ceased their stutter, becoming spotlights, as the thumping bass of the disco transformed itself into a muffled heartbeat.

Luxor's brood surged forward, yowling like banshees. Sonja met the first one head on, driving her switchblade into its chest. She glimpsed a moment of pain and confusion in the vampire's features before it folded around her fist like a punctured pool-toy. Before she could pull the blade free, a vampiress in seventies retro bell-bottoms and a macrame tube-top slammed into her, knocking her off her feet. Sonja rammed her palm into the vampiress's chin as she made to rip out her throat, snapping her lower jaw like a piece of celery. The vampiress shrieked her displeasure and tried to plunge a hooked thumbnail into Sonja's right eye. Sonja dodged the attack, biting off the vampiress's thumb and spitting it back into her face.

A vampire dressed in black leather pants joined the fray, kicking Sonja in the side of the head with a steel-toed Doc Marten. As he drew back his foot to deliver a second blow, Sonja snagged his bootlaces and yanked, jerking his feet out from under him. She scrambled back up, driving her elbow into the vampiress's gut. The hilt of the switchblade jutted from the dead vampire's rapidly decomposing chest and it came away with a sucking sound. The retro vampiress landed on Sonja's back, clawing at her face with three-inch-long fingernails. Swearing under her breath, Sonja reversed her grip on the knife, ramming it into the creature's left eye. She yowled once and let go, dropping onto the floor to spasm like a hooked fish at her enemy's feet.

Morgan seemed to be holding his own ground with a lot less sweat. As Sonja watched, he plucked one of his attackers out of midair and, with a practised turn of his hand, twisted the vampire's head completely around, so that it was looking at Sonja from between its shoulders. The vampire's eyes blinked, more surprised than pained, then went gray. Morgan tossed the dead thing aside as casually as he would discard a broken toy.

Before Sonja could decide whether to aid him or join with his attackers, the leather-pants vampire was back on his feet, slamming his head into her gut like a billy goat. The force of his blow drove her into the wall, cracking the plaster. Sonja rammed the silver blade into the back of his neck, between the third and fourth vertebrae. The vampire dropped, his body twitching and jerking as the silver toxins swept through his central nervous system.

Sonja looked up in time to see Morgan twist the head off the final member of Luxor's suicide party and hurl it in the direction of the packed dance floor. Despite everything, she really had to admire the guy's style.

Kill him.

She was tired. The battle had taken a lot out of her and it was more and more of a struggle to remain in high gear. Assessing her condition, she could tell she'd sustained a skull fracture and four broken ribs, possibly a ruptured spleen. Nothing she couldn't handle, really. But there was no way she could take down a vampire of Morgan's power. Part of her was even relieved that she would not be forced to act on what had, only minutes before, seemed the only sane thing to do.

Kill him.

She stood there, nursing her splintered ribs, and it suddenly occurred to her that it was the Other's voice, and not her own

– nor that of the vanished Denise – that was the most strident when it came to her obsession with Morgan. At first the three voices had been united, equally strong in their hatred, in their desire for revenge. But, over the years, Denise's voice had flagged, and now she discovered her own passion fading as well, leaving only the Other's disembodied voice the strongest and most vehement.

Kill him or die, the Other growled. *Kill him or we're all doomed.*

'Shut up,' she whispered. 'I'll do it when I'm good and ready.'

When she looked up again, Morgan was gone. But the jeweler's case he'd presented to her was lying on the ground at her feet, the thorny crucifix glinting up at her.

Silver. It was really silver. Considering the horror vampires held for the metal, it must have taken a great deal of courage on his part to even touch the case, much less carry it on his person. She found herself oddly moved by this show of bravery. She bent down and picked up the crucifix, dangling from its velvet choker.

He might be a murdering inhuman monster, but at least the guy had taste.

She grimaced as something deep inside her (the spleen?) began hemorrhaging. She had to get out of the club and drop back into human time if she wanted to keep out of the morgue. She hated waking up to find some coroner splitting her open like a Christmas goose.

She waited until she was out of the fire exit before slipping out of overdrive. There was a chorus of shrill screams as the vampire's head landed amidst the dancers. The owners of the Cherub Room would no doubt have a hard time explaining to the cops where the hell six horribly mutilated – not to mention inexplicably decayed – corpses were doing in their club. Screw 'em. That's what they get for letting just anyone in.

17

Why didn't I kill him?

He was standing right there. I could have killed him. It wouldn't have been easy, it wouldn't have been clean, but I could have done it. I could have at least *tried*.

But I didn't. And the funny thing is, I didn't even *want* to.

This wasn't like the first time I saw him after my transformation. Back then I'd wanted to kill his ass but good. But something in me short-circuited. There is a dominant-submissive switch that gets thrown whenever a broodling wants to destroy its sire. But it's not infallible. It takes willpower and determination to overcome it, but it can be done. But that's not what happened to me tonight. It's not like I couldn't move against him. I just looked at him and whatever it was eating my belly simply disappeared.

Maybe it's because he doesn't *look* like Morgan anymore. He doesn't look like the Morgan of my nightmares. He doesn't look like the Morgan who killed my friends. He's . . . changed. I never believed such a thing was possible for vampires, but seeing Pangloss in his final hours has made me unsure. There's so much I still *don't* know about my kind, about the world we exist in . . .

The only part of me that seems to be certain about Morgan is the Other. It wants him dead with lilies on his chest. But I can't figure out why. Morgan is a vampire. The Other is his creation. So why does it want to kill him? The Other is the part always eager to wreak havoc on those weaker than itself. The part that revels in hurting people. So why does it want to destroy Morgan, a creature that shares the same interests? I've spent my existence fighting the Other, trying to ignore its needs and desires. What should I do now?

Perhaps Morgan is right, perhaps it's time for me to put my

vendetta aside. It no longer really concerns me. Do I want to turn into a pathetic, vengeful moron like Luxor or Pangloss? For immortals, the Nobles seem to be a particularly petty group, constantly warring with one another over perceived slights.

With everything that's happened lately – Judd, Palmer, Lethe, Pangloss – maybe I need to take some time out and reassess what's going on. I . . .

Shut up. Shut up.

I'm *not* going soft. I'm *not*. It's just that I'm tired. I'm so damn *tired*.

I need to think. Need to sort out what I'm feeling. What's important to me.

Bullshit!

I'm *not* falling in love with him! That's bullshit and you fucking well know – what do you mean, it's *her* doing?

Denise is dead.

From the diaries of Sonja Blue

All in all, it went quite well. I could have done without Luxor's kamikaze squad, but in the end that worked to my advantage. It seems to have weakened her resolve against me. Good. It will make the seduction easier.

I have seduced thousands upon thousands of women over the centuries. Casanova was a rank amateur, compared to myself. There is little genius in coercing a woman to surrender her virtue. I, on the other hand, rob them of far more than their maidenheads. Oh, yes, they bleed, but in a far grander style. Yes, I have lured a legion of fair women to their dooms, but none was as deadly and as dangerous as my precious Sonja.

I must be careful that she does not scent the truth behind my motivations. She must believe that my affections are sincere. And, in part, that is the truth. I *do* love her.

I must confess I was proud of her tonight. The way she handled Luxor's dog soldiers was poetry in motion! She is indeed a prodigy. To think she's only twenty-five years old! Most vampires don't attain such skill and self-possession until they're well into their first century! She is strong, like a samurai blade tempered in the forge of a master smith. No wonder Luxor feared that she and I might team up against him!

Together, no Noble would dare stand against us. She has never scuttled under rocks or into dumpsters to hide from the sun. But neither has she submitted to the will of another. That is why she must die.

If only there was another way. The thought of destroying her pains me, but not as much as loving her does. I can only hope my dress rehearsals have been successful in preparing me for what I must do.

This will not be easy for me. In fact, it may very well prove to be the hardest thing I've done since I broke free of Pangloss's fealty, five hundred years ago. I take no pleasure in what I must do. Although she is the one who ruined my face, forcing me to walk the earth for the rest of my days a sneering one-eyed freak, I will not rejoice when she is no more. She is the only thing I have ever loved, and I must kill her. I *have* to kill her. There can be no other end to this. I am Morgan, Lord of the Morning Star. I will be slave to nothing living or dead.

Not even love.

From the journals of Sir Morgan,
Lord of the Morning Star

There was another barbed-wire rose and parchment note

tacked to the refrigerator when she woke up. No doubt Jen's work again. However, judging by the bloodstains on the carpet and the crimson fingerprints on the wall, he hadn't been entirely lucky in dodging the booby traps this time.

Sonja removed the note and read it, deciphering the spidery script that seemed both calligraphy and a spirograph drawing – the secret language of the Pretenders.

Morgan wanted her to meet him on the top of the Empire State Building.

How romantic.

The observation deck of the Empire State Building, the most famous once-tallest skyscraper in the world, was officially closed to the public. But nothing is off limits to creatures who can step between the cracks of perceived reality.

At street level the wind had not been particularly note-worthy, but one hundred and two storeys above the sidewalk was a different matter. It grabbed at Sonja's clothes, tugging on them like a persistent child, while her hair fluttered about her skull. Even with the windbreaks and protective barriers designed to keep suicides from plummeting down onto Fifth Avenue, the strength of the elements could not be denied.

Morgan was waiting for her, balanced on one of the railings, his hands clasped behind his back, looking out over the city that lay spread before them like stars reflected in a still pond. The wind made his opera coat flap and snap like a banner. He spoke to her without bothering to look over his shoulder to see if she was there.

'I knew you would come. Do you still wish to kill me?'

'What else is there to do? I don't play cards.'

Morgan laughed and turned to look at her, his twisted smile growing wider. 'You *do* have a sense of humor, then?'

'About some things. You're not one of them, though.'

He pointed at the thorny crucifix hanging from her neck. 'You honor me. I take it you liked my little token of affection?'

Sonja shrugged. 'I'm wearing it, aren't I?'

Morgan nodded and returned to looking out over the city. 'It's beautiful, is it not?' he said, gesturing with a sweeping movement of his left hand. 'The city, I mean. It's alive, you know. Not like a human is alive. More like a simple one-celled organism or a sponge. Hundreds upon thousands upon millions of humans eating and drinking and shitting and fucking and dying in such a small physical space – their minds and life forces united on a subconscious level, connecting them on a wavelength unacknowledged but not unfelt. Then again, perhaps a better metaphor might be that of a herd of cattle. Have you ever seen a stampede?'

'Only in the movies.'

'It is a fearsome thing, even for creatures such as we. It is nothing more than nature stripped bare, naked and unreasoning. The smallest thing can trigger a stampede – sometimes nothing at all. If the cattle are edgy, the slightest shift in air pressure can turn them from docile, cud-chewing cows into mindless, raging beasts. The effects can be as devastating as a tornado or an earthquake – and just as sudden. This city is like that. It is constantly on the brink of a stampede.'

'You're not telling me anything I don't know.'

'Am I not? I'm sorry. I don't mean to be pedantic.' Morgan pointed in the direction of the Lower East Side. 'Right now a drunken stepfather, enraged by his wife's refusal to give him sex, is strangling her three-year-old son. He's going to put the boy's body in the incinerator chute of his housing block to avoid detection.'

Morgan hopped down from his observation point and trotted to the opposite side of the deck, waving a hand in the direction of Central Park. 'Police are still searching for the body of an eighteen-month-old child of tourists from Iowa, reported snatched from his stroller by a wild-eyed Negro. In truth, the child was beaten to death three days ago by his parents and buried in a shallow grave in their backyard.'

Spinning on his heel like a demented weathervane, Morgan dashed towards the southwest corner. 'A balding closet queen with some political clout is chatting up a surlily handsome young man in a discreet piano bar in the West Village. The surly-looking young man has raped and killed eight older gay men over the last three years, chopping up their bodies and wrapping them in plastic garbage bags before tossing them out on lonely highways upstate.'

Morgan swerved again, like a compass needle being drawn to true north. 'In Harlem there is a dark, stinking one-room apartment with no electricity, no running water, no heat, no furniture, no food. There are eight children, ranging from nine months to seven years old, locked in the apartment while their respective mothers and fathers sell themselves or each other for crack.' He grabbed one of the pay telescopes mounted on the edge of the railing and swung from it like a child on a monkey bar, the delight in his face rendering his scars momentarily invisible. 'God, I *love* this town!'

Kill him, you stupid bitch! Don't stand there staring at him like a love-struck cow – slit his throat from ear to ear!

Sonja bit her lip until the blood came. The Other's voice stung her like scorpions and whips, but she refused to act. She had spent so many years fighting its influence that resistance to its demands had become automatic.

'You seem troubled, my child. Is something wrong?'

Morgan was watching her. His good eye seemed concerned, but its damaged twin was what drew her attention. It had been a long time since she'd had to rely on simple physical cues to decipher another's thoughts and emotional state. There was no way she could easily tap into his mind – Morgan's skill at psionic cloaking was equal to her own.

'Why did you ask me to meet you here?'

'Because I wish to continue our conversation from last night, my dear. And this time I doubt we'll be interrupted quite so rudely.'

'Nothing has changed between us, Morgan. I'm going to kill you, no matter what.'

'If that's the case, why aren't you killing me now?'

'I . . . I just don't feel like it right now.'

Morgan clucked his tongue at her. 'Come now, child, don't insult me by telling me such a wretched lie. You may be an angry girl, but you're not *stupid*. You possess a rational brain, of that I've no doubt. Perhaps you've stayed your hand because you've come to realize that there is no longer any point to your vendetta?'

Sonja fixed him with an angry glare, but the sight of his dead eye made her look away. 'What makes you think you know what's going through my head?'

'A parent knows its child – even a prodigal, such as yourself. There is a current that exists between us – do you not feel it? You and I are simpatico, far more than any get I've spawned. We are left hand and right hand, the tide and the shore, yin and yang. We are the same, you and I.'

'I'm nothing like you!'

'Do you drink the blood of living things?'

'Yes.'

'Have you ever taken pleasure from the pain and sufferings of others?'

'I—'

'Be truthful!'

'Yes, but they deserved—'

'Do you find humans blind and ignorant sheep, dragging the rest of creation with them on their mad dash to extinction?'

'Not all of them—'

'You are exactly like me! The one difference is that you still cling to the ghost of your humanity! You've somehow gotten it into your head that humans are to be pitied and envied instead of used. Why should you hold yourself to ideals that the vast majority of humans have discarded? Our kind do not *create* evil. Humanity does that all on its own. But we of the *enkidu* – and others of the Pretending races – are not averse to manipulating human misdeeds to suit our needs. We did not invent the Nazi concentration camps, or the Russian gulags, or the Khymer Rouge killing fields, or the

219

Serbian rape camps, but we would be fools to turn our backs on such fertile sources of . . . nourishment.'

'I've never had anything to do with anything like that—'

'Haven't you? Then why do you prefer to spend your time in the inner city? It's not just a matter of camouflage. Don't you feel a *high* every time you prowl a ghetto neighborhood – the more crime-ridden the better? Does it make you feel more *alive* – more *alert* – to trawl for prey in the most hopeless sectors of town? Oh, I'm sure you're telling yourself you're stalking those neighborhoods because that's where your prey is most likely to be. But there's more to it than that, isn't there? A lot more.'

He was right. She'd never been willing to admit it to herself before, but now there was no denying it. It was like he knew her, knew her in a way no other had before. The intimacy was both disturbing and compelling.

'Do you know what it's like to be lonely, Sonja?' Morgan's voice was quiet but intensely personal, as if they were standing by a country lake instead of high atop a skyscraper. 'Do you know what it's like to be surrounded by people but to be painfully, horribly *alone*? Do you fear that you might someday disappear into the emptiness that once held your heart?'

'Yes.' Her voice was so small she wasn't even certain she'd actually said the word aloud. Perhaps she hadn't.

'You know nothing of loneliness,' Morgan hissed, his voice suddenly growing a hard, rusty edge. 'You won't even have an *inkling* of what it's like for another century or two! To stand outside the flow of time and watch those you once called friends, confidants, and lovers wither away and die like leaves on a tree – knowing that no matter how many servants and consorts you surround yourself with, in the end you will always be alone. And the most horrible thing of all is that you will come to realize that you have no equal. There is no one who will ever truly fulfill your needs, challenge your expectations, or understand what drives you.

'The humans who are drawn to our kind are far from worthy companions. They're attracted to our inhumanity –

our monstrosity, if you will. They love us for what we are not, not for what we are. Even the brightest and most loyal renfield is little more than a pet. One that you will outlive and, in time, forget. How could it be otherwise?

'As the years bleed into decades, the decades lengthen into centuries, your memory will become so vast you'll be bored by everything and everyone. Nothing will be new. No sight will be unseen. No act undone. Without diversions and stimulation, the Ennui will eventually claim you. Meddling in the affairs of humans provides us with a certain amount of stimulation, but even that wearies after a while. That was why I spent so much time and energy trying to create my own breed of vampire. A desire to have my progeny rule the earth was a motivating factor, I'll admit to that. But mostly it was an attempt to keep myself . . . *involved*; to provide myself with new challenges.

'Of course, it failed horribly, largely because of your interference. I've realized in the years since then that my plans were foolish, perhaps even dangerous. Anise and Fell were made of weaker stuff than yourself, but they proved themselves stronger than I had imagined possible. And *that* is what prompted me to thinking that I have been surrounding myself with inferiors. All vampires do so – we naturally fear those as strong as ourselves. In vampire society there are only two positions – slave and master. To not be one is to be the other. We tend to ensure that our gets will be subservient. We rarely infect those who show signs of the inner strength, intelligence, and ambition that, in time, will result in Nobles. For a vampire to assert its will and claim its place in the hierarchy, it must break free of its Maker. And few of us are willing to pay for companionship with our very existence.'

'You didn't kill Pangloss.'

Morgan fell silent for a moment, his face unreadable. 'Pangloss . . . did not need to be killed. When the time came, he recognized me as his better. He surrendered his control over me in exchange for his continued existence. As I said, ours is a society of masters and slaves. That is why, in the five hundred years since I threw off his yoke of obedience, Pangloss was never able to do me genuine harm.'

'Perhaps it was because he loved you.'

Morgan barked a humorless laugh.

'His last words were of you.'

Morgan did not look surprised, but instead seemed to take it as his due. 'He's dead, then?'

'The Pangloss you knew no longer exists.'

Morgan shrugged. 'He no longer concerns me. What concerns me is you. I have found in you a strength unparalleled in others of my kind. You possess a freshness, a vitality, I consider most invigorating. Perhaps it is your extreme youth, as the *enkidu* measure such things, that inspires me. But when I look at you, when I am with you, I feel as if the world has been remade anew and that I am its conqueror.'

'What are you saying?'

'Only that I have had numerous brides in my past, but I have yet to take a queen.' Morgan gestured to the winking lights that stretched as far as the eye could see. 'We could rule the vampire and human worlds alike, you and I. With your immunity to silver and ability to travel during the daylight hours, we would be invincible. Every Noble would be forced to swear allegiance to us and submit to our will. We will be unstoppable. We will be *forever.*'

'What makes you think I'd go along with it?'

'I don't. But what else have you to do?'

'I could kill you.'

'And then what? Will you marry? Raise children? Prepare for retirement? Will killing me turn you back into Denise Thorne? Once I'm gone, what then will provide you with a reason for your existence? Will you continue mindlessly killing vampires simply because you have grown accustomed to it? Or will you succumb to the Ennui, as did Pangloss?

'You must cast aside your childish understanding of how the world works. *All* Nobles have blood vendettas against one another, but none of us truly wishes the other's demise.

222

Otherwise we would soon grow tired of the game and find ourselves withering away from boredom. You, on the other hand, are a genuine psychopath, killing the very thing that provides you reason for continuing.

'I blame myself, in part, for your madness. After all, if I had been there for you, schooling you in the nuances of Noble society, you wouldn't be as confused as you are now. Child, you have been acting on instinct out of ignorance and self-loathing, doing what comes naturally to our kind but without understanding the why and wherefore of it all.

'Tell me the truth, Sonja, don't you weary of constantly battling with yourself? Don't you long to surrender the burden of conscience? Don't you weary of forever being on guard against losing control?'

Sonja's eyes seemed to look somewhere far away. 'Yes,' she whispered.

'Then cast away your hatred! Put aside your weapon! Embrace me as a queen would her king, and the struggle will be over! We were meant to be together, Sonja. Ignorance and fear have kept us apart for these many years – but no longer! Do it, Sonja. Just do it.'

His words were so soft. So sweet. So soothing. Some of what he said made no sense, but a lot of it hit home. Sonja felt something within her soften and begin to give way. She suddenly felt so tired. So very, very tired. All she wanted was to curl up and fall into a deep sleep.

The Other dug its fingers into her forebrain, shrieking and spitting like an enraged mountain lion. The pain that filled her head was so huge there was no way she could even scream.

Stupid cunt! He's reeling you in like a fish! Morgan's an expert at finding vulnerable spots and manipulating them to his advantage! All this sweet talk about 'queens' and 'equals' is nothing but bullshit! Vampires are either masters or slaves! He said so himself! He's setting you up, girlfriend, and you're falling for it like the proverbial ton of bricks! Wake up, damn you! Wake up and kill him – kill him now!

Sonja staggered backward, away from Morgan, as another bolt of agony ripped through her gray matter. Purple-black stars exploded behind her eyelids.

Why are you doing this? Is it Palmer? Is it Lethe? Is this how you're trying to punish us for killing Judd? By letting Morgan turn you into one of his fuckin' gets? If you think I'm gonna sit on the sidelines and let you do that, sister, you've got another thing coming!

Morgan worked to hide his smile as Sonja spun away from his grasp, clawing at her temples and snarling like a wounded thing. A quick check of her aura revealed a spiky nimbus pulsing about her skull, alternating strokes of red and black. Morgan was reminded of sea snails battling one another. The only thing he'd ever seen like it was back in old Bedlam, when the gentry paid the Master of Lunacy to watch the madmen 'at play'. In any case, his little game had paid off. He'd succeeded in pitting the divided elements of Sonja's unstable personality against one another.

Sonja doubled over and vomited a gout of blackish blood onto her boots. Morgan wrinkled his nose in distaste. The bottled stuff.

Inside Sonja's head the scene was hardly as prosaic as what was going on outside it. Sonja found herself floating in a great blue-black void. Although she was in her own mind, her imago – her self-image – was that of her physical body in every detail. She hung in midair, uncertain which was up or down. Not that it mattered. The blue-black nothingness folded in on itself, like a piece of paper being wadded up by a child, and just as rapidly *unfolded*.

She was standing on a vast, empty ice field. The wind howled like an angry thing in her ears. A huge, pockmarked moon climbed the starless sky, barely clearing the glaciers on the horizon. The ice gleamed darkly, like the shell of an insect.

Where are you, damn it? she thought, honing her mind until it was a tight, hot beam, scouring the ice floe's surface like a laser sight. *Answer me – where are you? You can't hide from me!*

The ice beneath her feet pushed upward and outward, sending her flying. She stared in amazement as the Other climbed forth. Although they had shared the same body, the same consciousness for twenty-five years, Sonja had no idea what her vampiric self looked like. She hadn't *wanted* to know.

The Other looked like one of the hag queens medieval parents had used to frighten their children into good behavior. Her skin was blue and her breasts hung flat and empty against her ribs. Her hands were like the grasping feet of a bird of prey and her talons were as long and sharp as knives. Although her appearance was more in line with that of a corpse, her lips were obscenely full and seemed to writhe with a life of their own, exposing blackened gums and teeth better suited to an attack dog. She moved like an ape, her red eyes burning with an endless rage.

I'm here.

Sonja got to her feet and pressed the eye of her switchblade. The silver blade leapt out, glinting in the moonlight.

Then let's dance, bitch.

The Other dropped onto all fours and scuttled forward like a great scorpion, her joints bending at impossible angles. Sonja tracked as she circled her, shifting to keep the Other in front of her at all times. Part of her wondered if this was what the few humans capable of perceiving the Real World saw whenever they looked at her and shuddered in revulsion.

The Other used this momentary distraction to launch itself, its claws tearing at her midsection as its fangs strained for her throat. And then all conscious thought dissolved and there was only the need for survival.

Morgan stepped back as Sonja dropped onto the floor of the observation deck, spasming in the grips of what looked to be a grand mal seizure. Foam flecked her lips and her limbs twitched as if someone was running powerful bursts of electric current through them. Morgan did not dare get any closer because she still held her switchblade tightly in one fist – and the blade was exposed.

The surges of psychic energy he'd seen earlier were stronger than before. Now there was sound as well as a light show. Squeals of psionic static ripped through his head like the scream of a dentist's drill. Morgan grimaced and placed his hands over his ears, even though he knew it would do no good.

He had almost decided against killing her at the last minute, but this was definitely changing his mind. Anything capable of such anarchic energy release was far too dangerous for him to allow its continuance. He glanced up at the 222-foot television tower that jutted from the very top of the Empire State, stabbing the sky like a hypodermic needle. The very air around its tip was beginning to boil. Morgan licked his lips in anticipation. This was going to be good.

The psychic membrane that binds the eight million minds that comprise New York City shudders and flexes in response to the psychic disturbance, triggering minor ripples in the gestalt. Or, to follow Morgan's metaphor, the herd looks up and sees the lightning tearing holes in the sky and begins to grow agitated without really knowing why. Something bad is coming.

Times Square:

Edgar Tremouille is pacing his tiny studio apartment overlooking Times Square. He chews his left thumbnail to the quick and continues gnawing until the blood comes.

Lenox Avenue:

The baby won't stop crying. Normally it doesn't bother Yolanda that much, but tonight it's really getting on her nerves. She wishes her mother would come home from work so she can go out and hang with her friends. She thought having the baby would make her happy. She liked the idea of having something that had no choice but to love her. But now she wishes she was still back in the eighth grade and able to go out when she felt like it. Little Rodrigo stands in his playpen and screams as he rattles its bars. Yolanda turns the TV up as loud as it can go and pulls the kitchen chair so close her nose almost touches the screen. She puts her hands over her ears and tries to shut out the sound of Rodrigo's angry, demanding cries.

Irving Place:

Normally, Sam's fun to be around. More than fun. He's Cindy's one true love. They met at a friend's wedding nine months ago. She was the bridesmaid and he was working the bar. One thing led to another, and now they're sharing an apartment on the Upper East Side. All their friends envy them their relationship.

'You two are so perfect for one another.'

'We've never seen a couple so happy together.'

Even strangers comment on the perfection of their romance. Sam is always understanding and supportive and affectionate towards her. But tonight is proving to be a major exception. He's in a really foul mood for no real reason, sitting in front of the TV and slamming down beers and not talking to her at all except to make hurtful comments about her weight and her taste in friends and clothes and her intelligence. Once or twice she caught him looking at her with this really weird look on his face. She stands in front of the kitchen sink, washing the dishes, she begins to think about their relationship. Sam is a struggling actor. Cindy works for an investment firm. Cindy is seven years older than Sam. They actually live on her salary, since Sam waits tables in order to keep himself free for any work that might come in from his agent. Although they both work eight-hour days, somehow she seems to be the one to find the time to wash the dishes, handle the laundry, and clean the apartment. The more Cindy thinks about it, the more unfair it seems. The more *deliberate* it becomes. She wonders if he isn't planning on dumping her for some cute young thing the moment he gets a serious break in his career. She is fuming hard enough to blow smoke from her ears as she dumps the silverware into the soapy water.

The Church of Our Father the Redeemer:

Father Ignatius closes his eyes and prays for the visions to go away. Holy men are supposed to have visions, or so the Bible claims. But the visions that afflict Father Ignatius are far from spiritual. In his vision his mother is sitting in her chair near the window, fanning herself and looking down through the chintz curtains at the street below where they once lived in Hell's Kitchen. She's sweating and fanning. Sweating and fanning. Her dress is open, exposing her massive breasts. Sweating and fanning. Sweating and fanning. She stares out the window like he's not in the room. His mother hitches up her skirt over her hips and, without taking her eyes off the street outside her window, begins massaging the thing between her legs. The room smells of animals. She twitches a bit and moans, as if she's hurt herself. Then she looks directly at Father Ignatius and smiles, exposing bare gums. She's missing her upper plate. His mother is seventy-two years old.

Sonja was straddling the Other, hammering its head into the black ice. The wind that blew across the frozen void shrieked wordlessly in her ears. She had never been so happy before in her life. Never before had she been able to truly let go of herself, to fight without restraint. It felt *good*. The same way that a long-distance runner feels good once her body has gone beyond simple exhaustion. It was a feeling of freedom, of being severed from time and place and identity. There was only the now of the act.

The Other snarled and slashed at her with its razored claws, ripping Sonja open from throat to crotch. It chuckled darkly as Sonja scrambled to shove her intestines back into her body.

He's planning to kill you. You realize that, don't you?

Sonja's body bowed upward, the muscles straining until she was balanced on the top of her skull and the heels of her boots. The psychic feedback grew louder, causing Morgan to grit his teeth in pain. He had not expected such a dramatic reaction to his tampering. With a squeal of psionic reverb, dark energy leapt from Sonja's midsection, hitting the television aerial like a reverse lightning strike. The wound in the sky began to swell even further, as if filling with pus.

The wind was picking up, growing even stronger than before. Morgan moved closer to Sonja's prostrate form. As he reached out for her throat, there was a loud crackle, the smell of ozone, and a burst of black electricity. He drew back his hand, snarling in pain. The fingers of his right hand smelled like roasted pork. He'd forgotten about the damned silver crucifix he'd given her! He cursed under his breath and pulled the gun from the interior pocket of his opera cape. Normally he had no use for such crude weapons of destruction. He either killed with his mind or with the hands of others. But Sonja was a very special case.

He sighted down the barrel, aiming at her head.

Too bad it had to be this way. She might have provided him with centuries, perhaps millennia, of interesting duels. But she was too dangerous. He'd told her so himself. She refused to play by the rules. To her, vengeance was more than a game to while away the decades. She was sworn to destroy him and, sooner or later, she would do just that. But, worst of all, she tempted him. Tempted him to love. And to love is to be weak and to be weak is to be a slave. And that was something Morgan could never allow to happen. Ever.

'Farewell, my perfect love,' he whispered, and pulled the trigger.

*   *   *

Sonja reeled her guts back in and snapped her body cavity closed behind them, careful not to cut off her spleen or her liver. She kicked the Other square in the mouth, sending teeth flying like Chiclets.

I've had all of you I can stand! I'm sick of hearing your fuckin' voice screeching inside my ear every damn day! You've ruined everything for me! Everything! And now it's time you paid!

The Other wiped the blood from her mouth and grinned crookedly. *You're a real ass, you know that? How about me – you think I've enjoyed being cooped up with a fuckin' goody two-shoes all this time? Always rolling around in self-pity, feeling sorry for yourself because you're a big bad monster? Go ahead, beat on me all you want! Kick me! Punch me! It won't make a damn bit of difference! You've already tried starving me out, but that didn't work either, did it? Face it, sweetmeat, I'm here and there's nothing you can do to get rid of me!*

The entire ice field shuddered, as if shaken by a massive earthquake. Both Sonja and the Other looked at one another.

Did you do that?

Fuck no!

There was a cracking sound, as if the world's largest piece of celery was being snapped in two, and a fissure opened up between them. There was a roaring sound and the moon overhead shattered into a thousand silvery fragments. There was another, larger shudder and the chasm widened even further, hurling the Other into darkness.

The sky directly above the Empire State Building looks strange even to casual passersby. The clouds churning about its tip resemble blossoms of ink jetted forth by a frightened octopus. However, none of the nearby weather services pick up signs of a disturbance on their radar screens. So everyone is at a loss to explain the thunderclap that shakes every window in the city at ten minutes after midnight. But the mysterious thunder does far more than rattle windowpanes. It splits the thin membrane of sanity that keeps New York from chewing its own leg off like a coyote in a trap. And then, to put it politely, all hell breaks loose.

Cindy comes out of the kitchen trailing soapy water behind her. In one hand she clutches a carving knife. Sam is still watching the TV, his back to her. The nape of his neck is the only thing she can see. It's like the rest of him doesn't even exist. If she squints her eyes a little, she can see the dotted line going across it.

Edgar Tremouille hears the screams coming from outside his window and goes to look. Screaming on the streets surrounding Times Square isn't particularly rare, but the sheer volume – and the sounds of crunching bumpers and smashing glass – hints at something besides the usual territorial dispute between hookers. As he leans out his window, a cab jumps the curb and plows into pedestrians on the sidewalk. The driver is hunched over his steering wheel and grinning like a fiend as the cab scatters drug dealers, hookers, drag queens, and tourists in every direction. A second cab slams into a car with Jersey plates. The drivers get out and begin kicking and punching each other in the head and the groin, shrieking like wild animals. A crowd gathers, their eyes too wide and their faces too empty to be human. The cabby grabs the guy from Jersey and rams his head through the windshield. As the cabby staggers back, blood and busted safety glass dripping from his hands, a Molotov cocktail sails through the air, smashing against the front of the Papaya King stand across the street, spraying the crowd with burning gasoline. There are screams and shouts of anger and the smell of burning hair and roasting flesh. Edgar Tremouille has seen enough. He goes to the closet where he keeps his rifle. The End Times have arrived. The Tribulations have begun. And it is time for the Chosen to make their stand. He starts out by sniping at the drag queens. They are the ones who disturb him the most. He tracks one in particular with his scope – the one he'd given twenty dollars to let him suck its dick a couple of months ago. Edgar regretted the act the moment it was done. And it especially bothered him that the drag queen recognized him and called his name whenever he walked by after that. He screams as he shoots the drag queen. He screams as he shoots each and every one. He doesn't know why. He's killing sinners, but it feels like he's shooting part of himself. When there are no more drag queens, he starts in on the blacks.

Rodrigo isn't crying anymore. The TV's still turned up real loud, but Yolanda doesn't hear it. There is a lot of noise next door – sounds like a domestic argument. A real knock-down-and-drag-out. Not that such things are rare where she lives. Yolanda decides it's time to take the garbage to the dumpster. She tosses an empty can of Raviolios and a dirty diaper into the bag. She rams her foot down on the refuse to make some more room. Rodrigo's hand pops up, the fingers already starting to stiffen. Yolanda tells herself it's just a doll. Just a doll.

Father Ignatius counts his rosary and thanks God for taking away the visions. However, the prayer beads are wrapped around the neck of an elderly parishioner who reminds him of his mother. The smell of animals fills the confessional.

The streets of the city seethe with madness long contained and left to fester for years, even generations. Pedestrians knock the coffee cups from the hands of beggars, kicking them in the kidneys as they scramble on their hands and knees to recover their scattered change. Firemen armed with axes battle any who try to put out the blazing fire stations.

Policemen fire tear-gas canisters point-blank at the heads of the rioters filling the street, while other officers wade into the crowd with nightsticks and drawn guns. After a few minutes the line between rioter and police dissolves, as the baton-wielding policemen start beating each other as well as the unruly populace.

The carriage horses at Central Park scream and rear back on their hind legs, desperate to jump their traces, as swarms of hungry people boil from the park's surrounding greenery, armed with rocks and sticks and appetite.

Windows smash as looters climb into Fifth Avenue storefronts to liberate merchandise. Waiters and busboys douse the patrons of five-star restaurants with alcohol and set them alight, turning them into living cherries jubilee and banana fosters. Nurses in neonatal wards go from incubator to incubator, disconnecting the life-support systems. Wild-eyed Hasidic men and women cry out to Mosiach and hurl cinder blocks from the roofs of their housing developments. Thousands of undocumented immigrants pour into the narrow streets of Chinatown, torching the sweatshops.

Gunfire is everywhere. Burning buildings dot the city like candles on a cake. The screams of the hunted and the hunters fill the night. Manhattan and its surrounding boroughs are tearing at themselves, locked in a blind, claustrophobic frenzy, like the berserkers of old who whirled themselves into a killing fury by slashing themselves with their own knives. Those unaffected by the insanity huddle in fear and wonder if it is the end of the world – or just the end of New York? For some, there is no difference.

Sonja struggled to get back on her feet. The ice field was bucking and shaking like a wild animal, sending pillars of ice shooting upward. The sky overhead had given way from perpetual night to a pulsing aurora borealis. She had to get out of this rapidly disintegrating limbo and back into her physical body. Whatever was happening to her material self was obviously pretty major. But every time she tried to concentrate and take herself back into the material world, another shelf of ice shot upward, blocking her path.

She had to get hold of herself. None of this was *real*. Not in the physical sense, anyway. She was inside her head, not trapped on an antarctic glacier. All she had to do was open her eyes and she'd be free . . .

There was a sound like a cannon going off and the ground beneath her exploded in a shower of ice. Stunned, Sonja stared in mute horror as the Other emerged from its icy womb. It was huge, its head and shoulders blocking out the sky. The Other smiled and reached for her with a claw the size of a Buick.

Sissster, it growled. *We can never be safe until he who Made us is destroyed. As long as he exists, we will be weak. Join us, sister. Join us so that we might be reborn yet again.*

18

Morgan's ears were still ringing as he picked himself off the floor of the observation deck. There had been a flash and something like a clap of thunder the second after he fired the gun. He was lucky the force of the concussion hadn't sent him flying over the edge.

He got to his feet and staggered over to where Sonja's body lay sprawled. Curls of steam rose from her like a turkey fresh from the oven. He wanted to rejoice over the fall of an enemy who had cost him so dearly, but the laughter refused to come.

Then Sonja sat up.

Curse the instruments of man's dominion! His aim had not been true! Instead of blowing her skull apart like an overripe cantaloupe, the bullet had grazed the right side of her head. Although she was missing her right ear and a fist-sized patch of her skull now gleamed wetly for all to see, she was still very much alive.

'Morgan?'

He quickly returned the gun to his pocket and knelt beside her.

'I'm here, child. Are you all right? You fell into a seizure.'

Sonja seemed dazed, as if waking from a drugged sleep. 'You were right, milord,' she whispered. The lenses of her sunglasses were cracked and she removed them with trembling hands. 'I have allowed myself to be led astray by misplaced hatred. Your enemies have worked to turn me against you for their own ends. I would see them suffer in your name.'

As Morgan helped her to her feet, she allowed her forehead to drop against his shoulder. Morgan struggled to keep his face from pulling into a triumphant sneer. All was not lost.

If he could actually break her to his will, her death could still be avoided. But if the fire in her belly was extinguished, if she became just another of his adoring brides, then there would be no reason to love her. What provoked his passion was her deadliness, her ferocity, her *threat*. Part of him found the prospect of crushing her will and keeping the physical shell as a reminder of his victory appealing. Yet another side of him hesitated.

Sonja's arms slid about his waist, pulling him closer. She looked up into his scarred face with eyes the color of blood. Eyes so very much like his own. 'Hold me,' she sighed. 'I'm so very tired, milord. Please hold me.'

'I will do so gladly, but only after you put aside your weapon.'

Sonja glanced down at the switchblade she still clutched in her hand. Her fingernails had dug so deeply into the flesh of her palm that blood dripped from her fingers. Her face contorting in disgust, Sonja hurled the silver knife away from her, sending it sailing over the edge of the observation deck into the night.

Morgan tightened his grip on her. She felt so soft, so vulnerable; it would be so easy to slide into her mind and crack her ego open like a rotten nut. He lowered his face and their lips brushed. She reached out hungrily for him, pulling him into a full embrace, her tongue searching for and finding his own. And their minds met and were one.

They were standing beside a meditation pool in a Japanese rock garden. Dappled *koi* swam just below the jade-green surface, mouthing crumbs of bread. Morgan's imago wore the costume of a shogun of the Edo period. Sonja's imago was dressed as Sonja always was. Her black leather jacket creaked as she pinched off another handful of breadcrumbs and tossed them into the pool.

Sonja looked up at Morgan and smiled. Her eyes were once more hidden behind slivers of mirrored glass, only now the lenses seemed to grow directly from her brow ridge and merge into her cheekbones. 'Are you going to try and kill me now? Is that why you picked such a comforting mindscape? So I would be lulled into trusting you?'

Morgan shifted uncomfortably, the corner of his mouth jerking fitfully. The features belonging to his imago were whole but he had grown accustomed to smiling with only half his face. 'I don't know what you mean, my love. You are my queen – why should I kill you?'

Sonja shrugged and resumed feeding the goldfish. 'I dunno. Because I'm dangerous? Because I'm a threat to your continuance? Because I trashed your plans for world domination? Because I fucked up your face? Because I killed your most trustworthy servant? Because I scare you? How about just because?'

'What if I was going to kill you? What would you do to stop me?'

'Nothing.'

'I don't believe you.'

Sonja shrugged again. The piece of bread in her hands had yet to dwindle. 'Believe what you like. But I won't stop you. I'll even give back your chimera. Assuming you still want it, that is.'

'Are you serious?'

'I'm not laughing, am I?' Sonja unzipped her jacket and reached inside the breast pocket, removing a small ivory statue. She dropped it onto the ground and the statue began to twitch and writhe, growing larger. Within seconds the three-headed tiger with the scorpion tail was standing beside her, lashing its barbed tail and growling.

Morgan reached out with one hand and the chimera began to melt and warp, like a chalk drawing caught in the rain. The chimera became a *yazuka*-style tattoo on his bared chest.

'There. You have your chimera back. I hope you're happy. You can kill me now, if you like. I won't stop you.'

He could tell she wasn't lying. He stepped back and drew his samurai sword from its scabbard. Instead of being forged from steel, the blade was made of black volcanic glass. He drew back the sword as if he was readying to tee off. Sonja watched him placidly for a moment, then resumed feeding the fish. The sword cut through her neck as easily as it did the air, sending her severed head arcing into the meditation pond. The body stood for a few seconds more, blood gouting from the stump like a fountain, before collapsing.

Morgan wiped her blood from the blade, marveling over the ease of it all, yet concerned by her failure to defend herself. After all, this was the woman who had wrested a part of his very self from him in combat and made it her own. He had expected *something* resembling a fight.

There was a thick, bubbling sound from the direction of the pool. Morgan glanced up in time to see the waters first turn red as blood, then black as ink. The *koi* bobbed to the surface, their gill slits straining as they gasped their last. The middle of the pool was aboil, as if an underwater geyser was about to erupt.

A female figure emerged from the heart of the pool, rising on the befouled water like Aphrodite from the foam. Her skin was black as polished night, her dark hair thick and wild, like the mane of a lion. Her teeth were white as pearl and curved into fearsome fangs and her tongue was long and narrow, like that of a cat. She had four arms and in each hand she gripped an instrument of destruction: a shield, a sword, a noose, and a submachine gun. Around her neck was a garland of skulls and about her hips she wore a girdle of severed hands. When she turned her head, Morgan could see three other faces: one was that of a virgin, the second that of a blue-skinned hag, and third was Sonja's.

The black-skinned demoness nodded to Morgan as if acknowledging a debt. When she spoke, all four of her faces chimed in. 'I thank you, father, for recreating me anew. Before I was separate and unequal. Now I am whole.'

Morgan wasn't sure what to make of the black-skinned demon-goddess that stood before him. Was she one of Sonja's tricks?

'Who are you? What are you doing with Sonja's face?'

As if in answer the black-skinned demon-goddess brought her blade against the shield, making it ring like a gong. Morgan cried out and clutched his ears.

'Don't you know me, father? I am your death.'

The demoness laughed then, her multitude of voices filling Morgan's skull. He watched, awestruck, as she began to grow, until she towered over him like a building.

'I am the Dark One! I am the Queen of Nightmares made flesh! And you made me, sweet father, as all children are made: out of ignorance and appetite. I am your daughter, Lord of the Morning Star, and your executioner.'

Panicking, Morgan's imago cast aside its human form in favor of something more suitable for battle. His skin became mottled and scaly as his head widened and flattened itself. His arms and legs were rapidly absorbed by his torso as his body first doubled, then quadrupled in size and length, until he was the size of a city bus. Hissing his defiance, Morgan flared his hood and rose to challenge his enemy.

The demon-goddess laughed and began to dance, her four arms weaving in rhythmic patterns. Morgan reared back and spat a stream of venom at her eyes, but she blocked it with her shield.

'There is no denying me, sweet father,' she chided. 'I am the Slayer of the Dead.'

Morgan struck again, hoping to plunge his fangs into the demoness's naked thigh, but she moved too fast, slipping her noose about his neck and yanking it tight. Morgan hissed and flailed, his body lashing back and forth like a bullwhip.

'I have been a long time being born, sweet father,' the voices chorused. 'And birthing is hungry work. I would feed now.'

The demoness carefully laid aside her weapons while keeping a firm grip on the head of the giant cobra. Morgan shrieked and hissed and struggled with all his might, but there was no escaping the noose. The dark-skinned destroyer licked her lips with her long red tongue, her eyes gleaming like polished skulls, and sank her fangs into the back of her captive's neck with a satisfying crunch.

Any who might have seen them then would have mistaken them for lovers, locked in a passionate embrace. And, on some level, that was the truth. But if they looked closer, they would see the crackling sheath of purple-black energy that pulsed around the couple like St Elmo's fire, and how the aura surrounding Morgan was beginning to stutter and pale, while Sonja's pulsed like a drum.

Sonja opened her eyes and found herself staring into the face of a dead thing. The illusion of life that Morgan had maintained for so many centuries had finally failed him. His skin was the color and texture of parchment. His once-dark hair was now white and patchy, like a dog with mange. His flesh had melted from his bones, leaving him little more than a dry husk, a pitiful scarecrow outfitted with fangs. Although he looked like an ancient pharaoh, his eyes still burned with stolen life.

'Enough,' he wheezed. 'Please—'

'No,' she answered, her voice that of the black-skinned demon-goddess. 'More. I need more. Give me the chimera. Give me your love.'

Morgan raised a stick-like arm in a feeble attempt to stay her, but it did no good. Undeterred, Sonja sank her fangs into what was left of his throat. The vampire lord shrieked as a dark fire burst from his eyes and ears, his brain spontaneously combusting. Sonja continued to feed, oblivious to how Morgan's limbs withered and drew in on themselves, disappearing into sleeves and pant legs. Only when there was no more to drain did she let him drop.

What was left of Morgan lay at her feet, surrounded by a mound of clothes. It looked something like a cross between a pickled monkey and a petrified fetus, the discolored skin pulled tight over brittle bones. Even though she had drained it of seven hundred and fifty-three years of stolen energy, the creature still clung to the pretense of life. It lifted its oversized head on its feeble stalk of a neck and looked around with blind eyes, its dry bones rattling like the limbs of a marionette.

'Forgive me,' it piped.

She brought her boot heel down on its skull, shattering it like a light-bulb, and stepped over the pathetic remains of the thing that had created her and climbed onto the ledge of the observation deck. Her hands seethed with a black fire laced with tongues of crimson. The energy she had stolen from Morgan coursed through her veins, filling her with euphoria.

Her body vibrated like a tuning fork, juiced on the ultimate high – the life-force stolen from the undead. Morgan's power surged through her body, amplified by the negative energy that hung over the city like a pall of smoke. She reached out and pulled the madness that had shaken the city back into herself. The wind was so strong now that the television tower groaned to itself like an old man. She grinned and stretched her arms upward, as if to embrace the stars. And she stepped off the ledge into empty air.

She called the winds to her and they came, bearing her aloft as if she was a leaf. She giggled in delight, like a child on a roller coaster, and opened her arms wide, spiraling high into the night sky. She sped along, oblivious to the dazed and frightened populace trembling naked and bleeding in the streets below her. Those forced from their homes by fire found themselves gathering in the open parks, waiting the arrival of the sun. Those who dared look up saw the silhouette of a woman streak across the sky, then quickly looked away.

Sonja shot upward, higher than the tallest buildings, like a sky diver in reverse. She was so jazzed on the energy pulsing through her she didn't care where she was going or who saw her. After years of ignorance and fear, she now knew the truth. She knew *who* she was. *What* she was. Tonight the last step in her creation had been reached. Her evolution was complete. She was The Angry One. The Shatterer. She Who Cannot Be Turned Aside. She was the Ultimate Predator: the vampire who feeds on vampires.

The Nightmare Queen began to sing its victory song, banging its sword on its shield as it danced on the body of its defeated foe. The faster she danced, the more intense the black fire surrounding Sonja's flesh became. Her ears were filled with the sound of drums and the clashing of swords and the ringing of bells. Flush with victory and the exhilaration of birth, the newborn Destroyer touched down atop the World Trade Center and roared a challenge to the world.

Deep within the bowels of the Black Grotto, Lady Nuit froze, the scalpel she'd been using to flay a stock analyst from Connecticut falling from her fingers and sticking, point-first, into the floor. The human chandeliers began to moan again.

'Shut those damned fools up!' Nuit snarled, her voice dipping lower as Luxor's features and testes slid from their hiding place. 'I just got them to quiet down! I've had enough of their complaining tonight!'

'Yes, milord,' said Jen, smiling behind his hand. 'I'll see to it immediately.'

The buzz wore off while she was out over the Atlantic Ocean. One minute she was filled with enough energy to pulverize continents, the next she was riding on fumes. The first thought that ran through her mind was: *Wow, wotta rush!*

The second was: *What the fuck—? I can't fly!*

She plummeted from the sky like Wile E. Coyote suddenly realizing he'd run out of cliff, falling a hundred feet before hitting the water. She couldn't even see the land.

Six hours later, a beachcomber on Coney Island stared in amazement as a woman clothed in a leather jacket, jeans and boots staggered out of the surf, a length of seaweed wrapped around her neck like a Hawaiian lei. Before he could react to the strange sight, a man appeared from out of nowhere and threw a blanket over her, hurrying her off the beach.

Part 3

When the Dead Return

'From fairyland she must have come
Or else she is a mermaiden,'
Some said she was a ghoul, and some
A heathen goddess born again.

John Davidson, 'A Ballad of a Nun'

19

It didn't take the jungle long to reclaim the house.

The porch is alive with creepers and other blooming vines. The hammock I once shared with Palmer is now a mildewed, tattered mess, hanging from the hooks in the rafters like a monstrous spiderweb. A couple of empty Tecate bottles lying on their side amidst the litter wink at me darkly in the afternoon sunlight.

The front door is unlocked but the frame is badly warped from the heat and humidity, making it somewhat difficult to open. I inadvertently yank it off its hinges trying to open it. Inside, the house smells of mold, rising damp, and rotten garbage. Small lizards skitter out from underfoot as I go from room to room. Some of the windows are broken, allowing leaves and other detritus access to the house, but it looks as if no one has set foot in it since I left, months before. I'm not really surprised. The locals are exceptionally superstitious when it comes to Señorita Azure.

I step out into the courtyard. It looks desolate, with dead leaves collecting in the corners and weeds poking their rough heads between the tiles. The fountain no longer burbles to itself and the stagnant water has grown a scum of algae.

The back of the house is even more overgrown than the front. The rapidly encroaching jungle has swallowed Lethe's old swingset and monkey bars. A wild pig and her piglets burst from cover at my approach, fleeing in the direction of the forest. I follow them, but not with the intention of hunting.

The pig path is still there, of course. It's been there for several hundred years, and it will be there for several hundred more. I climb to the top of the neighboring hill, where the ruins of the ancient Mayan observatory once stood. I dust off one of the tumbled limestone blocks and sit on it, lotus-fashion, and cast my mind into the jungle.

Hours later, as the sun begins to sink, I receive an answer to my summons in the form of a man emerging from the jungle.

He wears a jaguar skin draped over one shoulder and an un-bleached linen loincloth. Jade earplugs stretch his lobes almost to his shoulders, and his lower lip boasts a similar ornament. Tattoos of Mayan sky serpents and jaguar gods swarm his naked torso and arms. His graying hair is pulled up into a warrior's topknot, adorned with the feathers of brightly colored parrots. In one hand he carries a machete and across his back is slung an AK47.

'Hello, Bill.'

'I don't go by that name anymore,' he replies. 'I'm called Chac Balam now. Lord of Jaguars.'

As he moves closer, I see that a disembodied hand rides his shoulder. It waggles two of its six fingers in my direction like antennae.

'I see you've still got Lefty with you.'

Palmer allows himself to smile. 'It would be hard to do without him. He's my good right hand. So to speak.' The smile disappears as quickly as water on a hot griddle. 'Why are you here, Sonja? Why did you come back?'

'Don't worry, I'm not here to try and force your return to my service, if that's what you're thinking. I just wanted to see you one last time, that's all. I wanted to tell you that everything's okay. I . . . I'm not the woman I once was.'

Palmer frowns and squints at me, looking for things only he might see. He nods, and some of the tension drains from his face. 'You *are* different. You're more – I don't know – *together*. It's as if the Other no longer exists.'

'Oh, she's here all right,' I laugh, thumping my chest. 'Just as Denise is still here. I guess you could say we have reached an understanding. Hard as it might be to believe, the Other actually saved my ass. Kept me from doing something really stupid. We no longer war amongst ourselves. What about you? Are you happy with your new life?'

'I've founded a guerrilla group, of sorts, composed largely of *campesinos* of Mayan descent. The government ridicules us in the media, but they're scared. They hunt us like animals, but they've yet to catch us. We keep our supplies and weapons hidden in the sacred cenotes. I guess you could say it's a back-to-Quetzacoatl movement.' He shakes his head and I glimpse some of the old Palmer, the one I used to know. 'I'm a pragmatic man. A reasonable man. You know that. But I had a dream not too long ago where I saw the world change. It was fierce and frightening, but not hopeless. It was as if the world was being reborn, not destroyed. All I want is for my people to prepare themselves for that day, away from the craziness and ugliness of the world that now exists. Sonja, am I crazy?'

'No. Just prescient.'

There is a movement in the trees behind Palmer, but he does not seem alarmed. He glances over his shoulder and nods, then turns back to me.

'I must go. Farewell, Sonja. Please don't misunderstand me when I tell you this, but I hope we never meet again.'

As Palmer slips back between the trees, I glimpse the figure that waits for him in their shadows. It is the girl, Concha. As she turns to go, I can see her belly is swollen with life.

It is almost dark by the time I get back to the empty house. I pause for a second, then reenter the building. *One last walk through*, I tell myself. *Just for old times' sake.*

The bedroom I shared with Palmer smells like old gym socks. The sheets on the bed boast large blossoms of fungus. Rats and mice have chewed their way through Lethe's collection of stuffed animals. The kitchen reeks of rotten garbage and whatever was left in the refrigerator when Palmer moved out. The pile of unopened invoices and bills of lading still sit atop the kitchen table. So does the black mask.

I pick up the mask and hold it so its impassive features are level with my own. Even though it has been left untouched for months, its surface still shines like a piece of polished onyx.

I feel her presence before I can see it, much the same way I'd been able to sense Morgan before he came into a room. The darkened kitchen is filled with a golden light that pours in through the windows facing the courtyard.

Auntie Blue.

The voice in my head is Lethe's, but it isn't the voice of a child. Still holding the mask in one hand, I step out onto the patio, shielding my eyes against her brilliance with an upraised arm.

The light fades as if someone has hit a dimmer switch, revealing a female figure at its heart. The woman is not the teenaged beauty Palmer described to me but a very, very *old* woman, her breasts hanging loose and her thighs and sex withered and wrinkled. I can hardly believe that this ancient crone is my three-year-old stepdaughter.

'Lethe?'

Yes, I was Lethe.

'What the hell happened to you?'

I underwent a sea change. As you did yourself.

'You know about—?'

We are agents of change, you and I. True, we are fashioned for completely different tasks, but our goals are the same. You are the Destroyer, I am the Maker. You're the sickle, I am the seed.

'That still doesn't explain why you're—'

An old woman?

'I wasn't going to be blunt about it, but . . . well, yeah.'

Everything is creation and destruction. Death and rebirth. It has always been so. Such was the case before the rise of man, before the reign of the great lizards, and the Unnamed Ones before them. Things are built, things prosper, things are destroyed. And the time has come for things to change again.

The last change occurred several hundreds of thousands of years ago, when a particularly clever species of ape was given a boost up the evolutionary ladder. However, mankind was led into a blind alley. In the beginning all humans possessed what is called 'sixth sense'. However, over the millennia, they have lost their awareness of the Real World, since it was in the interest of the enkidu and the vargr and other Pretending Ones to manipulate the breeding stock to ensure that they would remain in control. But by doing this, the scales of nature were thrown horribly awry.

Once stripped of its awareness, mankind became more of a danger than any Pretender ever dreamed. At first mankind flourished. Then it metastasized. It grew like a cancer, stripping the earth for its needs, stoking the very fires of destruction. Born blind and deaf, it cannot see the damage it does, the harm it inflicts. And, with every generation, it waltzes closer and closer to the brink of extinction – and with it, the destruction of the Real World. The time has come for the game to be set aright.

For too long have the enkidu preyed upon the hearts and minds of man. It is time for the playing field to be leveled. It is fitting, in its way, that by tampering with a system already out of balance, Morgan's dream of shaping a race in his own image would result in my creation.

The universe is Positive and Negative. Give and Take. Chaos and Order. If there is too much of one element, then the center can no longer hold. The Natural and Supernatural Worlds spawned us – the first of our kind – in an attempt to set things right. You are the Destroyer, the one who must prepare the way by slaying the demons that would challenge the race to come. You are the midwife to the rebirth, making sure the way will be clear. And I am the Creatrix, the Madonna, the Magna Mater – mother to the new flesh.

I have mated with twenty-five men, all of whom possessed the ability to see beyond. And I have borne twenty-five sons. Unlike myself, they shall live a normal mortal span. Each shall have the inner sight, to varying degrees. Some will be powerful psychics, others will merely have a knack for finding other people's car keys. All of them, however, will be aware. And, thanks to genetics and charisma, all twenty-five shall be highly attractive – at least as far as the females of the species are concerned. Should all twenty-five of my sons succeed in spawning four times each – and I doubt that will be a problem for them – and their descendants do likewise, within ten generations there will be twenty-six million of them. By the thirteenth there will be over one

billion. By the fifteenth generation Homo sapiens will be no more —
there will only be Homo mirabilis.

'Twenty-five? And Palmer—?'

*His was the first of my sons. The child has been adopted by the
British Home Secretary and shall grow up in the seat of power.*

'You damn near broke Palmer's mind, using him for stud like
that.'

The old woman who was once Lethe stares at me with flat,
golden eyes as if I've commented on the weather.

His seed was needed.

'Yeah, well, whatever.'

*My time here is short. My corporeal self is deteriorating. Soon I
shall be without form, reduced to energy alone. I merely wished to
see you—*

'For old times' sake?'

The old woman smiles, and for a second I glimpse my stepdaughter's face hidden within the sagging flesh and wrinkled skin.
The light emanating from her begins to intensify, until she glows
like a tiny star.

*They will need you to make them safe, as you made me safe. You
are their midwife, as you were my own. Watch over my children,
Sonja.*

'Like they were my own.'

Jen yawns and stretches behind the wheel of the Land Rover as
I climb back inside.

'About bloody time! I thought you'd never get back!'

'I ran into some old friends.'

'Anyone I might know, milady?'

'No. And stop calling me "milady". My name's Sonja.'

'As you wish, milady.' Jen points to the mask I'm still holding
in one hand. 'What's that?'

I glance down at the thing in my hands. The empty eyes stare
up at me, the lips parted as if in anticipation. I lift it to my face.
The world I perceive from inside it is limited in its view and
claustrophobic. I remove it and hurl it out the window.

'It's a mask. Something to hide behind and scare others with.'

Jen turns the key in the ignition and the engine comes to life. 'Where to next?'

I shrug and kick back in the passenger seat, resting my feet on the dash. 'It's a big world out there, Jen. Surprise me.'

'As you wish, milady.'

From the diaries of Sonja Blue